THE SHOOTOUT

England Dan got to his feet and worked his way back into the forest, hunting for any trace of Poke Jensen. A flash of movement set him off. Firing steadily, he chopped a bush to ribbons. Another quick move ejected the spent brass. He hunted for more ammo, then grabbed the one resting atop his ear and slid it home. The Webley snapped shut. With one round. As he faced Poke Jensen.

"I wanted to see who I was going to gun down," the outlaw said. He came from behind a tree to the left of the bush England Dan had "killed." With a contemptuous move, he holstered his piece. He began walking forward. His hand hovered over his pistol, ready to draw.

England Dan had no doubt the man's draw was spectacular. Not a hint of fear showed on Jensen's face. If anything, he was enjoying himself as he anticipated making another kill. If he had notched the handle of his six-gun, it'd look like a colony of termites had enjoyed a buffet.

"Come on out and let's shoot it out. You and me. Like men. Or is that asking too much of you?" Poke Jensen stopped when he came within ten yards.

England Dan backed away. A showdown with Jensen would end badly for him. He had a single round in his gun. Jensen had five. Jensen had to have been fast to have survived as long as he had.

He stared at Jensen and he was talking himself into believing that he'd lose any contest, he was ha...

Jensen's hand flashed. England Dan lifted his pistol and fired. Poke Jensen cleared leather and fired.

England Dan staggered and fell, but not from lead ripping through his heart. His involuntary retreat had caused him to catch his heel and lose his balance. Whether that saved his life was a fact to be debated around many campfires.

RALPH COMPTON

LOST BANSHEE MINE

A Ralph Compton Western by
JACKSON LOWRY

BERKLEY
New York

BERKLEY
An imprint of Penguin Random House LLC
penguinrandomhouse.com

Copyright © 2020 by The Estate of Ralph Compton
Penguin Random House supports copyright. Copyright fuels creativity, encourages
diverse voices, promotes free speech, and creates a vibrant culture. Thank you for buying
an authorized edition of this book and for complying with copyright laws by not
reproducing, scanning, or distributing any part of it in any form without permission.
You are supporting writers and allowing Penguin Random House to continue to
publish books for every reader.

BERKLEY and the BERKLEY & B colophon are registered trademarks of
Penguin Random House LLC.

ISBN: 9780593100677

First Edition: July 2020

Printed in the United States of America
1   3   5   7   9   10   8   6   4   2

Cover art by Chris McGrath
Book design by George Towne

THE IMMORTAL COWBOY

This is respectfully dedicated to the "American Cowboy." His was the saga sparked by the turmoil that followed the Civil War, and the passing of more than a century has by no means diminished the flame.

———◦———

True, the old days and the old ways are but treasured memories, and the old trails have grown dim with the ravages of time, but the spirit of the cowboy lives on.

———◦———

In my travels—to Texas, Oklahoma, Kansas, Nebraska, Colorado, Wyoming, New Mexico, and Arizona—I always find something that reminds me of the Old West. While I am walking these plains and mountains for the first time, there is this feeling that a part of me is eternal, that I have known these old trails before. I believe it is the undying spirit of the frontier calling me, through the mind's eye, to step back into time. What is the appeal of the Old West of the American frontier?

———◦———

It has been epitomized by some as the dark and bloody period in American history. Its heroes—Crockett, Bowie, Hickok, Earp—have been reviled and criticized. Yet the Old West lives on, larger than life.

———◦———

It has become a symbol of freedom, when there was always another mountain to climb and another river to cross; when a dispute between two men was settled not with expensive lawyers, but with fists, knives, or guns. Barbaric? Maybe. But some things never change. When the cowboy rode into the pages of American history, he left behind a legacy that lives within the hearts of us all.

—*Ralph Compton*

CHAPTER ONE

SOMETHING MORE THAN grinding hunger tied England Dan Rutledge's stomach in a tight knot. Hunting had been terrible. Summer this year in the Superstition Mountains had been drier than usual, making the deer and rabbits that bothered to stay in the high country skittish. Most of the forage the animals usually ate was dried and sparse, forcing them to go lower in the mountains. That made every hunt more difficult if he wanted to follow all those possible meals on the hoof.

Worse, England Dan hated to leave his partner in their mine alone.

It wasn't because of any danger, but John Cooley slacked off when he didn't have his partner constantly urging him to work harder or even to work at all. England Dan hardly blamed him. The Trafalgar Mine was playing out, and they both knew it. The amount of gold they pulled from the tons of ore they moved decreased monthly. Getting a single ounce for that work amounted to reason for celebration. Mostly there wasn't that much and hadn't been since last fall.

He tramped up the trail toward their mine, not paying attention to where he stepped. A low-hanging branch knocked off his bowler as he failed to duck in time. Cursing, he put down the two scrawny rabbits he had bagged and picked up the hat. A quick swipe of his forearm brushed off dirt. Or most of it. The hat had seen better days since he bought it in London, and his British Army officer's jacket had been patched so many times, it was more repair than original cloth. The epaulets had been ripped off when he was cashiered, and the gold braid had long since turned black from oxidation and filth. His cavalry boots needed polishing, and the gun belt strapped around his waist, carrying a well-used Webley-Pryse, showed empty loops where spare ammunition normally rode. He wore a bandolier slung across his left shoulder, but the cartridge loops in it were as vacant as those in his gun belt. Ammo cost money.

There wasn't anything about him that didn't have the "rode hard, put away wet" look.

England Dan sank to a rock and worked more on the bowler. His collision with the tree limb left a sticky patch of pinesap. Using his thumbnail, he flicked it off. The gob landed in the dirt, perfectly domed and mocking. Detritus survived. His future was less well formed and murky.

He looked up suddenly when strange voices drifted downslope. Cooley often talked to himself and sang off-key when he worked. Answering himself in a different tone was brand-new. This turned Dan wary. Perching his bowler securely on his head and brushing his unkempt gray-streaked sandy hair out of his eyes, he drew his six-gun and came to his feet slowly. Every sense strained. He made out two distinct voices rumbling from off the trail. He took a deep whiff of the air and caught the scent of tobacco. Someone with enough money to buy fixings for a smoke moved through the undergrowth.

Choosing to rummage about in the dried bush rather than take the trail sent a new thrill through him. His feeling of impending disaster proved accurate. The only men who crept up on the mine like this were claim jumpers.

A shot in their direction would solve a couple problems. It spooked men too cowardly to present themselves at the mine, and it warned his partner. Unless Cooley was actually working deep in the Trafalgar, he'd hear and know something was wrong.

England Dan carefully broke open the Webley and saw four of the six chambers carried live rounds. Four bullets to fight off an unknown number of would-be thieves and murderers. An astute claim jumper had no reason to leave the miner alive. For the first time, he wished his hunting hadn't been so successful, if two rabbits merited such a label. His marksmanship was far better than his partner's, but he had taken a dozen shots to bring down this pitiful bounty.

He had to do better with the claim jumpers.

Slipping through the brush as quietly as possible, he found a deep footprint in the soft ground under a tree. He measured it against his own. He stood six feet tall. If the footprint was to be believed, the man making it was at least a head taller and a hundred pounds heavier. To verify his guess, he found a second print and tried to put his feet in each. He held back a moan as he strained his crotch. The stride, even if the man was running, showed him to be a giant.

England Dan ran his finger over the six-shooter's trigger. Four rounds, even of the potent .455 slugs, might not be enough to bring down a man this size.

A brief thought flittered across his brain. Turn around. Leave his partner to his fate. He heaved a deep sigh and continued up the slope. John Cooley might do that. England Dan Rutledge wouldn't. He was made of sterner stuff, even if his father, the earl, thought otherwise. Cooley was his partner, and partners watched out for each other.

He crouched low when he caught sight of their cabin. No smoke puffed up from the chimney. Wherever Cooley was, he had abandoned the cabin to go there. Working around the cabin, he chanced a quick glance inside. Empty. He moved past a small mountain of black tailings to get a better look at the mouth of their mine. It was fifty feet upslope. The ore cart wasn't at the end of the track running into the mine. That told him what he needed to know. Cooley was working to fill that rusty bucket deep inside where they had found a new vein.

If his partner dug like a badger a hundred feet into the mine, he'd never hear anyone moving around outside.

But England Dan did. The crunch of feet against gravel alerted him to a man darting to keep from silhouetting himself at the mouth. Moving like a marmot, England Dan popped up, took in the situation and dropped back. One man armed with a rifle had dashed across the front of the mine while another tried to position himself above the opening.

That one physically matched the tracks he had found. A guess of six feet six was shy of the truth by three or four inches. The only thing he lacked to be completely intimidating was a gun. He didn't sport iron at his waist or carry a rifle like his partner. England Dan stroked his Webley's hammer, appreciating the worn crosshatch there intended to keep a thumb from slipping. It was a double action, but he had been trained to cock it and fire like a single action to keep from pulling the trigger repeatedly in the heat of battle and unexpectedly finding the cylinder empty. It was his only advantage in this fight.

The man with the rifle pressed into the rock beside the mine opening signaled his partner. The behemoth above made an impatient gesture with a hand the size of a ham hock. As if that was the order he'd waited for, the rifleman swung around and began firing into the mine shaft. Bullets whined off the walls, tearing deep into the mine. The sparks from a few ricochets leaped backward past the gunman, causing him to duck.

"Go in!" The giant's voice rumbled like thunder among the tall peaks.

"I don't know if I got him."

"Is he still digging?"

The rifleman shoved a finger in his ear and wiggled it around. He shook his head and peered up. "I can't tell. The report deafened me."

"Go find out. Get in there!"

The man stared at his rifle, jacked in another round and plunged into the mine. From where he hid, England Dan couldn't hear any sound in the mine. The fusillade had been short and intense. Cooley could have been cut down before he knew what happened.

"Please, be taking a break like you always do. Sit down and—" He hadn't realized he was speaking aloud.

The giant let out a deep-throated bull roar and reared up. He held his arms out at shoulder level, fists clenched, eyes searching wildly. England Dan reacted without realizing what he did.

Four shots tore through the air in the man's direction. A fifth tug on the trigger landed on a spent chamber.

England Dan cursed as he looked up. His marksmanship was good. Graduating from Sandhurst had taught him not to panic in battle. Nothing had been said of hitting his target four times and so much lead having no effect. The giant of a claim jumper roared and pounded on his chest, then jumped down. The only hint that the four .455 caliber rounds in his chest bothered him appeared when he landed hard off-balance and collapsed to one knee. He shook himself like a wet dog and got to his feet.

The snarl on his face chilled the miner to the core of his being. As crazy as it was, England Dan might have stood his ground and fought. Those bullets in the man's chest had to wear him down eventually, but the claim jumper's partner came rushing from the mine, waving his rifle around.

"Who fired? I knew there was a second one of them varmints."

The giant grunted incoherently and pointed downhill in England Dan's direction. It was time to retreat.

This had never been covered in any of his military studies. To retreat meant failure. The British Army never lost a fight except for that bloody fool, Cornwallis. Their forces might be cut down to the last man, but they never lost. England Dan had developed his own set of more pragmatic tactics while stationed in India. He turned and bolted. Rifle slugs danced around him, adding speed to his "advance to the rear."

He came across a game trail and feinted left, as if heading farther downhill. Footprints in the dry dirt showed his direction. With a powerful jump, he reached up and caught a tree limb. A hard kick swung him around in a circle so his belly pressed into the branch. He pushed himself to a squatting position, hidden among the foliage.

"He came this way. There's his footprint. Come on!" England Dan felt like a hound on the hunt.

"You go. I don't feel so good." The giant turned this way and that, as if looking for a way to escape.

England Dan hoped the monster's innards had been ripped apart by his bullets and he slowly bled to death. The two claim jumpers had intended to flush Cooley from the mine if they didn't plug him by firing wildly into the shaft. They hadn't given him a chance. For all Dan knew, his partner was bleeding to death in the mine—or was mercifully dead already.

He slipped the Webley into his holster, slid the leather thong over the hammer and drew a wickedly sharp knife sheathed at his left hip. If either of the thieves passed beneath him, he'd drop down and slit their throat. Hiding like a coward galled him, but he intended to stay alive. The mine still had a few ounces of gold waiting to fall under his pick. Defending his property and his partner—and himself—was a matter of honor.

Killing the claim jumpers was a matter of survival.

Scooting along the limb, he positioned himself directly over the game trail and waited. And waited. Straining his every sense, he tried to locate his attackers. The rising wind in the treetops drowned out small noises along the ground. From the way the clouds were gathering, a rare thunderstorm was preparing to dump tons of water on him.

Taking a deep breath, he sought the hint of tobacco. Nothing. A trace of moisture replaced any distinctive scent. Thunder sounded in the distance. The knife hilt turned damp as his hand sweat with strain. His fingers began to knot.

Stretching his body along the limb, he chanced a look along the trail in both directions. An incurious fox danced about on the path. England Dan dropped and startled the fox, but the animal would never have poked his nose out of hiding if the claim jumpers had been nearby. A few quick wiggles got England Dan into the undergrowth, where he could burrow open a small tunnel through the brush to peer at the mine uphill.

The claim jumpers were nowhere to be seen. Neither was John Cooley. Digging in his toes, England Dan began creeping up the hill until he reached a spot a few yards from the mouth of the mine. No sound came from inside, but he heard crashing and glass breaking from the direction of the cabin.

He gritted his teeth, got his feet under him and let his fury explode. Legs pumping hard, he ran to the cabin. The door had been ripped off its hinges. Inside lay total destruction. The claim jumpers had destroyed everything. The larder had been dumped out. All the food—what little there had been—was gone.

Rage built and he loosed a roar that echoed from the mountaintops. England Dan brought his anger under control and searched the ground for tracks. Only one set showed. The giant could have never hidden his tracks. He was too heavy. Stride long and alert for any trap, Dan set off along the trail curving eastward around the mountainside.

"Got you," he snarled when he came upon the huge man sitting on a rock, holding his chest. "Give back everything you stole!"

The giant grinned. Two front teeth had been broken, and the rest were blackened. He lifted his immense hands, each larger than a quart Mason jar. Balling them into fists, he raised them like a prizefighter.

England Dan circled. His opponent remained seated. With a roar he lunged forward, using the long-bladed knife as if it were sword. A huge gash appeared on the claim jumper's forearm. He hardly reacted. England Dan kicked hard with his back leg and lunged again. This sent the tip of the knife into the giant's chest. For a moment, the man didn't stir. Then he casually batted the weapon away. The bloody knife clattered a dozen feet away.

"I will kill you!" The words came out amid bubbling pink froth on his lips and a deep rattle from his chest.

The giant tried to stand, but his legs gave way under him. The bullets had worked their leaden death magic internally. The knife cut had to have been as close to fatal as possible without actually killing him instantly. England Dan dodged inside the man's tree-trunk arms and began hammering away with his fists. Hitting a man on the jaw was a good way to break fingers. He had been in enough bar fights to know this. His target lay just under the giant's chin. Three quick punches drove into the man's Adam's apple.

That ended the fight. Gurgling and gasping for breath, the monstrous man grabbed for his throat. He turned red in the face as he choked to death. In seconds he toppled over. A few feeble kicks and then . . . nothing.

England Dan stared at the body. His chest heaved, and his heart threatened to explode in his chest. For all his army training, he had lost his sangfroid, as his colonel used to call it. The threat of dying always robbed him of his composure. This time he had avoided injury or death. But the next time? He vowed to keep his calm.

"They stole purt near everything, but they didn't find our gold stash."

At the words, England Dan scooped up his knife and faced his partner. Cooley held a small leather sack in which they hid the product of all their hard work. It had been stashed away from the cabin.

"But all our supplies are gone."

"You fixed that one real good. I never saw a man so big. How'd you do it?"

"Where'd you get off to? The other claim jumper went into the mine after you, but he came out so fast, he could never have found you."

"Dan, old man, you're plumb loco if you think I was going to do anything but hide. I had a pick. He had a rifle. Then there was gunfire from outside the mine." Cooley shook his head. The few strands of brown hair remaining on his skull remained plastered in on his pate by a sheen of sweat. "You done good, though. You chased off his partner. And this one? Well . . ." Cooley poked the dead man with the square toe of his boot. "Those spots on his chest. You shot him four times?"

"It took a knife thrust and a sound pummeling to stop him."

"This is gonna make one fine story when I tell it back in town. If I draw it out long enough, the boys'll buy me a half dozen drinks."

England Dan snatched the bag with a tiny nugget and a few dozen gold flakes. He opened the drawstring and turned it to catch the sun's rays. "At least we're not entirely broke. We need to replace our food, though."

"You get anything from the hunt?" Cooley searched the giant and found a folding knife, which he tucked into his own pocket. "I hope so. I ain't gettin' anything off this one, and I worked up a powerful hunger."

"Two rabbits," the Brit said. He cleaned his knife on the giant's pant leg, replaced it in the sheath and went back downhill to find where he had dropped his kill.

He grunted and fought to keep his temper in control. The rabbits had been devoured during the fight. From the tracks, the fox had snaked him out of his dinner.

"It figures. Nothing else is going right," he said to himself. Then he hiked back to the dilapidated cabin, hoping to find something, anything, overlooked by the claim jumpers. There wasn't a scrap left. To work off his anger, he rehung the door. Dinner would have suited him better.

CHAPTER TWO

ᕦ

"Y ES, SIRREE, IT surely was a good thing those owl-hoots didn't steal Mabel." John Cooley bent over and patted the mule's neck. The animal turned a large brown eye to him and let out a derisive snort, then devoted full attention to the rugged trail toward Oasis.

"They'd still be trying to get her to move," England Dan Rutledge said. He tramped along, leading the mule.

"You sound mighty sour, Dan, my man. Is it because I have to ride after bangin' up my leg?" Cooley held it out and pointed to the torn pants leg. "If I hadn't dived for cover when the claim jumper started shooting into the mine, I'd be pushin' up daisies for certain sure."

"It's a scratch. Hardly bled."

"I can walk if you want to ride, Dan. I'd be in some

pain, but for my partner, I'd do that. Help me down, will you, so my leg doesn't collapse under me?" Cooley held out his hands for support. His partner ignored him. A small smile crept onto Cooley's lips. Dan thought he was so superior because he was some kind of royalty back in Britain. That kind of snootiness didn't cut it in America and certainly not in Arizona Territory. John Jacob Cooley was as good as any son of an earl or count or whatever Dan's pa was.

"Too bad we don't have Mabel staggering along under five hundred pounds of gold," England Dan said. He patted the pocket of his decrepit military jacket where he carried their actual stash. If there was an ounce there, it'd surprise Cooley. He'd toiled for close to three weeks to scrape that much out of the failing mine.

"If you wouldn't go off on your weeklong hunting expeditions, like you did back in Britain, riding to the hounds and all, there'd be more. You can't expect me to do all the work in the mine." Cooley spat. "Since I do all the work in the mine, why can't I rename it? What's Trafalgar Mine mean, anyway? Trafalgar? That's not a good American name, not like the Davy Crockett would be."

England Dan grumbled about starving without the game he shot, then lengthened his stride to get farther away.

"What? You're tryin' to run off? There's nothin' wrong with the name Davy Crockett. He was an ancestor of mine. A famous one, but you wouldn't know anything about our history, would you, you bein' a furriner and all?"

"You yammer on about him enough for me to know every instant of the man's life. Because he got killed is no reason to change the mine's name."

"Oh, but it's just dandy to call the mine after a fight between some Brits and Frenchies?"

"And the Spanish. Lord Nelson beat them all. It was a victory, not a massacre like what Davy Crockett got himself into."

"He died a hero." Cooley began to stew. His partner had turned testy after the claim jumpers stole their victuals, but there was no call to badmouth Davy. None at all.

"Finally," England Dan said, pointing. "There's town. I swear, it's farther every time we come here."

"I've worked up quite a thirst. Join me in a tot of John Barleycorn?" Cooley tried to pacify his partner's ire with some British talk.

"I've got to see if my money's come in. If it has, I'll stand you a shot of whiskey rather than that popskull you usually swill."

"You do that," Cooley said. "Life's hard as a remittance man, ain't it? All that waitin' for money to arrive wears a man down."

Rutledge glared at him. "If it wasn't for the money the earl sends me, we'd have lost the Trafalgar a long time back."

"Yeah, he pays you to stay away from England. My pa's dead. Ma, too. All I have is knowing I've got Davy as an ancestor. That's better than the few pennies your pa sends you every month."

"You don't say that when you're eating the food bought with my remittance." England Dan jerked at the mule's reins. Mabel balked and Cooley lost his seat. He tumbled to the ground. He stretched cramped legs, barely keeping his balance. His partner tossed him the reins. "You see to Mabel while I go to the telegraph office."

"Let me have our poke so I can see to that chore." Cooley waited until his partner pulled the leather bag with their meager gold from his pocket. He tossed it over. Cooley snared it deftly and tucked it into his own coat pocket.

Without another word, England Dan stalked off.

"You don't have to go away mad. I swear, I don't understand you, Dan. I don't." Cooley settled down when his partner ignored him. "Come on, Mabel. I'll see to gettin' you some grain. Maybe even an apple. You'd like that, wouldn't you? Just remember which of us takes care of you."

Cooley stabled the mule and wandered Oasis' main street. The town snuggled up close to the western slope of the Superstition Mountains and would have dried up and blown away if it hadn't been for the dozens of marginally profitable gold mines in the nearby hills. He wished the Trafalgar Mine was more than eking out an existence. Stories of fabulous strikes abounded, but he never knew personally any of the prospectors who found the mines or the miners who worked them.

Cooley stopped in the door of the Thirsty Camel Saloon and looked around. Only a handful of men leaned against the bar. Only three cowboys played poker at the single green-baize-covered table in the rear. It was a slow day in Oasis.

Pushing on into the smoky interior, he went to the bar and planted his elbows on the beer-stained wood. From the far end of the bar, the barkeep signaled he'd

be right there. Cooley waited impatiently. The bartender owned the Thirsty Camel and most of the town.
He claimed to have been in the French Foreign Legion
and had named many of the town's more important
businesses after things he had seen down in Algeria.
Cooley doubted Ray Hendrix had ever been out of
Arizona, must less joined the foreign legion, but it
made for a good story. Cooley appreciated a good tall
tale now and then. He wished his partner did. Dan was
such a moody stick in the mud.

"Didn't expect to see you so soon, John." The bartender reached under the bar and dropped a shot glass
in front of his new customer. With a smooth move, he
drained an ounce from a half-filled whiskey bottle. He
waited for his customer to pay up.

Cooley ran his fingers up and down the sides of the
glass, causing the amber fluid inside to ripple and reflect light. The sight and smell tormented him.

"My partner's on his way. He said he'd buy me the
first drink."

"England Dan's an honest bloke." Ray Hendrix
laughed. "If he said the drink's on him, he'll pay."

Cooley closed his hand around the glass and lifted
it. All the way to his mouth he studied the liquor, sa-
vored it and then downed it fast. The potent brew
burned the length of his swallow pipe to his belly. He
choked and slammed the glass down.

"What are you putting in that rotgut? It's got the
kick of a mule, and I don't mean my old mule, Mabel."

"I added a few more drops of nitric acid to give it
some body. Glad you appreciate it."

"Rusty nails for color, grain alcohol and now nitric
acid. You know how to distill the good stuff, Hendrix."

He waited to see if the barkeep offered a second drink on Rutledge's tab. When he didn't, Cooley spoke sotto voce to sound as if he shared a secret but loud enough so the men on either side of him at the bar overheard. "It's been a tough few days, what with killing a claim jumper and running off another one."

"How's that?" The patron to his right sidled over. "Claim jumpers, you say? What happened?"

"Well, I don't know if I ought to be spillin' any of this. Not until I go tell the marshal."

"Marshal Obregon left town last week. He got a better job over in Bisbee." Hendrix shook his head sadly. "Leaves Oasis without a lawman."

"I heard Obie hung up his gun and went to work in the copper mine," the customer said. He tapped his glass on the bar. Hendrix refilled without question. Cooley moved his glass over beside the other one. The barkeep hesitated, then filled it when the other man nodded curtly.

"You sound like you knew him real good," Cooley said. "How's that?" He squinted as he studied the man who'd bought him another drink. "I don't recollect seein' you in town before."

"I travel around a lot and got to know some of the law. Obie Obregon's a good man. A stickler for details, but a good man unless you cross him."

"Like you did?" Cooley read people well. This drifter rode close to crossing into the illegal, unless he missed a guess. He wasn't one to judge, especially if he had enough free whiskey to wet his whistle.

"Now, why'd you go and say a thing like that?" The man glanced at Ray Hendrix, but the barkeep had moved on to tend another customer. He was likely beyond earshot. "You have to excuse my lack of manners. I've been out in the desert so long, I'm not used to speaking with other human beings." He thrust out his hand. "The name's Yarrow."

"Pleased to meet you. I go by the moniker of John Cooley." He shook the man's hand and noticed how the trigger finger had a callus but the palm was a stranger to hard work. His own hand was more like rough horn than flesh from all his digging and toting and sorting through tons of ore.

"Come on over and let's set a spell." Yarrow pointed to a table at the empty side of the saloon where they could talk without being overheard. Cooley wanted to know what the man's pitch was.

Yarrow took a bottle with him and put it in the middle of the table. Cooley helped himself again. Already feeling a bit woozy from the extra-potent tarantula juice, he leaned back and tried to get a better idea of the man he drank with. His brain spun all around. It didn't matter. He was getting all the booze he could drink.

"You have the look of a man who knows this part of the territory real good." Yarrow scooted his chair around, poured Cooley another drink and waited for an answer.

"I do. My partner and I been diggin' in the ground in the Superstitions for nigh on three years now."

"Done good, too, less I miss a guess. You have the look of a successful gold miner."

"Well, now, I can't say we're the most successful, but we've done all right. Me and my partner work hard at our claim. We call it the Trafalgar Mine. That's named after 'bout the most famous battle ever fought. The

Brits whupped up on the French and Spanish, you know. We named it for successful fighting."

"I'm sure it's yielding gold galore for you, but it's not the best mine in the mountains." Yarrow looked around and lowered his voice. "You ever hear of the Irish Lord?"

Cooley stared at the man, focusing his eyes on him as best he could. "'Course I heard of it. They took tons of gold from that mine. More. But it's like that Lost Dutchman. It's . . . lost." His breathing came a tad faster and his mouth turned to cotton as he thought about the reported riches from that mine. Some folks had all the luck, finding a claim that rich.

"You do know the story. Nobody knows what happened to the owner. Fact is, he kept the location all secret-like, but I came across a gent who found the mine and drew a map to it." Yarrow poured another drink. "Now, I'm not inclined to go hunting for it. I got business over in Santa Fe that's more important."

"More important than tons of gold?" Cooley squinted. His head spun around, but he was thinking good enough to know there wasn't anything to take a man away from the Irish Lord Mine. That nobody knew its location made it all the more valuable.

"I got me a pretty señorita waiting for me. For too many years I've been on the trail, drifting hither and yon, letting the wind blow me to the next town. But Maria, now, Maria's worth settling down for. Her pa's a rich hacienda owner. Marrying into that family'd mean a lifetime of money. He's got more head of cattle than you can count. And she'd surely keep a man warm on those long, cold Santa Fe winter nights."

"But the Irish Lord. The gold . . ."

"It'd take me a long time to find it since I don't know these hills, not like you. Lookee here." Yarrow pulled a folded sheet from his vest pocket. He carefully opened it but put his hand over the center to keep Cooley from seeing the details. "I got this from an old prospector who was on his last legs. Now, I tried to save him. I did, but he was too far gone. I brung him into Oasis, but he was dead by the time I got him to the sawbones."

"He gave you this map?"

Yarrow nodded sadly. "He did that very thing. It was his way of rewarding my charity in trying to aid him."

"How do you know it's for real?"

"Well, John, let's just say the map wasn't all he gave me for my kindness."

"Gold?"

"There's gold and there's gold by the pound. That's what's in the Irish Lord."

"So you struck it rich?"

"I did, but I need more. You see, Maria's papa demands a big dowry. The gold I was given almost gets me there. A few dollars more and that'll impress him enough to let a gringo like me marry into a Spanish family that's had a land grant from the Spanish Crown for close to two hundred years."

"I see. So you're sellin' the map?" Cooley tried to look around the man's hand that was still pressed down. Yarrow lifted it just enough for him to see an X mark.

"It pains me. If I didn't have such a purty filly waiting for me, I'd spend a month or two hunting for the mine. It's reputed to be the richest ever found in these hills."

"I've heard tell that it's the richest in all of Arizona," Cooley said. "That's why I can't figger why the owner'd disappear. Nobody's heard of him or the mine in almost a year. Most folks say the mine played out, and he moved on."

"There's enough gold left in that mountainside to make a dozen men richer than Crocker or Standford. The railroad barons will seem like paupers compared to a clever man who—" Yarrow stopped in midsentence and folded the map. He started to tuck it into his pocket.

"Hold on there, partner. Why'd you all of a sudden change your mind about sellin' me the map?"

Yarrow studied Cooley closely, then shook his head. "You have a mine already." He hesitated. "Even if the Irish Lord is a richer one, you already have all the gold you need."

"All I need?" Cooley hiccupped. The room swam about from so much whiskey downed so fast. "Not all I want. I got money to pay for the map. If you're sellin', that is. You might not want to share your bounty."

"I told you my plans over in Santa Fe. I might keep the map and toss it into Maria's dowry, but her old man's already so rich, even this much gold might not mean anything to him."

"You said it's the biggest find in all Arizona. What man's not yearnin' for a piece of that?"

"When you own half of northern New Mexico Territory, gold doesn't mean as much. You know ranchers. To them land is the real coin of the realm. No, this isn't for you."

"I got gold. Lemme see the map." Cooley fumbled with the bag holding the pitiful few gold flecks and dropped it on the table.

Before he could pick it up, Yarrow snared it and had the drawstring open to inspect the contents. "This is a fair amount of gold. I like you, John. I do."

"Then you'll sell me the map?"

As if pulling teeth with pliers, Yarrow fingered the map, then pushed it across the table. Reluctance showed in his every move.

"Take it, old son. Take it and get so filthy rich, you'll be able to buy me out when you're done. The Irish Lord Mine's that rich a strike."

Greedily, Cooley pulled the map to get a better look at it.

"I can't tell from this where the mine's situated. There's a dotted line and an X. But where do I start the hunt?"

"Those mountain peaks are the key." Yarrow tapped a line of inverted Vs. "You know the Superstition Mountains. Finding them will be as easy as falling off a log." He pushed the almost empty whiskey bottle toward Cooley. "Drink up. There's a shot or two left."

Cooley had trouble pouring. He spilled more on the table than he got in the glass. Closing one eye helped. He started to ask Yarrow a question about the lost mine, then swung around. The drifter had vanished.

But that was all right. Cooley had the map and wasn't going to share it with Yarrow. The man had no idea how valuable this mine was. No idea.

Cooley held it up and stared at it through one blurred eye. He was going to be rich. Him. No need to share his good fortune with his partner. As he turned the map around to get a better perspective on it, he jumped a foot.

"Cooley! You infernal buffoon!"

England Dan Rutledge stormed over. Maybe he'd have to share after all.

CHAPTER THREE

ENGLAND DAN RUTLEDGE froze as he came out of the general store when a gunshot echoed down the street. He opened the box of cartridges and hastily loaded his Webley. It felt better knowing he had six rounds in the cylinder. Tucking away the partially empty box in the crate of supplies he carried, he looked up and down the main street. Other than the distant report, Oasis stood empty and unexcited.

The clerk came out and stood beside him. He carried a shotgun and looked more irritated than frightened.

"You heard it, too?" Dan thought he had turned a tad jumpy after everything that had happened up at his mine. Having the clerk with him made him feel better. He wasn't imagining danger.

"Ever since the marshal left town, we've had to keep order ourselves. I complained to the mayor that he ought to hire a new lawman, but he's a cheapskate and won't spend the money." The clerk snorted contemptuously. "If you ask me, he's putting the money in his own pocket."

"You need a vigilance committee." England Dan had heard how effective they were out in San Francisco.

"Too much trouble for most of these do-nothings. I'm thinking on following Marshal Obregon over to Bisbee. That's a lively town. Not like Oasis has become. My cousin says he sells more out of his bakery down the road from the copper mine in a week than I do with all my merchandise in a month."

"Maybe his bread's better quality."

The clerk glared at England Dan and went back into the store, his finger stroking the twin triggers as if he wanted to discharge both barrels. Nobody had a sense of humor anymore, though England Dan hardly blamed the clerk if random shots rang out all the time. He edged out and looked around. The jailhouse looked deserted. Without a marshal there was no reason to keep it open.

With a deft move, he hoisted the supply crate to his shoulder and went to the livery. The stable boy was nowhere to be seen. He dropped the crate and put his gear on top of it. Mabel had quite a nose and would pick through the food if he didn't do something to keep the mule out. He added some grain to the trough in her stall, then stepped out. His belly grumbled, but the cotton bale in his mouth made him decide to get a drink first. The telegraph office had handed over two months' worth of his remittance from his pa.

He felt a pang of guilt living off his family like this;

then it evaporated. The earl paid him to stay out of England for a reason. He was the second son and something of a disgrace. Going to royal court in London required a certain amount of pomp. That dignity vanished if a duke or prince inquired after him. Dan resented his older brother, Syngin, who would someday inherit the vast estate and the title, but Syngin carried special animus for his younger brother. He fit in perfectly with polite society and was shown off like a prize heifer. Introducing a sibling who had been drummed out of the army was simply not done.

"Solicitors," he grumbled as he walked to the Thirsty Camel Saloon. "If anyone deserved to be exiled . . ."

He forgot about his family when he entered the saloon and looked around. Only a few patrons used the bar to support themselves. The solitary drinker flopped across the table at the side of the room stirred and asked for another bottle. Before England Dan could move an inch, the barkeep called out to him, "You owe me three dollars."

"I haven't had a drop." England Dan looked around and stared at his partner, who was sitting at a table off in the corner alone, peering over at something and swaying slightly.

"He said you'd pay."

"He's put away that much? In less than an hour?"

"Him and his sidekick, yup, they did."

"I'm his partner and—" England Dan stopped talking and shook his head. Somebody had hit up Cooley for a drink or two and then left without paying his fair share. "What'd he look like? The one who was drinking with him?" He jerked his thumb in Cooley's direction.

"Never saw him in town before. He had enough trail dust on him from a week or longer in the saddle. Tallish fellow, not as big as you, though. He wore a denim shirt and had a yellow bandanna. Don't remember much more'n that. He wore his six-shooter slung low like a gunfighter, but he didn't cause any trouble, so I left him alone." The barkeep tapped his finger on the bar to get England Dan's attention. "Three dollars."

Dan found the money in his pocket and slammed it down on the bar. His remittance fee was decreasing faster than expected. Almost two months of money to keep them working at the Trafalgar had disappeared between buying the replacement supplies and Cooley's wild bender.

"You want a drink?"

England Dan ignored the question and marched across the floor. "Cooley! You infernal buffoon!"

His partner jumped and looked around wildly, relaxing only when he saw England Dan.

"You got some explaining to do, Cooley. Why'd you get so drunk so fast? And who was it you were drinking with?" England Dan started to ask another question, then clamped his mouth shut. A terrible thought came to him. "Where's the gold? Our take from the last month?"

"You won't b-b-believe my good luck. I b-b-bought a map to our future. We're gonna be filthy rich, old man. So rich we can set ourselves up in fancy houses with all the women we want." Cooley hiccupped and wiped his mouth.

"What have you done?"

His partner leaned over. The reek of booze was almost enough to make England Dan drunk. Cooley carefully put the map on the table. A quick swipe smoothed out the wrinkles.

"I b-b-bought us a mine worth a fortune. As you'd say, a b-b-bloody fortune."

"This?" England Dan spun the map around and stared at it. The penciled mountains and what might have been a river faded to almost invisibility. Only the groove cut in the paper showed what had been there originally. England Dan traced a trail of tiny dots to where an X rested beside what could have only represented a mine. "What is it?"

Cooley leaned over even farther and tried to whisper. His voice rang out loud and clear. "That's where we find the Irish Lord Mine."

The bartender and two drunks at the bar snickered. England Dan reached down and touched the butt of his Webley. That'd shut them up, but it wouldn't relieve the embarrassment he felt because his partner had fallen for such a transparent confidence scheme.

"Nobody knows where the Irish Lord is, and the owner's not been seen or heard from in a year."

"This is where it is," Cooley said positively. He tried to press his finger down on the map and missed.

"The mine played out, or the owner left for some other reason. Maybe he died from the plague, and anybody going into the mine'll suffer the same fate. More likely, claim jumpers killed him, like they tried to do to us. The hills are filthy with those vermin."

"Played out? The Irish Lord? But it's the most valuable mine in the whole danged territory. We know where it is. We follow the map and dig around and we're rich, Dan. Rich!"

The men at the bar outright laughed now. England Dan glared at them. They turned away and whispered among themselves, but he knew what they were saying. They knew he had a fool for a partner, too.

"He took all our gold? All of it?"

"It's worth it, Dan. We'll be rich when we find the mine."

"Where is it?"

"In the mountains. It's on the map! What's wrong with you?" Cooley's eyes went wide with surprise at his partner's inability.

"Where do we start? Where's the start of this trail? How do we find it? The Superstition Mountains cover a hundred fifty thousand acres. There's nothing on this so-called map showing where it is in all that rock."

"This. This here mark. That might be Weavers Needle."

"Or it might be nothing. That looks more like a smudge." England Dan held up the map and frowned. "It could be a drop of dried blood."

"He got it off a dead prospector."

"Don't insult me. I don't care what lies he fed you."

"Lies!" Cooley sagged back. "You mean, this isn't a map to the Irish Lord?"

England Dan knew it was a map to somewhere, but not a single feature on the map carried a legend. It made no sense that the owner of the Irish Lord had drawn a map to his own mine. The mine had been so rich, he had never recorded the deed for fear of claim jumpers, or so went the tale.

"What's the name of the man who took our gold?"

"I know that hoity-toity, upper-class Brit tone. You're not gonna start shootin', now, are you?"

"I'll get our gold back. Don't worry. I'll give him back this . . . map." England Dan slammed his fist down on the paper. He controlled his anger and folded the map and put it into his vest pocket. Rising, he towered over his partner. With a single grab, he caught Cooley's collar and pulled him to his feet.

His partner danced like a marionette for a moment, then got his balance. Even with most of a bottle of whiskey sloshing about in his gut, he walked on his own from the saloon.

"You gents come back real soon," the barkeep called. This brought a new round of laughter from the others.

England Dan ignored them. Outside he grabbed Cooley by the shoulders and turned him this way and that.

"You see the thieving varmint anywhere?"

He shook his partner so hard, Cooley's teeth chattered. This sobered him enough to brush England Dan's hand off.

"If you think he rooked me, tell the marshal. You're too mad. You'll fill him full of holes when he was only helpin' us out."

"He stole our gold by giving you a fake map. And the law left town. This isn't something I'd ever take to a marshal. They'd put him in jail and take the gold as evidence. It'd be a month before the circuit judge came by for a trial, if Oasis is even on a circuit anymore." He muttered under his breath. With his luck, the trial would be held in Prescott or some other place so far off, it would take weeks, if not months, to get a verdict.

The longer they strayed from the Trafalgar Mine, the less gold they mined.

"Let's go hunting for him." England Dan shoved Cooley down the street and made him look into every store they passed to search for the cowboy. He began to think they were on a snipe hunt. If too much time slipped by, finding the crook would be impossible. After going down one side of the street, they worked back up the other.

England Dan looked around when two shots rang out. Oasis was a real shooting gallery today. If he caught the confidence man who'd rooked his partner, there'd be even more gun smoke in the air.

England Dan pulled Cooley back to keep him from getting ridden down by a vaquero astride a big black stallion. The rider tipped his head down to give them the once-over. The huge sombrero he wore cast shadows on his face. All England Dan saw was a huge mustache with dancing tips. Then the vaquero rode on, studying everyone along the street, sizing them up.

England Dan heaved a sigh. With the run of luck he was having, there wouldn't be thieves come to steal their supplies but real claim jumpers. He had no desire to shoot it out with a half-dozen desperadoes digging in his blue dirt and stealing his pathetic gold.

"I don't know where he'd go," Cooley said. "To the bank? Or the mercantile?"

"To the livery stable to get his horse and get out of town," England Dan said. He shoved Cooley in that direction. There had been a couple horses in stalls next to Mabel. Since the stranger was passing through town, one of them had to have been his.

He held his stride down to one that Cooley could

match. His partner chattered incessantly, saying how England Dan didn't know what an opportunity he was passing up.

"He'll take the map back and return our gold. If you think it'll make you rich, you ride out with him."

"I don't want a new partner. Dan, this is for *us*."

England Dan knew a shortcut to the stables and veered off the main street down a debris-littered alley. Vermin paid him no attention as he passed. He posed no danger, but the rats squeaked and ran for their lives when a large black cat pounced from behind a rain barrel. England Dan vowed to emulate the cat. It had caught a victim by the neck. Powerful jaws closed and ended the rat's miserable life. He'd do the same to the man who had swindled his partner.

He stormed on and left the alley before he realized Cooley wasn't with him any longer. Impatiently gesturing, he called out, "Get a move on. He'll leave town, and we'll never find him."

"Dan." Cooley's voice cracked with strain. "He ain't gonna be leavin' town anytime soon. Not ridin' his horse."

"What are you going on about?" He spun and saw his partner standing beside a pile of garbage where the cat had caught its meal. Cooley pointed with a shaky hand.

England Dan retraced his steps and saw a booted foot sticking out from under the pile. He kicked away some of the debris.

"Is that him?" England Dan asked, but he knew the answer. The barkeep said the sharper had worn a denim shirt and a yellow bandanna. Like the one the dead man lying in front of him had tied around his neck.

"I didn't do it, Dan. I didn't!"

A quick search of the dead man's pockets showed he had been robbed. The bag with their gold was nowhere to be found. England Dan had heard two shots as he left the saloon. The corpse had a pair of bullet holes in his chest.

Someone had beaten him to the draw by a few minutes. And someone had his gold.

CHAPTER FOUR

"WHAT A LOUSY place to die." Lars Jensen hooked his knee around the saddle horn as he looked down Oasis' main street. A quick move pulled off his floppy-brimmed black felt hat and beat it against his thigh. A week's worth of trail dust rose and turned to dancing diamonds in the sunlight. Swiping off the sweat from his forehead with his dirty sleeve didn't make him feel any better.

Finding the son of a bitch who had stolen the map would.

Settling his hat again to keep the late-day sun out of his eyes, he dropped to the ground. His horse let out a relieved whinny. They had been on the trail since sunup, and resting for even a few minutes had been out of the question. If he didn't retrieve the map stolen from Rusty Rivera, there'd be a much longer nap ahead. A permanent one looking at the wrong side of the sod. Poke wasn't the kind to be charitable, even to his kid brother. Luckily there was some time to find what had happened to the map before Lars faced him.

Yuma Penitentiary was all the way across the state, and Poke wasn't due to be released for another week. But after spending close to six months in that cesspit, he'd want a bath and a shave, some whiskey and a woman.

And the map his partner on the cavalry-payroll robbery had made so he could find where the loot had been hidden.

Jensen walked slowly down the middle of the street, taking in every detail. A cruel smile curled his lip when he saw how the townsfolk took one look at him and ducked inside. He knew he cut an imposing figure. He was half a head taller than most men and fifty pounds heavier, even the ones who worked the mines. His shock of blond hair was a perfect gold and set off eyes bluer than the Arizona sky. But his looks appealed to the ladies. It was the way he carried his six-gun slung low and tied down at his right hip that sent the men scurrying away like cockroaches. He had the look of a man who was used to shooting down anyone in his way. Truth was, he had lost track of how many men he'd gunned down, and that didn't keep him from getting a good night's sleep.

He looped his horse's reins around a large iron ring at the corner of the saloon and went in. If the lowlife thief he hunted was anywhere, this was the place. He never slowed as he entered. The light from behind turned him into a shadow. Jensen let the few customers in the bar study his silhouette and realize trouble had marched in. When he saw the bartender move to where he likely kept a pistol hidden under the bar, he strutted over and leaned down. He needed information, not gunplay. Not right now.

"Beer. I got a desert thirst that needs quenching."

"Well, mister, there's plenty of desert around here. You come in from Bisbee?" The man wiped his hands on a towel, made sure the mug was clean enough and then pulled the beer. It hissed and foamed. Jensen had never seen anything that looked better, not even that whore over in Mesilla who had let him slurp up tequila poured into her belly button.

"You always run off at the mouth like that?" Jensen growled just enough to make the barkeep blanch. He enjoyed watching the effect he had on others. It came in handy. Having to shoot a man wasn't as much fun as intimidating him. Usually.

"No, sir, I . . . sorry to have offended you."

Jensen lifted the mug and drained it. He let out a huge belch and dropped the empty mug back to the bar with a loud clack. He had properly trained this dog of a bartender. The man refilled the mug without asking if his customer wanted another. Jensen poured this straight down his gullet, too, then gestured that he didn't want another.

"You want whiskey instead? We got—" The barkeep turned even paler when the polar-cold eyes fixed on him. "Sorry. No more talking. It's my nature, part of the job. I—"

Jensen reached across the bar and grabbed him by the front of his canvas apron. Using his impressive strength, he lifted the man onto the tips of his toes and shook him just a little to keep his attention. Sometimes fright made their minds wander.

"I'm looking for a cowboy. He'd be new to town, within the last day or so."

"What do you want with him?" The barkeep immediately regretted the question. Jensen twisted his fist and pressed up under the other man's chin. Choking, he turned red.

Jensen judged what the man could tolerate, then loosened his grip. "We got business. Leave it at that."

"There was one fellow. He spent a while talking with a miner. John Cooley. They was over there at that table." A shaking hand pointed. Jensen didn't bother looking. The other customers who'd been at the end of the bar had crept out the back way. Other than the barkeep, there wasn't anyone else in the large, empty saloon.

"This Cooley fellow. Was he real friendly with the newcomer?"

"I don't think they knew one another, but they got to be friendly. Shared a bottle. Cooley got drunk, and his partner dragged him out. England Dan was real mad."

"Why's that?"

"The other fellow stuck Cooley with the tab. I made England Dan pay for it all. Him and Cooley they got a mine—"

"I don't care about them. The fellow drinking on Cooley's dime, did he wear a yellow bandanna?"

"N-now that you mention it, he did. He left. Close to ten minutes back." The barkeep shifted his pointing finger to the front door.

Jensen released his grip and turned to leave.

"Wait, mister. You owe me for two beers!"

Jensen glared back over his shoulder, then smiled. Men had soiled themselves when he gave them that

look. The barkeep was made of sterner stuff. He only
turned whiter than a bleached muslin sheet.

"Get Cooley's partner to pay for it."

He stepped outside and considered where his quarry
would have gone after leaving the saloon. Crossing the
street, he went into the general store. His instincts were
good. The yellow bandanna had bought some chaw using a fleck of gold. Jensen had no interest in looking at
the speck of gold, but he did because the clerk insisted
he look at it. It humored him to know that was supposed to keep him from shooting up the store—and the
clerk.

It worked good enough. He left the clerk with a
whole hide and a store without holes in the ceiling.

When he stepped back into the bright sun, he turned
toward the livery stable. This was the only other place
where he'd likely find the map-stealing no-account.
Barely had he taken a dozen steps than the back of his
neck began to tingle. He stopped and looked around.

"Got you!" Jensen saw a flash of yellow and a man
running down the alley. He lit out after him. The man
ran fast. Jensen sprinted out of need. He had to retrieve the map. If he was this close to success, he wasn't
going to fail.

He closed the distance between them and reached
out his long arm. He gave the fleeing man a hard shove
that caused him to lose his balance. Tumbling facedown, the man skidded a few feet in the dirt and garbage. As he came to a halt, he reached for his gun.
Jensen stepped over him and stomped down hard. His
boot broke bones in the other man's gun hand. He
howled with pain.

"What are you doing! Take my money. I won't put

up a fight!" the man whined pitifully, making tiny mewling noises as he clutched his busted wrist.

Jensen rolled him over and plucked the six-shooter from his holster. He tucked it into his own gun belt and turned his freezing glare on the man.

"Here. Take it. It's all I got." With his left hand, the man fumbled out a small pouch. He dropped a few coins and a pair of greenbacks in his haste to fork over his worldly riches.

"I want the map." Jensen stuffed the money and gold sack into his coat pocket. "You stole it off Rivera. I caught sight of you looting his body, but you got away from me."

"I . . . Was he your partner?"

"I hardly knew him, but he was supposed to give me the map. Where is it?"

"I saw you searching him. I thought you were just a scavenger. A vulture like me."

"Robbing dead men's nothing to brag on, but we all do it. Give me the map."

"I don't have it. Honest!"

"The *map*!" Jensen drew his six-gun and pointed it at the other man's face. That usually lubricated a tongue and got the truth flooding out.

"He took it. I . . . I sold it to him."

"Him? Cooley?" The name stuck in his head from what the barkeep had told him.

"I don't know his name. He was just another drunk. That's where I got the gold. I . . . I spent some of it on tobacco. Got me some chew. You want that? Take it!"

He was just wasting his time now. Without another word, Lars Jensen pulled the trigger and sent a bullet drilling into the man's chest. A second slug, just an inch higher, went through his thieving heart. He had learned all he could and still didn't have the map. Poke wasn't going to like that.

He went to the mouth of the alley, then ducked back as a man rode past. Jensen lifted his six-gun and started to pull the trigger but held his fire. The rider bent forward, spoiling the shot.

By the time the rider passed, his chance at an easy kill gone, Jensen knew better than to stick around. That federal deputy marshal had been on his trail for the better part of a week. The more he tried to lose him, the closer the lawman got. He stuck to him like a dab of tar.

Jensen ran back down the alley past the cowboy he had killed. He turned the corner and went for the livery.

His horse shied when he approached. It needed watering and grain, but that had to wait. Right now he needed to concentrate on finding some galoot named Cooley.

Cooley had to have the map. But he wouldn't keep it for long. Lars Jensen would see to that because his brother, Poke, wanted it. And he wanted it bad. If there was anything Lars had learned over his life, it was never deny Poke Jensen anything he wanted.

Especially if it was a map to a thousand dollars' worth of stolen cavalry payroll.

CHAPTER FIVE

W E'VE GOT TO tell someone. We can't leave a body
to rot, not in the middle of town." England Dan
Rutledge turned over and over all the things to do.
None of the options satisfied him. The man who had
rooked his partner had been robbed, killing along with
him any chance of getting their gold back.

"There's no law in Oasis," Cooley said. He backed
away uneasily. "Leave him be. This isn't any of our
concern."

"If there's no marshal, maybe there's someone at
the jailhouse who can tell us what to do."

"You got a dollar you can loan me, Dan?"

England Dan scowled. He fished around in his
pocket and pulled out a crumpled greenback. It was
worth buying off his foolish partner if it kept him out
of more trouble. Cooley bobbed his head up and down,
took the proffered greenback and left without a word.

England Dan stared at the corpse. It hadn't moved.
Flies buzzed around and bugs pushed past the flaccid
lips. His partner was wrong. He had to do something,
even if it wasn't his business.

By the time he got to the main street, Cooley had
vanished. He considered asking the barkeep for help.
The body was in the alley between the Thirsty Camel
and the empty store. He shook his head as he realized
Ray Hendrix had no reason to help. The body wasn't
inside his establishment, and he would loudly dispute
any responsibility beyond his swinging doors. With a
deep growl, Dan set off for the marshal's office. There
might be somebody there who could do more than direct him to the undertaker.

He stopped and stared when he found the jailhouse.
It was an adobe building with thick walls and vigas poking out in front along the edge of the flat roof. There had
been an attempt to put up an awning to shade the entrance, but the lack of maintenance had long since
caused the few yards of canvas to flap loose and turn
into ragged streamers. The door stood open, but what
made him hesitate was the black stallion hitched to the
rail beside the jail.

Approaching cautiously, he peered into the dim interior. The vaquero who had almost run down Cooley
looked up from the stained desk. Wanted posters were
spread in front of him like cards on a faro table. He
pushed up the huge sombrero and glared.

"What do you want?"

"You the new town marshal?"

England Dan moved his hand closer to the butt of
the Webley slung at his side. The vaquero looked more
like a bandido than a lawman.

"I'm just passing through." He pointed to the posters. "I keep up on who's on the run."

"You a bounty hunter?"

"You ask a powerful lot of questions. I'm no bounty hunter." He pulled back his embroidered short jacket to show a badge fastened to his shirt.

In the light leaking in from behind him, England Dan made out the words. "You're a federal deputy marshal."

"So you're able to read. Good for you." He let his jacket slip back into place. "That didn't answer my question. What do you want? I'm not going to throw out any drunk or break up a fight."

"It's too late for that. I found a man in an alley with a couple bullet holes in his chest. He'd been robbed."

"How do you know that?"

The question put England Dan on guard. Saying anything about the gold or the map might land him in jail instead of whoever had shot down the swindler. "His gun wasn't in his holster. One pocket had been turned inside out."

"That pocket didn't get that way because you searched the body, now, did it? You found the body and thought to steal anything because the dead man wasn't going to spend that silver dollar or use that six-shooter."

The deputy's mustache twitched as he talked. England Dan worried that this was a tell, and the lawman was getting ready to shoot him down on suspicion of murder.

"Nothing of the sort. I'm just a citizen who thought to do his duty. Sorry to have bothered you." England Dan backed away. The deputy had done nothing to hint that he was a back shooter, but then anybody could pin on a badge. There wasn't any reason he had to believe the vaquero just because he said he was a federal lawman.

"Hold your horses." The man heaved to his feet, glanced at the wanted posters, then hitched up his gun belt as he came around the desk. "Show me the body. It's out of my jurisdiction, but it just might be the owl-hoot I've tracked all the way from Mesilla."

They walked side by side, both silent. England Dan kept his distance because of the broad-rimmed sombrero taking up so much space around the deputy.

The crunch of their boots on the dried street finally wore on England Dan. He asked, "What's the man wanted for? The one you're hunting?"

"I don't have time to list every crime he's committed. Him and his brother are a regular tornado blowing across the territory. Lars Jensen shot a man in the back over in Mesilla. Then he held up a stage and stole a bag full of US mail off a Butterfield stage. That's what got my boss interested in him. Nobody steals mail and gets away with it."

"Lars Jensen, you say?"

"You know him?"

"Can't say that I do, but the name's sort of familiar."

"His brother's Poke Jensen. He got locked up in Yuma six months back for some crime or other. I never paid any attention. It's Lars Jensen I want."

"You are a single-minded man, from the sound of it."

The deputy stopped and stared at England Dan. He glared for a moment, then grinned and thrust out his hand. "Alberto Gonzales."

"Dan Rutledge." He held his tongue. Telling Deputy Gonzales about the bogus map and John Cooley's part in it only muddied the water. "I'm a miner up in the hills above town."

"You have the look of a Brit cavalry officer." He took in the shoulders of the jacket where the epaulets had been ripped off. The gold frogs on the front hung torn, and holes throughout the jacket sorely needed patching.

"I'm a long ride away from that part of my life. Digging gold from the ground is what I do now."

Alberto Gonzales nodded and looked around. "Where's the body? If it's not him, I want to get this over with so I can get back on Jensen's trail."

England Dan went down the alley and stood a few feet away from the dead body. Gonzales came up and hardly glanced at the body.

"That's not Jensen." He spun and stalked off.

"Wait! What're you going to do about him?"

"You take care of it. You found him."

"But, Deputy Gonzales, I don't know him. I never laid eyes on him before I found him."

"It's not my job." Alberto Gonzales turned the corner and headed back toward the jailhouse.

England Dan stared at the dead man and shook his head. He had been a trained officer in the British army, even if he had been run out. Dealing with the unexpected had been a requirement when he served in India. But then there had always been someone higher in the chain of command or a local official to deal with dicey matters. Simply walking away from the dead man was an obvious solution to his problem. Let someone else find the body and solve the problem.

He walked straight across the street, found a cross

street and went down it to the edge of town. Hiram O'Dell was the town undertaker. England Dan had had few dealings with the man, but those that he'd had were never pleasant. The undertaker's sour disposition was understandable since most of his customers ended up in the potter's field.

England Dan went into the office and almost backed out. The heavy incense O'Dell burned to cover the stench of death in the parlor made him wrinkle his nose and choke.

"You finally kill that good-for-nothing partner of yours?" Hiram O'Dell pushed apart heavy curtains and left the viewing room.

If England Dan ever killed Cooley, the body'd never be found. Burying him in Oasis was as alien an idea as paying for the planting.

"There's a body in the alley outside the Thirsty Camel. You'll have to get paid from the city since the man didn't have a dime on him."

"I'm sure you checked." O'Dell looked down his nose at the man who had brought such bad news.

"The federal deputy marshal will back me up on that."

"What marshal?"

"His name's Alberto Gonzales, and he wears a huge sombrero. He's on the trail of an outlaw from over in Mesilla."

"So he's not our new marshal." O'Dell sneered. "Obregon was hardly up to the task. There's no reason to think a deputy from over in New Mexico Territory would do better."

"Tell the mayor to pay you. That's what the money from all those fines is used for."

O'Dell said something England Dan didn't hear. He

bade the undertaker a good day since that was about the worst insult he could deliver without getting profane, then left. The late-day hot sun burned away. After all that had happened, it was time to leave Oasis and get back to the mine. The Trafalgar had another six months' gold in it. All that he needed to do was put his back into it and keep his malingering partner working.

As he went looking for Cooley, he worried that his partner would demand possession of the map supposedly showing the location of the Irish Lord Mine. This was the sort of myth Cooley bought into easily. While he didn't doubt such a mine existed—or had at some time—he had never heard of anyone who knew the owner or had ever seen so much as an ounce of gold from the mine. He knew the legends of El Dorado. England had its own myth in the quest for the Holy Grail, and the Irish talked about wee folks and pots of gold at the ends of rainbows. That was more what Cooley wanted. To hunt and find that pot of gold.

"Irish Lord Mine," England Dan scoffed. "The Leprechaun's Mine's more like it."

He prowled the streets and circled back to the Thirsty Camel a couple times, thinking his partner had wanted the dollar for more liquor. The barkeep denied having seen Cooley again, and England Dan believed him. There was no love lost between him and most of the Oasis residents, but Ray Hendrix was usually polite and not surly like O'Dell or dismissive like the federal deputy.

England Dan stepped out from the saloon and looked around. The only place Cooley could have gone other than the Thirsty Camel, where he'd need money, was on the edge of town opposite the undertaker's parlor. England Dan started walking, taking time to rest in the shade along the way. His feet ached, and his entire body felt like a giant raw nerve from the afternoon heat. More than that, he dreaded the chore ahead of him. Getting his partner out of the cathouse would take some diplomacy on his part. Madam Morgan wasn't anyone he wanted to cross. She was a formidable woman in her own right, and she hired bouncers who could pick him up and tear him in half without breaking a sweat. At this time of day, the bouncers weren't likely on duty. That gave him a small hope of convincing Cooley to leave without their interference. Madam Morgan was protective of her customers and the money they spent in her establishment.

The two-story brothel stood away from several other buildings, all boardinghouses. England Dan wondered what the owners of those more legitimate hostels thought of the goings-on next door. Madam Morgan ran a bawdy house, after all, serving liquor to her customers and making little attempt to rein in her soiled doves' antics. If nothing else, he supposed, it provided a subject for endless discussion at the dinner tables of the boardinghouses nearby.

The building was well tended. The railing carried a fresh coat of whitewash, and the chairs set at the far end of the porch looked comfortable. He almost went to see just how comfortable. After all that had happened, he was bone-tired, but he had lingered on his way to the brothel. If he sat down here, Madam Morgan likely would charge him for the pleasure.

"You're not who I expected." The buxom woman stood in the doorway, peering myopically at him with fists resting on ample hips. Madam Morgan wasn't a bad-looking woman considering her size, but stories about her using a straight razor on lovers who disappointed her abounded. England Dan looked past her. Two bouncers moved around just behind her. Both of them carried sawed-off shotguns.

"I'm looking for my partner." He made a point of looking past Madam Morgan. "What's going on?"

"I thought you were Hiram." She moved close to study his face. "Don't worry your head none about it. Everything's as fine as frog's fur now."

"Hiram O'Dell?"

"Don't go getting too curious. While you're waiting for Cooley to finish up, you want to see what some others of my girls have to offer? I have a couple new ones since the last time you were in. One of them might be able to fake a Brit accent. Isn't that what you want, you British rake?"

"I want for me and my partner to clear out of town."

"After everything that's gone on today, I understand. It's getting so a lady can't run a peaceable establishment where a gent can relax and enjoy himself." Madam Morgan spoke more to herself than to England Dan. She looked up and past him. She waved and called, "Around to the side, Hiram."

The undertaker drove a black-painted wagon. He gave England Dan a sour look, then yeehawed and snapped the reins to get his team pulling around the building, hidden from sight. Whatever had happened in the brothel had left behind a dead body. That wasn't so unusual since the Cyprians were the most likely in any town to commit suicide, but England Dan felt something more had gone on. The two armed bouncers showed that. If a girl had killed herself, they'd move the body out quietly without drawing attention to it. He almost asked Madam Morgan if she wouldn't have buried the body out back and never called for the undertaker.

"I want to get Cooley. Don't make me start up a ruckus."

"You always were a pain in the butt, Dan, but I have a soft spot for you and that ornery partner of yours." Emotions washed over her. Her bosoms heaved up and down as she came to a conclusion. "Go on up. It's on your head if you disturb him in flagrant delgado."

"In flagrante delicto," he corrected automatically.

"You Brits, you know everything," Madam Morgan said sarcastically. She signaled her bouncers to let him pass. "They're up in room five."

England Dan touched the brim of his bowler by way of thanks and pushed past her, though not before enduring a quick pinch to his butt. He carefully watched the two men with the shotguns to be sure they'd gotten the word from their boss. They reluctantly let him go up the steep stairs unhindered.

He stopped at the head of the stairs while Hiram O'Dell wrested a body from the room opposite Cooley's. The naked man had been shot repeatedly. A cold shiver ran up England Dan's spine in response to the wounds. They seemed so callous. He shook it off and went to room five when the undertaker dragged the man's body toward the back stairway.

"It's me, Dan. Open up. We've got to get out of town. Come on, John. Finish up and get your drawers on."

He heard a mumbled conversation. It didn't take a

genius who knew Latin to guess what was being said, both by his partner and his partner's temporary bed partner.

The door was flung open. John Cooley clutched his shirt to his chest and tried to get into his trousers. He stumbled and fell back into the arms of a half-naked woman. Given other circumstances, England Dan would have appreciated the sight more. She was blonde and, while not beautiful, definitely cute with a button nose and pouty lips and bright green eyes. Her other attributes were equally on display, and she made no effort to cover them. A bold smile and a hip cocked to one side with her hand resting on it made her appeal about complete.

"You owe me a dollar, John."

"Here, Mandy, here, my darlin'." Somehow Cooley found the greenback dollar and handed it to the woman. She fielded it easily. The way she slipped it between her fingers like a gambler showing off his dexterity with a poker chip impressed England Dan. Cooley had gotten his money's worth with this one.

He turned and almost fell over O'Dell as the undertaker dragged another body along the hallway.

England Dan looked at the dead woman. His throat constricted, and his stomach knotted. He looked back into the room at Mandy, then at the dead woman.

That was when Mandy let out a soul-curdling shriek and pushed past Cooley to drop to her knees beside the lifeless woman.

"Mindy! What happened?"

England Dan stared. Mirror images: blonde hair even done in a similar fashion, finely boned cheeks and a swanlike neck. If the prone woman had opened her eyes, he didn't doubt they would be emerald green, too. Blood colored the thin muslin shift but no longer spread in a sanguine bloom. Her vitality was gone, snuffed out by a bullet. He forced himself to look at the woman crying bitter tears. There wasn't a whit of difference between the two women, other than the one who'd been with Cooley was alive while the other lay unmoving and cold to the touch.

CHAPTER SIX

L ARS JENSEN VAULTED into the saddle and turned
his horse's face to get out of Oasis. Before he had
gone a hundred yards, he slowed and let the horse
come to a halt. He had to feed and water the horse or
it would die under him. He dared not let that happen.
Without the map, Poke would shoot him. And without
the horse, the deputy marshal would run him to ground
before sundown.

He urged the horse in the direction of the feed mercantile. Around behind the store, he let the horse
drink from a rain barrel. A fifty-pound sack of feed sat
out where he could run a knife through the burlap.
The grain spilled out. The horse perked up and abandoned the water in favor of eating the grain. Jensen put
his hand down flat on the dock behind the feed store,
spread his fingers and began moving the sharp tip between fingers, slowly at first and then with greater

speed. The click-click-click drew the attention of the store owner.

"What are you doing? That's not your feed. I set it aside special for Mr. Contreras. You owe me ten dollars!"

Jensen never slowed as he stuck the knife deeper and deeper into the wood with every stroke. When the owner came toward him, he flipped the knife around and drove it deep into the man's thigh.

The owner let out a strangled cry of pain. "You stabbed me!"

"I'll kill you if you don't leave me alone. I might kill you even if you do because you annoy me." Jensen wiped the blood from the blade, using the other man's own pants leg. When the owner began limping away, Jensen lifted the knife and brought it down hard. The man spread his legs wide to keep from being stuck again.

"You just keep on feeding your horse, mister. You can have all the grain you want." Clutching his bleeding leg, he dragged himself back to the doorway. Using the jamb, he pulled himself partially erect. Leg dragging, he fell through the door into his store. He slammed the door behind him.

Jensen chuckled when he heard a locking bar drop into place. That took care of another problem. His horse was fed and watered now. It had rested for a spell, so it was ready to hit the trail, only he couldn't do that. Not yet.

Without the map he was a dead man. Poke wasn't the kind to forgive and forget, not with a thousand dollars at stake. It was his brother's fault all this had happened, but explaining that to him wouldn't work too good. Poke had a fierce temper. After being locked up in Yuma for six months for another crime, he'd want to claim what was his from the payroll robbery that had been a complete disaster.

The best Jensen could tell, Poke's partner in the robbery had been Barton Beeman. Poke had decoyed the cavalry patrol away, and Beeman had hidden the gold. Somewhere along the way, he'd been all shot up and was dying, so he drew the map for Poke. Rusty Rivera had come along and agreed to deliver the map. Whatever had happened to Rivera left him dead in the desert, the cowboy with the yellow bandanna taking the map and everything else before Jensen reached Rivera.

He had almost caught up with the cowboy while he had the map. But he had passed it along to somebody named Cooley. That was all he knew.

"Cooley. How many of them can there be in a nothing town like Oasis?"

He looked over his shoulder at the barred door. Chances were good the grain store owner knew this Cooley. Or he knew someone who could get Lars aimed in the right direction. Going around to the front of the store wasn't high on the list of smart things to do, not with Deputy Gonzales prowling around.

Having the lawman on his trail was a stroke of bad luck. What he had done to get such a bird dog after him hardly mattered. Any of a half dozen crimes might have set Alberto Gonzales on the trail. Killing the lawman from ambush seemed the best way of eliminating the problem. But that would be like kicking a wasp nest. A half-dozen federal marshals would be set on his tail for such a crime, but so what? Dodging a dozen

wasn't that much harder than hiding from one dedicated marshal like Alberto Gonzales.

Lars Jensen checked his six-gun and made sure all
six chambers were loaded. He usually rode with the
hammer resting on an empty. The time had come to
have the extra round. His eyebrows rose when he saw
that there were three empties. He hadn't reloaded after gunning down the cowboy with the flashy bandanna. Remedying this took a few seconds. The weight
at his hip now felt good, right, ready to throw down on
a federal deputy or . . .

"Cooley. That's the name of the galoot who has
the map."

Jensen gathered up some spilled grain and wrapped
it in the burlap. He slung this over his horse's rump for
feed later. Leading the horse back to the main street,
he made a beeline for the Thirsty Camel. As much as
he wanted another drink, he had a job to do, a man to
find, and time was running away from him like a
scalded dog. He whipped the reins around a hitching
rail and went inside.

The barkeep rushed for the far end of the bar and
grabbed underneath. The two patrons bellied up to the
bar paid no attention.

"I'm not here to drink," Jensen called. "Has Cooley
been back?"

"You clear out. Go on. Shoo!" Ray Hendrix laid his
six-gun on the bar and tried to look tough.

Jensen almost threw down and shot him just for prac-
tice. The memory of Alberto Gonzales riding along,
alert and ready to find himself a fugitive from the law,
stayed his hand. He left without a word. Chances were
good the barkeep wouldn't tell the deputy about such an

insignificant showdown. He might brag about chasing off a gunman, but who'd believe him?

If Cooley hadn't come back to the Thirsty Camel to dip his beak once more, he was likely to find other pursuits. Jensen mounted and rode to the hotel. From its deserted appearance, Cooley wasn't here to find feminine companionship. Jensen sat astride his horse, thinking on the subject, when a man came out of the hotel.

"You. Yes, you," Jensen said when the man recoiled at being called out. "I'm looking for a young lady for ... well ... you know." He let the man fill in the requirements. "Where might I find my choice of such ladies?"

"You want Madam Morgan's. A two-story house on the other side of town."

"Sounds like the very place I want to be." Jensen wheeled his horse around and trotted off, wondering if the man had lied just to send his annoying interrogator on his way.

When Jensen laid eyes on the house, he knew he'd been steered right. A half-naked woman in an upstairs window waved to him. He waved back and rode around to the side of the brothel. As he dismounted, a man came from the door, working to button his pants.

Jensen hardly looked at the man. His eyes fixed on the partially clad blonde leaning indolently in the doorway. She smiled at Jensen, licked her lips slowly and then blew him a kiss.

"My luck's improving," Jensen said as the woman disappeared back into the brothel.

"You'll have to wait. She's got a regular waiting in the parlor." The exiting customer saw he'd buttoned his fly crooked and tried again. He never looked up at Jensen as he struggled with cloth and fastener.

"Who might that be?" Jensen sucked in his breath.

"Some miner named Cooley. Mandy and him'd get hitched if he ever struck it rich. She just takes his money a dollar a throw."

"Sounds as if you are benefitting from his lack of gold. Me, too."

"She's a favorite, but there's something even better. There's a—"

Jensen pushed past the man to go in the side door. Listening to some local's exploits bored him, especially when the lovely woman was his way of finding the man who had the map. If she met up with Cooley, that would make it easy to identify the miner. Jensen wasn't likely to forget the charmer. If he'd had time, he'd sample her charms and make her forget the yokels.

"Whoa there, big boy." An obese woman blocked his way into the parlor. "You got to check in first with me. I'm Madam Morgan, and I run this fine establishment." She laid a meaty hand in the middle of his chest. "Oh, you got muscles, don't you? You're gonna be real popular with the girls, but you deal with me before making a selection."

He peered past this meaty roadblock and saw the blonde stroking a man's stubbled cheek over in the parlor. She whispered something that caused the man to grin lewdly. The customer tried to grab one of the woman's breasts, but she danced away and shook her finger at him. This admonishment gave Jensen a good look at Cooley. Then the whore laughed and let the miner circle her waist with his arm and lead her off. Jensen heard the click of boots on stairs going up. A slamming door told they'd reached their location in record time.

"What room're they in?"

"Now, you have to wait your turn," Madam Morgan said. "They're our most popular ladies, and for good reason. Mindy, there is—"

He pushed hard and sent Madam Morgan reeling. She caught herself against the wall. Her smile vanished. Her otherwise handsome face turned downright ugly. She pulled out a straight razor and swished it back and forth in front of her. From the way she held it, this wasn't the first time she'd used the vicious weapon.

"You don't go pushin' me like that. Get out!" She came forward, brandishing the razor.

Lars Jensen sized her up, then swung hard. She tried to cut his left arm but only sliced away a patch of his coat. His fist struck her on the side of the head and knocked her back again. Dazed, she shook her head to clear it. Jensen was impressed. He had knocked out men with a softer punch than that. He ran his fingers over the hole she'd cut in his sleeve. If he hadn't been so close to retrieving the map, he'd have shown her the error of her attack.

He swung around and started up the stairs to find Cooley. He didn't expect her to come after him, and she didn't.

"Clarence, fetch Gus and Brutus!" Madam Morgan's voice came out ragged. She was still stunned from the punch.

From some hidden nook, a young boy darted out. He stared wide-eyed at Jensen, then bolted out the front door. Jensen had no idea where Madam Morgan had sent the boy, but if it was to fetch help, the effort would be wasted. He took the steps up two at a time. A twist opened the door on his left. An empty bed showed he had the wrong room. Pivoting, he opened the first door on his right.

It took him a second to figure out the tangle of arms and legs. The whore had dark hair.

"Hey, you, get out!" The man in the bed twisted around. "I paid for another ten minutes."

Jensen slammed the door and went to the next room. He threw open the door. The briefest glimpse told him he had the right place. The blonde was naked to the waist now, discarding even the immodest blouse she had worn downstairs. She looked at him with shocked eyes so green they looked like sparkling gemstones. The man was caught with his pants down around his ankles. He hadn't shucked them off yet, or maybe he never intended to go that far.

"Where is it?" Jensen stepped into the room. He shoved the soiled dove aside when she came to shoo him out of the room. A huge hand closed on the man's long johns and twisted them into a knot. Lifting, Jensen heaved and dumped the miner onto the bed so hard, it creaked once, then collapsed.

From the bed down on the floor, the man looked up. Fright replaced his initial irritation at being interrupted. "Wh-what do you want?"

"I want the map, Cooley. Where is it?"

"Map? I don't have any map. And I'm not—"

Jensen kicked hard and twisted. He wore half-mounted spurs with knobbed rowels. The spur cut across the man's face and opened a deep gash on his cheek. Again, the wound was more frightening than dangerous. It worked to set the man gibbering.

"The map, Cooley. Give me the map."

"Quit saying that. I don't have no map! I'm not—"

The whore attacked Jensen then, nails like claws raking down his arm. He whirled around, and she staggered. He saw the expression on her face and knew she was a fiercer opponent than the man with the bleeding cheek.

"This isn't your fight, girlie." He took a step away and held out his hand to warn her away.

That did nothing to stop her naked fury. She came at him again. Most of those he had faced were crazy old coots, drunken cowboys or those who thought they could win a quick reputation by taking him on. The woman should have been as smart as she was beautiful, but that didn't stay his hand. With a single easy move, he drew and fired point-blank. The slug hit her like a sledgehammer. She straightened and then fell backward as if she stood at attention. With arms extended high over her head, she slammed into the floor. She had died before she even knew the danger she faced.

Jensen turned and cocked his pistol. Aiming between the man's eyes produced another reaction Jensen had seen many times before. The man's weathered face turned ashen.

"The map. Give me the map, Cooley."

The man's eyes darted toward saddlebags on the table that had been beside the bed. Jensen pulled the trigger. This slug tore through the man's skull and knocked him back. Unlike the woman, he had known what was in store for him. The fright was something to behold, but Jensen had no time to appreciate his handiwork. A second shot ended the man's life. He grabbed the saddlebags and dumped the contents onto the floor. A spare shirt tumbled out into a puddle of blood from the whore.

Jensen sorted through the contents. A smile bloomed when he found a pack of papers. He tore off the ribbons holding the papers and leafed through. Anticipation turned to anger when he reached the last of the pages. Nothing but legal documents. Nothing that looked like a map hastily drawn by Barton Beeman lay among the items.

Moving like a striking snake, he grabbed the trousers around the man's ankles and heaved. Cloth tore. He went through the tatters, searching for the map. The man's shirt and vest failed to deliver up the map, too.

Jensen stepped away from the bodies and let his towering rage take control. He emptied his pistol into the man's corpse. It didn't make him feel any better. Cooley had hidden the map before coming to the cathouse. That made no sense. Had he passed it along to someone else? Why would he do a thing like that when the stolen payroll was all his for the taking?

"Upstairs. I heard gunfire. Take him down, boys. Don't be gentle. He's a threat to all the girls." The madam's voice crackled with fury.

Jensen snarled. The kid had run off to get the madam's henchmen. He took one last look around the room in case he had missed a hiding place for the map. Seeing nowhere that looked plausible, he opened the gate on his Colt and began punching out the spent brass. Each shell clattered to the floor as he walked. From the ruckus downstairs, at least two men were arguing about how best to kill him. His empties removed, Jensen began reloading. When he had all six chambers filled, he started for the stairs. Killing a few more men would help him let off steam. ·

A load of buckshot tore past his head. He ducked

and backpedaled fast. It was one thing gunning down someone waving around a six-shooter. Madam Morgan's bullies were using more firepower than he had. Opening up the way, they had shown how eager they were to shoot something.

As eager as he was to fire back, he still had to find the map.

After running down the hall, he reached the backstairs. A quick peek down didn't bring another load of buckshot. He dived down the stairs and kicked open the side door. His horse waited impatiently for him and kicked its hooves in agitation. As long as he'd ridden the nag, it had never gotten used to gunfire.

He jumped into the saddle and got a deep seat, then galloped away. He heard shouting behind him, but it died down as he put more distance between himself and the brothel. That had been messy. It'd get messier if he ever found Cooley's partner. He had to be the one with the map.

CHAPTER SEVEN

~

"TWINS," ENGLAND DAN Rutledge muttered. "Identical twins." He stared at Mandy in wonder. She had been with Cooley while her sister was with some other customer. "It could have been you that got gunned down."

"Nobody'd want to shoot me." John Cooley had turned pale as the undertaker removed bodies. "I haven't done anything to anybody."

"You fooling around with somebody's wife? Have you been cheating on me?" The partially naked Mandy stamped a bare foot. With her hands on her hips, she looked and sounded like an aggrieved wife.

"There's only you, my sweet." Cooley finished buckling his gun belt and nervously fingered the Colt at his side.

England Dan wondered if gunfire was so common that Mandy and Cooley had ignored her sister and her customer getting mowed down. He was glad he never patronized the house.

England Dan wished his partner would stop playing with his gun. Cooley wasn't much of a shot. More than once he had accidentally discharged his six-shooter trying to clean it. He had to be a lover and not a fighter, but chances were good that he was no great shakes at that, either.

"We'd better hightail it," he said. England Dan turned and plowed straight into Madam Morgan. She had one of her bouncers standing guard behind her. The sawed-off shotgun was a formidable weapon. In Gus' hand it looked insignificant. The man was almost as big as the giant who had tried to rob Dan's mine.

"You take the tart with you," the madam said furiously. She glared at the blonde. "This is the first trouble I've had since coming to Oasis. I might have known you and your sister would be the cause of it."

"Mindy was shot dead, Madam Morgan! How could any of this be her fault? It had to be Justin's fault. Maybe he crossed a jealous husband."

"Justin wasn't hitched, and the man who did the killing's nobody I ever laid eyes on before."

"Then you know me and Mindy aren't the cause."

"Clear out. You got ten minutes. Then Gus helps you along your way."

"Not him," Mandy said in a choked voice. "He's big." In a voice almost too tiny to hear, she added, "And he enjoys hurting me."

England Dan spoke up. "There's a federal deputy marshal in town. Tell him about this. The killer might be the man he's tracking."

"No!" Madam Morgan blurted out. "No lawmen in

this house. They're nothing but trouble. Local marshals always shake me down, and the federals expect everything to be on the house. And then they both cause all kinds of trouble with the other customers. Who wants to spend some time in a bawdy house with a peace officer giving you the once-over?" She shook her head. "Them two will get buried all right and proper but nothing more. No law. Ten minutes and you'd all better be out of here." She herded Gus ahead of her down the stairs.

"Out the back way," England Dan said. He wasn't sure if Mandy had any belongings with her or was even fully dressed yet. She looked almost as naked wearing a yellow dress with a scoop neck and a hemline at her knees as she did without a stitch on.

"I'm coming with you," she said, gripping his partner's arm. "You got to protect me, Cooley. You lost me this job. You got to take care of me."

"Watch after her, John. I'm going to find Deputy Gonzales and see if the killer's not the outlaw he's hunting."

"Why? Is there a reward? Madam Morgan is right, Dan. Leave it be. Go pokin' that hornet's nest, and you'll stir up the owlhoot that killed Mindy."

"I don't care if there is a reward. He shouldn't be riding free after murdering two people in cold blood."

"Cold blood, hot blood, what's the difference? Mindy and that Justin fellow are dead no matter how it happened." Cooley licked his lips. "I'll head on back to the mine."

"*We'll* head on back to your mine," Mandy said.

"Take Mabel," England Dan said, "and there's a crate of supplies. Take that, too."

"Who's Mabel? You *are* cheating on me!"

England Dan wondered at the blonde woman's possessiveness. She rented herself out and yet demanded that Cooley be faithful. There were too many things he didn't understand, and this was a lesser one. He followed them down the backstairs and outside. He waited to be certain Cooley and Mandy headed for the livery stable before he circled around the brothel, not sure what he sought.

A youngster sat huddled at the far end of the front porch, his back pressed against the wall and his knees drawn up so he could hug them close. If he tried any harder, he would curl up into such a small ball that he'd disappear. That was likely his intent after everything that had gone on.

England Dan settled down beside him and said nothing until the boy began to squirm.

"What do you want, mister? Madam Morgan said I ain't s'posed to talk to nobody."

"Well, that works out, then. I'm pretty much a nobody." England Dan fell silent until the void had to be filled with words. "Was you upstairs when that big blond fellow pushed Madam Morgan and then stomped up the stairs?"

The boy swallowed hard. "I didn't see. Brutus wouldn't let me go up, but I saw Mr. O'Dell taking out bodies. Mindy was shot dead."

"By the big blond owlhoot?"

"Had to be him. Never saw anybody look so mean. He had to be to cow Madam Morgan like he done."

"You liked Mindy?"

"She was all right. She and her sister—they're twins, you know. That means they look exactly the same. She and Mandy never talked to me, but they sure were pretty." A flush rose. "I saw both of them as naked as jaybirds. I wasn't supposed to. Madam Morgan said not to look, but I couldn't help myself."

"They're beautiful. You think either of them knew the big blond fellow?"

"Not from the way he acted. I never seen him 'fore. Madam Morgan never had, either. When I described him to Gus and Brutus so they'd know what they was up against, they had no idea who he was, either."

"If a deputy marshal comes around, you tell him what you saw, no matter what Madam Morgan said about talking to anybody else. Deputy Gonzales is likely after him for other crimes. If he's not stopped, he'll keep killing folks."

"Even Mandy? That'd be a cryin' shame."

England Dan allowed as to how that was possible. He sat for a spell longer, then got up and began the hike back toward the jailhouse that he supposed Alberto Gonzales had made his own. When he got there, the deputy was nowhere to be found. He sat at the desk, turned over a wanted poster and carefully wrote out on the back what had happened at Madam Morgan's. The penciled report might catch the lawman's attention, or he might ignore it. England Dan did what he could to emphasize that he thought the killer was the same outlaw Gonzales had followed from Mesilla. This was all he could do.

Weighing the sheet down with a lawbook he found in a desk drawer, he decided it was time to clear out of town. Something ate at his gut about the shooting at the bordello. The shooter had thought the man with Mindy was Cooley. Confusing the twins was easy enough, and an innocent man had died because of that. But what had Cooley done to be such a target?

"He got the man he wanted," England Dan said, trying on the idea for size. The words rang hollow. Why would he have killed Justin? The man was a clerk who had lived in Oasis for as long as England Dan had been working the Trafalgar Mine. Still, this made him feel a bit better.

"Lars Jensen," he said. "That was what Gonzales called him. Killing Justin might have satisfied the outlaw's bloodlust and let him go on his way. Yeah, that's it. Jensen is in Mexico by now."

He gave the jailhouse a final look. The deputy hadn't left any trace behind. If Jensen was heading for Mexico, Gonzales must have been on his trail. As comforting as that idea was, England Dan doubted it. Stepping out, he pulled down his bowler so the narrow brim shaded his eyes. He took a deep breath and started walking. It was a long way to the mine. If he walked fast enough, he might overtake Cooley and Mandy before nightfall and help himself to some of the victuals he'd bought earlier.

By the time it got too dark to walk, he had put close to ten miles between him and Oasis. His legs ached, and he was too tired to hunt for a rabbit or a marmot for dinner. He gathered berries and found a few other plants that tasted good when boiled into a stew but that were a tad bitter when eaten alone. A stream gurgled pleasantly and soothed his ruffled nerves. The trip to town had been as harrowing as chasing off the thieves stealing the supplies from the mine.

He spread pine needles on the ground, snuggled down to hollow out space at his hip and shoulder and felt almost comfortable. Lying back, he began drifting to sleep, but the image of the giant he had killed at the mine haunted him. Somehow he worried the Goliath hadn't been stopped and had clawed his way out of his grave to go after Cooley, killing wantonly.

He came awake with a start when he dreamed hands were reaching for him. With his Webley out and pointed, it took him a few seconds to realize he had been dreaming. Another few seconds passed, and he realized he had the drop on a dark shrouded figure sitting cross-legged beside him.

"You snore." The dark figure began laughing. It built until his entire body shook with mirth. He rolled over on his side and kicked his feet. Starlight revealed moccasins on those feet. By now England Dan knew who his sentry was.

"No Shadow, calm down." He sat up and holstered his six-gun. Reaching out and shaking the Indian did no good. No Shadow continued his maniacal laughter until he suddenly stopped.

"You have food for me?"

"I don't even have food for myself. But there are a few berries on a bush. Over there."

The Indian crawled on hands and knees, snuffling and barking like a dog. England Dan heaved a sigh of resignation. No Shadow was of the Mogollon tribe, and he roamed the Superstition Mountains on his own for the most part. Sometimes he joined a larger band, usually hunters who tolerated him because he was plumb loco. England Dan never understood what the Indians thought of him. Being crazy didn't seem to give him special privileges, but the tribe didn't avoid him, either. For his part, England Dan wondered if No Shadow was anywhere near as loco as he acted. It was a convenient way to beg for food and not be obliged to repay favors.

It wasn't hard to see Cooley playing the same role, if he thought it would be easier than scrabbling in the mine for a few ounces of gold dust.

"What are you doing out tonight?" England Dan lounged back. He was awake now, and getting back to sleep with No Shadow prowling about wasn't going to be easy.

"Hiding. I fear him."

"What are you talking about?" England Dan sat up straight. Lars Jensen came instantly to mind. "Do you mean a big, tall blond fellow?"

"Blond? You mean with yellow hair?" No Shadow shook his head, then shook all over like a wet dog. "I hide from Big Owl. He hunts again." The Indian came up on his haunches and turned his head back and forth, sniffing the air like a bloodhound.

"Is he one of your tribe? Did you get in trouble with him?"

"He not human." No Shadow sank down and stretched out, his chin on his folded hands in front of him. "He is a man-eater. All over he roams. I heard him." He let out a long, mournful howl. "His cries bewitch."

"How's that? They scare you away?"

"No!" No Shadow moved to sit cross-legged again. "You hear his cries and accept his curse. He is your chief forever. He lures you and then eats you!"

"What's this ogre look like?"

No Shadow barked out a laugh and shook his head. "How can any know? They go to him and get eaten. Nobody lives. All that remains are skeletons. Gnawed-clean bones after Big Owl gorges himself."

No Shadow fell silent. England Dan had nothing more to ask about Big Owl, but he found himself straining to hear tiny sounds in the night. Nothing close to them moved or made any noise. That was to be expected since they were the intruders, but in the distance, a wolf howled, and other less identifiable sounds echoed through the mountains. He tried to figure out what made those noises but couldn't.

"These are the Superstition Mountains," he said more to himself than to No Shadow.

"You think I am crazy." No Shadow swayed back and forth. "Not when I speak of Big Owl. He preys on Indian and round eyes, but he prefers Indians. We taste better."

England Dan knew better than to ask how No Shadow had come by that fact. "How long's Big Owl been after you?"

"A week. I left a hunting party of my people to lure him away. Every night I hear his cries but do not go to him." No Shadow whipped out a knife. It flashed in the dim starlight. England Dan shifted to reach his six-shooter if the need arose, but the Indian only brandished the weapon for emphasis, not for killing.

"If I kill Big Owl, I will be chief!"

"How are you going to do that if the man-eating ogre can mesmerize you?"

"I do not know what that means. He hunts. If he is distracted by other prey, then I can kill him." The knife rose and fell, buried to the hilt in the soft earth. "It is a terrible thing to kill a god."

"Big Owl is a god?"

No Shadow fell silent and wrapped his arms around himself, trying to make himself as small as possible.

England Dan understood the urge. As they sat in silence, straining to hear Big Owl's hypnotic call in the distance, an idea popped into his head. He pulled out the map Cooley had bought from the dead cowboy.

"You roam all over these hills. I have a map but don't know where to start."

He spread it on the ground, positioning it so the starlight lit it enough to read. Some odd notion came and went that doing this would reveal secret writing or give him the clue needed to orient the map. It looked like the same map, only fainter than when he saw it in sunlight. The mountains were obvious but the dots and the X were almost invisible.

No Shadow took his time crawling over on all fours. He sniffed at the map. England Dan pulled it back when the Indian tried to lick it. This won him a deep growl. He almost whacked the Indian on the nose like he would a dog but held back. When No Shadow settled down, he spread the map out again. This time the man ran his finger over the inverted Vs showing mountain peaks.

"I know this place. It is far away. On the eastern side of the mountains."

England Dan considered this and realized he had been thinking wrong about whoever drew the map. He thought they had used Oasis as a starting point, or at least had shown the mountains from the west. Deputy Gonzales said Jensen had come from Mesilla. If Cooley was the one Jensen was looking for, this map had to be the key. Had he been looking for it this whole time? If this map did in fact show something of interest to the outlaw, it stood to reason that he'd approach from the east.

"Where?" He tried not to sound too eager.

"Mule Springs. The mountains look like this from there." No Shadow stabbed his finger down on three of the Vs on the map. From that, England Dan knew now he could find the trail into the mountains and get to the Irish Lord Mine.

He folded the map and secured it in his large coat pocket. He lay back and turned over what No Shadow told him. The map might be to the richest mine in the Superstition Mountains, or it might be a different kind of treasure map, one that Lars Jensen would willingly murder to get. That wasn't a comforting thought, but it explained why the outlaw seemed to dog Cooley's footsteps. Jensen didn't know whom the yellow bandanna'd cowboy had sold the map to, but everyone in town knew Cooley. The deaths at the brothel could have been confusion over which whore Cooley had chosen.

"Twins," he said in wonder. Life and death hung on such a thin strand.

Without knowing exactly when, he drifted off to a fitful sleep, only to be awakened by a shrill keening. He drew his pistol and looked around for the source.

"Is that Big Owl?" No one answered. No Shadow was gone, and Dan was alone.

Alone with a supernatural man-eating ogre prowling the mountains, hunting for its next meal.

CHAPTER EIGHT

ARE WE THERE yet? I'm tired of riding this old mule." Mandy tightened her grip to keep from getting thrown off when Mabel bucked. "She doesn't like me."

"Don't insult her," John Cooley said, tramping alongside. "She understands what you say."

"She's a dumb ole mule." Mandy pouted.

"I was cussin' her out once, and I'm sure she understood. She turned around and kicked me halfway into tomorrow. See?" Cooley pulled up his shirt and showed the outline of a horseshoe on his stomach. "That's her right back hoof that caught me."

"I wondered how you'd got that. I just thought it was an injury from doing something heroic." She batted her eyes at him and smiled. For him it was like a second sun had come out and beamed down on him.

"I reckon it was heroic enough. It's not like bronc

bustin' or anything like that, but Mabel's quite a handful if you don't know what you're doin'."

"So you have a way with animals?"

"Only if you're the wild animal," he said, trying to swat her rump. He missed, hit the mule and caused Mabel to buck again. Cooley caught the blonde as she was tossed off into his arms. They stood that way a moment before he let her down.

"That creature will be the death of me. I could never live if it kicked me like it did you."

"I'm tough," he said, "but you don't have to worry your purty head none now. That's the trail up to the Trafalgar Mine."

"It's about time." Mandy began the long, steep climb, letting Cooley deal with the mule.

He dutifully followed, trying to balance the crate with the supplies his partner had bought. If Mabel kept bucking, he'd have to carry the heavy crate up this slope and he'd be sweaty and winded by the time he reached the summit. That wouldn't do, not with Mandy thinking so highly of his physical prowess.

He stoically marched along, but the climb was easier because the woman went ahead. He appreciated every twitch, how the hitch in her get along seemed so effortless, the white flash of her legs and arms, the way the sun turned her tangled hair into a river of molten gold. He was one lucky galoot to have her. That Mindy had to get herself killed was a pity, but fate could be cruel. Everything was working out just fine for him.

He wondered, if he asked, would Mandy marry him? It wasn't as if other girls from Madam Morgan's cathouse didn't get hitched. Most of them married away to ranchers with big spreads or powerful men who owned entire towns. Mindy had more than once pondered marrying Clyde Farley. Farley owned the third-largest sheep ranch in the south of Arizona. Sheep were smelly and cattlemen disparaged them, but year in, year out, Farley sold mutton and wool for good money. While the cattlemen sold their beeves for meat and leather, that was a single sale. Farley produced enough wool annually from the same sheep to keep his empire intact. He'd even hired a couple Basques from Spain to come help tend his ever-growing flock.

Cooley knew he'd never be that rich, but mining gold wasn't smelly. That sheep stink had kept Mindy from marrying Farley, though the way everything turned out, she would have been better off smelling like lanolin than getting a bullet in her lovely chest.

Her sister was flightier, but Cooley thought Mandy was better looking, even if the two had been identical twins. There were small things he appreciated.

"Is this it? *That's* where you live?"

"Yup, me and Rutledge. It's all messed up now. The thieves I told you about searched it and threw everything all around inside. But I'll get it cleaned up."

"It's only got one room. You expect me to sleep in there with both of you?"

"Could if you wanted," he said. He recognized the set to her jaw and the way her lips thinned. She wasn't happy with that. "I got the big bed. Me and you will fit just fine. Dan's cot is across the room."

"My room back at Madam Morgan's was a lot more comfortable. I had a bed with a real mattress, and there was a tub out back and—"

"And when I dig enough gold from the mine, you can have a grand bed. One of them beds with posts

comin' up at each corner. It'll have a feather mattress
and a canopy over it. You'll sleep like royalty."

"What do you know of royalty?"

"Well, now, Dan's tole me a lot. His pa is a count or
earl or something important back in England. He's always goin' on about how the kings and princesses live
over there in huge mansions with servants and butlers."

"His father is royalty? That makes him royalty, too."

He didn't like the direction this was taking. Cooley
quickly set her straight.

"He ain't in line to inherit the title or any of the
mansion the family lives in. He's a remittance man.
His pa sends money every month so he won't go back
and be a nuisance. His brother's the one who'll inherit
it all. His brother's got some weird name like Syngin.
Not any kind of name I ever heard of, even among the
Indians."

"Syngin," Mandy said, letting the name roll off her
tongue. "That's what I'd call exotic. Is his brother
married?"

"You keep Mabel from runnin' off while I get the
supplies into the cabin." Cooley grunted as he hefted
the crate to his shoulder. He saw Mandy reluctantly
tend to the mule. That stopped her wild fantasies about
the Rutledge family, both here and over the Big Pond.

He didn't have to kick open the door. It hung on one
hinge because Dan hadn't done much of a job repair-
ing it. The claim jumpers had gone through the cabin
like a tornado, throwing things around and breaking
anything that was glass. He hoped Dan had bought a
new kerosene lamp. The chimney on the old one had
been broken, though the wick and the reservoir had
escaped undamaged.

As he put the crate down and began unpacking it, he considered spending a night in the cabin with only the fire in the stove for light. He wasn't a reader like Dan. Being in the dark with Mandy was a whole lot more fun than trying to figure out all those words.

He perched on the edge of the table. If he wanted to keep on having fun with the lovely girl, there'd have to be a lot more gold pulled from the Trafalgar Mine. The truth was only too obvious, both to him and to his partner. The mine was playing out. The vein they had found and followed hadn't been that large, but it had been enough to keep them going. The past month or two, no matter how much they worked, the vein narrowed down and would peter out entirely before much longer. What was he to do then? Mandy wasn't cut out to sit around the cabin all day and then listen to him complain about the hard work and teeny specks of gold all night long.

Cooley patted himself down, looking for the map. Then he remembered Dan had it. That had set off a passel of unfortunate events, all centered around men being gunned down. Men and Mandy's sister. That told him there was something about the map that was worth a mountain of gold.

"The Irish Lord," he said softly. Visions of nuggets as big as his fist came to him. He vowed he'd have a wedding ring made from the first nugget he pulled out. It'd be an ounce or two of the finest gold anybody had ever seen. All he needed to do was use the map to find the lost mine and he'd be rich enough for Mandy.

More than rich enough. She'd get more than that four-poster bed. He'd buy her a mansion sitting atop Russian Hill in San Francisco.

"What do we do now?"

He looked up. The woman stood silhouetted in the door. The sun behind her limned her trim form. The way she stood, one hip cocked and a hand supporting her as she leaned against the doorjamb was about as sexy as anything he had ever seen.

"Dan's got to get here anytime now, though we made good speed because of the mule. It'll take him a day longer. Then we get to pullin' the gold from the mountainside."

"A day? It'll be that long before your partner gets here?"

"You're my partner, Mandy, my love." He pointed. "That's my bed. See? It's as big as I said."

"It's nowhere as big as the one I had back in town." She crossed the cabin to test it. It had a straw mattress.

"It's not as big, but it has something the other doesn't."

"Now, what would that be?"

He caught her up and spun her around, careful not to smash her into the table or walls. He set her down on the bed gently as she squealed with delight.

"It's got the two of us in it."

After a pleasant interlude, they lay together on the bed. Mandy stirred, then poked him in the ribs with her thumb.

"Aren't you a miner? You can't be a layabout and expect the gold to jump out of that hole in the ground." She sat up, stretched and gave Cooley a twinge of longing.

But she was right. As much as he wanted to spend the rest of the day here, or until Dan showed up, the mine had gone untended for almost a week. The ore went nowhere, but the gold that had to be spent to keep everything running waited. He stroked her golden hair until she stood and began dressing. Watching was a treat, but having her poke him again wasn't.

"You're a lazy oaf, John Cooley. You get up there and do mining things."

He climbed into his clothes. Looking around the cabin, he wanted to put everything into order. Then he remembered he had a woman here now. If she was going to be supported by the gold he teased from the mine, it was only fair she earn her keep.

"Get to cleanin' up the cabin," he said. He tried to kiss her, but she ducked and stepped to the far side of the table. "I'll dig up a ton or two of ore. That ought to crush down to a few ounces."

"Do it," Mandy said. She looked around with obvious distaste but set to picking up and cleaning the debris left by the robbers.

Cooley hitched up his drawers and stepped outside. The day had turned cloudy and dull. That matched the way he felt. Mandy expected things of him, more than England Dan ever did. But then he never felt any guilt when he dodged work and let the Brit do it. He had to keep Mandy happy, or she'd leave him.

He trudged up the slope to the mouth of the mine. He rummaged around in the ore cart and found a pair of heavy canvas overalls and pulled them on. They protected against cuts and nicks from the rock and saved his clothing. Putting his back into it, he got the ore cart rolling along the tracks and followed it into the mine. Within a few feet, the light from the mouth became too dim to see. He fumbled around on a rocky ledge, then found a hard hat and a half-dozen miner's candles. Beside them on the ledge lay a piece of flint and steel.

He worked a few minutes to get a spark and light the first candle. He settled it on the hat and pushed deeper into the mine. When he came to the end of the stope, it took several minutes for him to find the vein he had been working. That difficulty told him this vein was almost played out. They'd have to follow another.

Or figure out the map and take over the Irish Lord Mine.

Thoughts of how much gold that legendary mine had and how he'd pull out nuggets as large as his head kept him working. Every stroke of his pick wasn't in the Trafalgar Mine but in the abandoned Irish Lord. The ore tumbled to the floor. When it piled up enough, he began loading it into the ore cart. Having to do all the work himself rankled, but his partner had to be back anytime now.

As he pushed the ore cart, an ugly thought made his swallow hard. Dan had the map. What if he didn't plan on returning to their mine and instead went after the Irish Lord on his own? Cutting out a partner doubled the amount of gold that'd go into his own pocket. He had never been happy getting money from his pa in England. Every time he took the remittance money at the telegraph, Dan moped around and was unbearable. Cooley had seen that more than once.

This was a way for the Brit to get rich. Going home he could lord it over his pa and brother. All he had to do was double-cross his partner, the one working the Trafalgar all by himself. Cooley's smoldering anger let him push the ore cart a tad faster than usual. As a result it shot from the mine and crashed into the block at the end of the track. The cart tipped over and the contents tumbled downhill to the crusher.

Cooley rushed to catch up, looked down and smiled at the size of the pile below, then froze. Not far from the pile, a horse reared and tugged at its reins. The small avalanche had frightened it.

But who had ridden the horse here? That wasn't his partner's. Dan wouldn't spend what remained of his monthly remittance to buy such a horse or the gear adorning it. The tack was decorated with Mexican silver worth a fortune. Tooled leather saddlebags flopped about on the horse's rump. Nothing about the gear spoke of England Dan Rutledge.

A wild thought that the horse belonged to the deputy Dan had run into back in Oasis came and went in a flash. A tall blond man strode back along the trail to the cabin, six-gun drawn. He hunted for whatever had spooked his horse.

Cooley fell to the ground as if all the bones in his legs had turned to water. The only one who fit the description of the man below was Lars Jensen. The man the Mesilla federal deputy was hunting had come to the Trafalgar Mine. And a thousand things piled into Cooley's head. Whatever crime Jensen was guilty of in New Mexico meant nothing if he was responsible for killing Mandy's sister. He was as likely to kill her now, for whatever reason. It had to be a grudge. Revenge for some old slight.

He reached down to his side. His six-shooter was back in the cabin with Mandy. There had been no reason to carry his piece into the mine. It weighed close to three pounds and got in his way as he worked. It was hard enough swinging an eight-pound sledge or using a pickax. It wasn't like he had to shoot at tommy-knockers or snakes or hibernating bears. More than once when he had started mining, he had lugged the gun with him and it had discharged. Dan had shouted at him, and he had almost shot himself in the leg. The only real time either of them needed their six-shooters was when claim jumpers came to rob them blind.

Cooley ducked behind the ore cart and shivered as if he had caught the ague. He tried to think straight. Nothing came to him. Mandy had his gun. She could take care of herself. He stood and stumbled on a rock, and the ore cart tipped back with a loud crash. Worse, it started rolling back toward the mine.

He popped up like a prairie dog and saw Jensen stop on the trail to the cabin and come running back. The noise drew him like carrion excited a buzzard. Panicked, Cooley ran toward the mine, then veered to the side and scrambled up the slope beside the mouth. Getting caught in the mine was surefire death. There were air chutes cut every hundred feet or so, but none of them was big enough to squeeze through. All Jensen had to do was stand at the mouth of the mine and start firing. Anyone inside would be turned into a bloody corpse in nothing flat. The claim jumpers had tried that but were too inept to do it right. From the gunman's looks, he wasn't inept.

Cooley flopped onto his belly as the outlaw got to the mine level. Jensen puffed and panted, showing how he had come from lower altitudes. He never looked up. If he had, he would have spotted the cowering miner. When he got to the mouth, he did exactly as Cooley had known he would.

"Come on out. You got what I want. There's no reason to get yourself all shot up over it."

"The map," Cooley whispered to himself. The outlaw wanted the map. To make the gunman go away he would have gladly tossed it down, only England Dan had it. Cooley pressed himself flatter and tried to make himself entirely invisible. He had heard Dan talk about lizards that faded into the background by changing the way they looked. He tried to become a chameleon.

He flinched when Jensen fired a shot into the mine. The bullet spanged off a wall and drove deep into the ground.

"It'll get worse. Come on out, and I promise not to shoot any more."

Jensen stood with his six-shooter aimed into the mine. If Cooley had actually been inside and tried to surrender, he would have died on the spot. As it was, he forced himself to keep from crying out as another bullet echoed inside the mine.

"My patience is all used up." Jensen edged forward, moving so light from behind him lit the mine shaft. He cursed and entered.

As he vanished from sight, Cooley slid down the hill, tiptoed to the trail leading down to the cabin, then ran hell-for-leather. His boots pounded hard on the ground. The sound might as well have been thunderclaps. They sounded louder to him. He skidded to a halt and looked into the cabin.

"Mandy!"

No answer. He reached around and grabbed his six-gun from the peg where it hung. Cooley strapped it on, then considered his options. Laying an ambush for Jensen was about the stupidest thing possible. The man was a killer. He had probably done that to dozens of men and knew all the tricks.

Cooley ran for the shed, where Mabel should have been peacefully chewing away at her fodder. He went cold inside. The mule was gone. Mandy must have ridden off when Jensen came into the camp, no thought to warning her lover of the danger. He swung around, hand on the butt of his pistol. Shooting it out with the outlaw meant somebody would die.

It didn't take a genius to figure out what the scene would be when the last of the gun smoke cleared. Cooley had never killed anybody in his life. He'd never even shot at another man. Looking along the trail Mandy must have taken, he began a stumbling run. If he caught up, the two of them could make better time astride Mabel. And if he didn't, Jensen would have an easier time following mule tracks but he wouldn't ever find a man on foot.

John Cooley put his head down and ran even faster.

CHAPTER NINE

"COOLEY," JENSEN SAID softly, repeating the name over and over as he rode up the steep hillside. He drew rein when he came to a poorly lettered sign proclaiming the area ahead of him to be the Trafalgar Mine, owned by Rutledge and Cooley. A smile came easily now. He had found the man who'd bought the map off the cowboy in the Thirsty Camel Saloon.

He drew his six-gun and checked to be sure it was loaded. His brother had always ridden him hard about that, ever since they were kids and had gotten into a shootout with a marshal in San Angelo. Poke had saved him that day. The lawman had had the drop on him. From the expression on the man's face, he had been going to pull the trigger and save the county the trouble of hanging a horse thief. Poke had snuck up behind and tapped the lawman on the shoulder. As he turned, his brother had shoved his gun into the marshal's belly and fired until his six-shooter came up empty.

That had been the first man Jensen had seen die. If Poke hadn't acted when he had, Jensen knew he'd have been moldering in a potter's field now. The lesson had been well learned. While he wasn't sure of the exact number, he thought seven, maybe eight men had eaten lead from his six-shooter since then. He pondered the matter a moment, going over the body count, then shook off coming up with a definite number. The one in question had slumped over the saddle and ridden off after a shootout near Eagle Pass. He hadn't bothered tracking him down to be sure he was dead because the man with his lead in his had crossed over into Mexico.

His victim wasn't a deer, after all. Not going after a wounded animal was cruel. A man could take care of himself.

Jensen slid his pistol back into his holster and urged his horse up the slope. The path was rocky. He wondered how Cooley and his partner ever got gold back to Oasis along such a poorly maintained trail. By the time he got to the top, he decided the mine wasn't producing enough to make that a problem. The pile of dross still trickled a few rocks down the side.

He considered this and looked up at the mine itself. An ore cart had dumped a load. Jensen frowned. If somebody was working the mine right now, the rock had to have just been dumped. From the look of the pile, it wasn't all that stable, and a vagrant breeze had disturbed it. Either way, checking the cabin off to his right made more sense than seeing if anyone was wandering about the mine shaft. He didn't want somebody sneaking up behind him when he was intent on finding the miner at work.

He started for the cabin, then spun, bringing up his six-gun when the ore cart fell back down and rolled out of sight.

"Take the high ground," he muttered, reversing course and starting uphill. Anyone in the mine could not only draw a bead on him; he could drop rocks on his head.

He slipped and slid on the poorly kept path, finally reaching the top, gasping for breath. When he and Poke had been kids, they had walked everywhere. As soon as they got the idea of stealing horses, they'd ridden. The longest he remembered walking after that revelation was from his horse to the door of a saloon.

A quick look around didn't show any hiding place near the mouth of the mine. He strode over and aimed his gun into the mine.

"Come on out. You got what I want. There's no reason to get yourself all shot up over it."

He waited a few seconds. Sounds came from deep in the mine. Maybe. He fired a round. The lead whined off a wall and finally fell silent far down the shaft.

"It'll get worse. Come on out, and I promise not to shoot any more." He tried to pick up any noise, but the report had partially deafened him. Canting his head to the side did nothing to help him hear if his threat had worked.

"My patience is all used up." He approached the mine slowly, wary of a trap. Hearing and seeing nothing, he cursed. Then he turned a little to let the light from behind him show the way. Poke would have skinned him alive the way he silhouetted himself. *Always know where the light is,* his brother had said—but then he said a lot of things.

Shooting off his mouth had landed him in Yuma Penitentiary for six months. So far, even though he had forgetten to check his pistol before a fight and ignored how he outlined himself against the sky, Jensen had avoided jail. This was Poke's second stint behind bars.

He pressed against the rough mine shaft wall and worked his way deeper until the light was too dim for him to see. Waiting a spell didn't flush out the miner. Jensen fired again and saw nothing but the long spark as the lead dragged itself along the hard wall. Backing out he stepped into the sunlight again and looked around. He heard feet hammering against hard ground. After rushing to the end of the ore cart's track, he thought he saw a flash of somebody heading for the cabin.

Slipping and sliding down the rocky path, he turned cautious at the bottom. Cooley had to be around somewhere. If he and the Rutledge mentioned as a co-owner were both in the cabin, they had him outgunned. Being careful kept him alive. He got off the trail and approached the cabin from a crazy angle by which he had to kick his way through half-dead, parched underbrush. With a final rush, he pressed against the splintery wall and found a knothole to peer through. The field of vision was too narrow. Somebody might have been waiting just inside the door, ready to gun him down.

Jensen reared back and slammed hard into the wall. It shattered, dumping him into the cabin. He landed on his belly, both hands on his six-gun. He looked around for something to shoot. The single-room cabin was empty.

Cursing, he got to his feet and brushed off splinters sticking in his shoulder and arm. He flung open the door and looked down the path toward a shed. An animal had been kept here. Dropping to his knee, he studied the tracks.

"A mule. They're trying to escape on a mule!"

He laughed all the way back to his horse. Even with the rugged trail, his horse would outpace a short-legged mule. Unless the trail turned rocky and worked its way around a mountain on a narrow ledge, he'd overtake Cooley in jig time. Jensen reloaded his pistol as he rode along; then he checked his Winchester to be sure he was ready for any fight.

Occasional glances down proved enough to assure him he was on the trail. Still-fresh mule scat told him he was getting closer, but he tugged on the reins and halted. Something caused the back of his neck to itch, a sure sign somebody was watching him. Carefully looking around, he saw nothing to warn of a trap. The sensation refused to go away even when he swiveled about in the saddle, whipped out his six-shooter and pointed it upslope into a tumble of rocks. Nothing moved there, and he hadn't seen or heard anything. If anyone had hidden in what was the best spot for an ambush, he would have flushed them out. All he heard was the soft whistle of wind through pines higher up on the mountainside.

Jensen remained motionless long enough to make anybody watching antsy. Nothing caused him to shoot. Not even a rabbit or a lizard stirred. He had seen a half-eaten marmot farther back along the trail. Scaring off a coyote seemed most likely, though why the scavenger hadn't taken the entire animal when disturbed was something not worth thinking on too hard.

He slipped his pistol back into his holster. Even a warning shot would have given his quarry a fright and lent more speed to the escape. A quick snap of the reins sent his horse trotting along. New hoofprints convinced him he was not only on the right path but within a few minutes of spotting the mule and its rider.

The trail curled around the mountain and opened into a broad green meadow ringed with pines and scattered stands of aspens. Those trees formed a perfect frame for a mule with a rider slogging across the open space.

He put his heels to the horse's flanks and galloped. Barely had he begun to close the distance than he saw another rider coming across the meadow. That rider was not only closer, but also galloping to reach the mule. Jensen slowed to see what would happen when the two got together. At first he thought they were intending to rendezvous, but the mule with the rider—it looked like a woman—veered away, trying to elude the newcomer.

She had no chance astride a mule. The rider caught up and grabbed the reins, halting the mule.

For the first time, Jensen got a better look at the horse rider. He swore and instinctively reached for his pistol.

"Gonzales. How'd you get here ahead of me?"

The Mesilla deputy pushed back his broad-brimmed sombrero and spoke at length. Then they both began gesturing, the woman pointing ahead and the federal lawman back in the direction he had come.

"Lady, you got more lives than a cat," Jensen said softly. He got a good look at the woman. How she had escaped back at the Oasis brothel was a poser. She had been with the man he had mistaken for Cooley. Now she was out here arguing with Alberto Gonzales.

The lowdown he'd had from the man back at the cathouse said this woman was with Cooley. That meant she could lead him to the map. Whether Cooley still had it or had given it to the woman for safekeeping, Jensen felt he was getting closer. And that was a good thing. Every day he wasted was one less day his brother spent in Yuma. When Poke showed up, and he would real soon, he'd want the map Barton Beeman had made to the stolen cavalry payroll. Over the years, Jensen had learned not to disappoint his brother. Ever.

He slid the rifle from the saddle scabbard, cocked the Winchester and snugged it against his shoulder. Firing from horseback was tricky, but he had little to lose. The deputy wanted the woman. That much was obvious from the silent playacting between lawman and whore. Even if he missed, he wasn't going to be much worse off than he was now.

Jensen drew back on the trigger. The rifle bucked and sent its .44-40 slug straight and true. Alberto Gonzales jerked, threw up his hands and fell off his big black stallion. Frozen with fear, the woman looked at the fallen lawman.

Rifle still pulled in to his shoulder, Jensen trotted forward. He tried to get a second shot at the fallen deputy. The woman knew things he needed to know. Gonzales was a thorn in his side. Jensen got off another shot, but it kicked up a tiny plume of grass and dirt, missing his target by a couple feet. Firing from a moving horse only wasted ammunition.

As he rode, he slid the rifle back into its scabbard. His six-gun came easily to hand. Riding past the fallen deputy let him get off a few more shots. Gonzales jerked and rolled over into a grassy depression. Jensen started to go back, then saw that the woman astride her mule was making tracks out of the meadow.

He turned to chase her down when a bullet whined past his head. A quick look back showed the deputy marshal had dragged himself around to rest his pistol on a rock. Another round made Jensen wince. It tore a few threads from his coat. The woman wasn't going to get away, and killing the lawman eliminated a lot of trouble.

He wheeled about and emptied his six-shooter at the deputy. Sparks flew off the rock where Alberto Gonzales rested his gun, but none of Jensen's bullets came close to ending the miserable man's life.

"Give up, Gonzales," Jensen called. "Stop shooting. You've failed. Make me mad and this is where the buzzards will dine on your dead body!"

For a few seconds he thought the deputy had given up. Then Gonzales reloaded and started firing again. One round whizzed so close that Jensen jerked to the side and lost his balance. He fell to the ground. The impact shook him up. His head buzzed, and his shoulder hurt so bad, he worried he had busted up something important. Jensen forced himself to sit up. The dizziness passed.

"You had your chance, Gonzales. I'd've ridden off, but now I'm going to kill you. I'll fill your worthless carcass full of lead and laugh while I'm doing it."

"You're a lowlife, no-account coward, Jensen. Surrender and I won't gun you down like a mad dog." Alberto Gonzales punctuated his call for surrender with several more bullets.

Jensen hadn't been counting, but instinct told him the deputy had to reload. He got to his feet and steadied himself. He started walking toward the rock where Gonzales had taken refuge. Rather than shooting as he came, he aimed and waited. Every step took him closer.

"You giving up, Jensen?"

The deputy popped up to shout the question. When he did, Jensen fired. For an instant, Gonzales said nothing. Then he vanished from sight behind the rock. Jensen kept walking, reloading as he got ever closer. He stared down at the prostrate lawman.

"Finally," Jensen grumbled. "I finally got you off my trail." He cocked his six-shooter and aimed to put another round into the helpless man. A curse escaped his lips. He lowered the hammer and rammed his six-gun back into its holster.

Running out of ammunition was a real problem. He had a full six-gun and only three more rounds in the loops on his gun belt. Nine shots. As much joy as emptying his gun into the lawman would give him, he had to be practical. He hopped onto the rock and looked around. The woman had disappeared, but he didn't worry about her too much. His largest obstacle lay dead on the ground.

He jumped down and grabbed the deputy's gun. Empty. Grunting, he rolled the body over. The gun belt was as empty of ammo as the discarded pistol. Jensen thought up some new pungent curses and stood. Even robbing the dead wasn't paying off for him. He put his fingers to his lips and whistled. His horse trotted over and waited for him.

Jensen swung into the saddle and used his spurs to get the horse galloping. It wasn't possible for the woman to get away, but his patience had come to an end. Trailing her had been amusing. Killing Alberto Gonzales had changed his mood since that wasn't as much fun as he expected. If anything, the lawman's death had been a letdown for him. There wasn't time to properly celebrate, and truth to tell, he hadn't enjoyed it the way he'd expected because Gonzales hadn't suffered enough. For all the trouble the deputy had given Jensen over the past few weeks, he should have lingered long enough to reflect on his mistakes.

As he rode, Jensen considered staking the deputy over an anthill. He'd heard the Apaches did that to their enemies. Or cut their eyelids off and force them to stare into the sun. All the stories excited Jensen, but he had never seen the Indians do any such thing. They'd all been shipped off to reservations and penned up. Maybe he should find a renegade who'd escaped and ask about their tortures. Or he needed only to wait for his brother. Poke had good stories. After his stay in Yuma, there might be new tortures to consider meting out to lawmen.

He reached the edge of the meadow. The trees were sparse here, and the exposed ground gave up tracks easily. Jensen swerved from the trail and followed mule tracks deeper into the forest.

Gauging the mule's stride showed how it had slowed to a walk. The woman had been lucky getting to woods, but the mule had shown its own mind now and slowed down. Jensen sniffed the air and listened hard. The sound of a small stream came from ahead. The breeze sneaking through the trees brought moisture with it that felt good against his face. His horse turned eager, wanting water. He held it back until he saw the creek.

Jensen kicked free and hit the ground. He let his horse rush ahead. He walked behind, alert. And he was glad he did. His horse drank greedily. The woman took this as her signal to rush forward. She held a small knife high overhead, ready to drive it into an exposed back.

Only Jensen had turned the tables on her.

The metallic click of his pistol cocking froze her. With the knife held high over her head, she turned and faced him.

Jensen sighted along the barrel, smiled and said, "Howdy. Me and you got things to talk about, missy."

CHAPTER TEN

ENGLAND DAN RUTLEDGE wanted nothing more than to sit beside a fast-running brook and soak his aching feet. Walking back from Oasis had tuckered him out. More than anything, he missed riding Mabel. The mule never complained and kept moving at a steady gait whether it was downslope or uphill all the way back to the Trafalgar Mine.

He trudged to the split in the trail. The right fork led to his cabin. The uphill path to the mine mocked him. So much work getting to the mine that refused to yield more than a few specks of gold a day. He touched the pocket where he carried Cooley's treasure map. The Irish Lord Mine had become legendary for the gold pulled from it. And the reason it was legendary was that nobody knew where it was. England Dan had the gut feeling it might not even exist, except in the gold fever–infected minds of prospectors and cowboys telling tall tales around a campfire.

A quick turn to the right and he started toward the cabin. He slowed and stopped. His hand went to his Webley. A hoofprint in the dirt was too large for a mule's shoe. A few feet farther away, a pile of horse manure drew flies. Fresh and far too much for Mabel to have dumped. A horse meant trouble. He started to yell to see if Cooley was all right, then clamped his mouth shut.

If Lars Jensen had tracked Cooley and the woman here, England Dan might be walking into an ambush.

He thumbed back the hammer to ready his six-shooter for a fight. Walking softly, alert in spite of being dog-tired, he slipped to the side of the cabin. He pressed his ear against the wall. No sound from inside. Edging along the wall, he got to the door. The squeak as he pushed it open would have awakened the dead. A quick look inside confirmed what he suspected. Cooley and Mandy were gone. Somebody had bashed in part of the back wall.

Searching the cabin didn't show any blood. Cooley and Mandy hadn't been killed inside, unless Jensen had strangled them. From what England Dan had seen of the outlaw, he'd use his pistol or a knife rather than his bare hands. Cooley might not have put up a struggle, but from what he had seen of the whore, she'd fight until her last fingernail was ripped out.

"His gun," England Dan muttered. "It's gone. Cooley hightailed it."

That thought burning in his brain, he hurried to the shed, where they stabled the mule. Mabel was missing.

A quick look showed the tracks in the trail leading around the mountainside. Both Mabel and the horse had gone in that direction.

England Dan wiped his lips as he considered what to do. Alberto Gonzales ought to be alerted if the man on horseback was Lars Jensen. But convincing the federal deputy of the rider's identity was a problem since England Dan couldn't say for certain who was chasing after his partner. Without realizing what he was doing, he started along the trail. A boot print in the dirt stopped him dead in his tracks.

He dropped to his knees and examined the outline. While he wasn't the best tracker who ever lived, he read these signs easily enough. Cooley had made the boot print. England Dan recognized the worn heel and the hole in the sole from following the tracks they made up to the mine, day after day.

Curiously, the tracks led off the trail and down the side of the mountain. Why Cooley hadn't stuck with the trail was a poser. All he could figure was that Mandy rode the mule and Cooley had tried to decoy Jensen away. That surprised him a mite. Cooley wasn't the kind to risk his own hide, but he had been smitten with the girl. That changed a man, even John Cooley.

England Dan slipped and slid a ways down the slope and found a rocky ledge that ran parallel to the trail twenty feet above him. He dropped to all fours and pushed his face low, trying to catch a small shadow off raised tracks in the dust. Finding nothing in either direction, he swung around and sat, thinking hard. Where Cooley had gone and how coming down here had helped Mandy get away were mysteries that needed to be solved.

England Dan looked back up. From here Cooley would have had no shot at Jensen, even if the man rode tall on his horse. He would have been better served to go upslope and shoot down if he wanted to ambush the outlaw. England Dan got to his feet and trooped along the narrow ledge, heading in the same direction as the mule and Jensen. Checking now and again for signs, he finally gave up. If Cooley had come this way, he had walked like an Indian and left no tracks. More likely, he had gone the opposite way to get away from any trouble.

That disappointed England Dan since it meant his partner hadn't changed one whit. He had looked out for himself and let Mandy fend for herself.

The ledge suddenly dropped off, leaving a four-foot gap between one side of the trail and the other. Jumping posed a problem since England Dan needed a running start. The ledge curled around the mountain and prevented him from getting much traction. Since the trail had petered out, he climbed back up to the higher track. When he pulled himself over the edge, he saw a steamy pile of horse dung. He was on the right course again. Lengthening his stride so he devoured the distance, he set a better pace than if he rode Mabel.

He tired himself out more than if he rode the mule, but he felt he was getting somewhere now. As fast as he walked, he stopped suddenly when he heard gunshots ahead. A quick touch on the butt of his six-shooter assured him he was ready for whatever went on ahead. Whatever it was, he doubted Cooley had any part in it. The first shots were from a rifle. Answering the long gun came sharp, loud reports that sounded nothing like Cooley's handgun.

Whoever shot it out had meant it. Volley after volley came. Then silence. That meant someone had given up—or had taken enough lead to die. England Dan's stomach turned over. If Jensen survived, England Dan would be walking right into danger. He plowed ahead, running now to reach the meadow. Ahead he saw a man drop down from his horse and kneel.

He was checking to see if his opponent was dead. The man stood, took off his hat and wiped sweat from his forehead. The shock of blond hair identified him. Jensen was the victor in this fight. England Dan raised his pistol, but the range was too great. Jensen stepped back up into the saddle and holstered his pistol. As he sat upright, he presented a perfect target—if England Dan had carried a rifle. Firing now only alerted the outlaw that he had another man to kill.

Jensen trotted off, never looking back. England Dan ran forward and vaulted over a ridge of rocks that the outlaw's victim had used for shelter. As he feared, he saw Alberto Gonzales sprawled flat on his back. A wound in his chest had spread, and blood soaked the lawman's shirt. That slug might have stolen his life, but more likely, from the way his face was entirely hidden by caked blood, a shot to the head had killed him.

Shooing away flies, England Dan knelt beside the deputy. His pockets had been turned out when Jensen searched the body. A discarded pistol and an empty gun belt showed what Jensen sought. England Dan took some grim pleasure that the owlhoot had run short of ammunition. How much, if any, he had taken off the deputy gave only a few more shots.

He reached over Gonzales to pick up the man's sombrero. Staring at the dead man's bloodied face unnerved him. Even leading his command in India, he had never gotten used to such wounds. He recoiled and sat heavily when he dropped the hat over the deputy's face, and the man batted it away and moaned.

"You're alive?" His voice came out in a hoarse whisper. "How can you be alive?"

One dark eye opened and fixed on him. Alberto Gonzales reached up and grabbed him by the lapel and pulled him down.

"Get him," the lawman croaked out. "Gun him down. He's a mad-dog killer. For me, shoot him."

"You need medical help." England Dan knew how lame that sounded. They were a day's travel away from Oasis. And finding a doctor there was harder than finding a sober man in the Thirsty Camel Saloon.

"Get him." Gonzales gripped even harder and pulled England Dan down so his bloody lips were inches from his ear. "I can make it, if I know you plugged him. For me. Reward. Get him."

Alberto Gonzales released the grip, and England Dan rocked back. He stared at the deputy, thinking he had died. But he hadn't. The man was as tough as nails. His chest rose a bit and fell fast as he gasped for breath. The few options he had became jumbled in England Dan's head. Without proper attention, the deputy was a goner. He had at least one lead slug in him that had to come out. But taking him anywhere was out of the question. They were in the middle of a mountain meadow, and England Dan wasn't up to dragging the deputy, even if he put together a travois.

He craned his neck. Jensen was disappearing at the far side of the meadow, riding into a thick stand of pines. England Dan stood and turned slowly in a full circle. Salvation lay in the opposite direction. The deputy's powerful black stallion edged toward them, smelling blood and likely still skittish from the gunfight. With the horse to carry the lawman, returning to the mine cabin would be far easier. There he could tend to the man's bullet wounds out of the hot sun. Better yet, in the cabin there wouldn't be the constant swarm of insects waiting to dine on almost-dead flesh.

Two fingers in his mouth, he let out a long, loud whistle. The black stallion reared, pawed at the air, then landed hard and turned its head to stare at England Dan. A second whistle brought it trotting over.

"Good horse, good Whirlwind," Alberto Gonzales grated out.

Taking the reins, England Dan walked the horse around to let it get used to him. The smell of its master's blood still spooked Whirlwind, but it settled down.

As he got the feel of the animal, England Dan considered how best to sling Gonzales over the saddle to return to the cabin. His train of thought was derailed when the deputy called out in a surprisingly strong voice.

"I'm all right. Track him down. Shoot him. Shoot him for me. I'll see you get the reward."

England Dan hesitated. Leaving the lawman was dangerous. His wounds might do him in at any instant, but Mandy had a killer on her trail. Mabel was no match for the swift horse Lars Jensen rode. He balanced the two choices. Alberto Gonzales was likely to die. Mandy could be saved but at great risk.

"Go," Gonzales urged. "There's a girl. Jensen is after her. Save her."

England Dan grumbled as he made the deputy as

comfortable as he could; then he positioned the sombrero to keep the sun off the man's face and chest.

"This is the best I can do right now. I'll save her. Don't you go dying on me. I'll be back as fast as I can."

Alberto Gonzales made a dismissive gesture and settled down, his chin on his chest. Again England Dan thought the man had died, but the labored breathing continued. He swung onto Whirlwind's back and let the stallion have its head. The powerful beast shot like a rocket, headed directly for the spot where Jensen had entered the woods.

Most horses England Dan had ridden were spirited, but none had the strength and speed of the deputy's black stallion. He couldn't help comparing this ride with being astride Mabel. That was hardly fair. The mule was surefooted, strong and usually uncomplaining. It performed chores Whirlwind would never do.

And the wind tearing past England Dan's face was something impossible to achieve riding Mabel. He slowed as the trees rose around him. The cool forest enveloped him and muffled sounds. He slowed to a walk and finally drew rein to better listen to the world around him.

A distant horse neighing had to have been Jensen on his mount. England Dan rode Whirlwind in that direction for a few minutes, then dropped to the ground. The forest floor was carpeted with fresh pine needles. He saw a few crushed patches where a horse might have trod, but he wasn't sure. The broken branches on some brush still oozed sap. He didn't have to be an expert tracker to know he was on the right trail. Someone had ridden past here only a short while earlier. This, along with the sounds ahead, put him on guard.

With an easy draw, he pulled his six-shooter and led

Whirlwind deeper into the woods. He tethered the horse to an oak limb when he heard movement ahead. Riding up on Jensen was a surefire way to get himself filled with lead. Sneaking ahead, keeping as quiet as possible, brought him to the edge of a clearing. For a few seconds he thought his ears had deceived him. Then he saw movement in shadows twenty yards off.

He drew a bead and slowly pulled back on the trigger. Common sense overrode his need to get even with Lars Jensen. Without knowing for sure whom he was about to shoot at, he could kill some stranger who was innocently riding through the woods. When his target stepped out into the sunlight, he jerked back on the trigger.

Jensen!

His reaction caused the bullet to sail high and harmless. Jensen reacted with the speed of a striking rattler. He swung around, six-shooter drawn. He homed in on England Dan like a bloodhound on the scent. Bullets ripped past the miner and drove him back. He squeezed off a couple rounds that did nothing to stop the outlaw's attack.

Taking refuge behind a tree, he heard Jensen's bullets hammer into the wood only inches from his head. He broke open his pistol and ejected the spent brass. Fumbling, he reloaded and waited. Jensen had to reload soon. When he did, that would give the chance for a full-out frontal attack.

The pause in the attack spurred England Dan to action. He whirled around the tree. From the corner of his eye, he saw the splinters blown off the trunk. Concentrating on Jensen, he rushed forward, ready to kill. He swung around, trying to find the outlaw. Lars Jensen had vanished like fog in the bright Arizona sunlight.

If there hadn't been a faint cloud of gun smoke slowly dissipating, he wouldn't have known anything had disturbed the forest's solitude. Working his way to the edge of the clearing, he looked around for an ambush. Try as he might, he couldn't find a trail to follow.

England Dan wrestled with the problem. He had no trail to follow. Mabel was nowhere to be seen or heard. If Mandy still rode the mule, she was running away and knew to hide from anyone after her. Jensen deserved to be brought down, but England Dan wasn't a lawman. Far from it. He felt an obligation to do as Alberto Gonzales had asked—to kill the outlaw. But he couldn't help but think back to the deputy, who was still alive.

For the moment.

If he wasn't tended to soon, a new grave would be necessary. Better to save him so he could recover and go after the desperadoes like Jensen. Even before he was back in the saddle, Gonzales had the authority to call in other federal agents who were all able to do more than England Dan ever could. He was a miner, not a marshal.

He backed into the forest. Guilt gnawed at him. He had been cashiered from the British Army in India for cowardice. At the time he had thought it was better to save a village than to launch a suicidal attack. The same dilemma gripped him now. Go after a killer and maybe get killed? Or retreat and help the injured federal deputy marshal?

"She's your problem, Cooley," he grumbled. "You're the one who brought her to the mine." He snorted derisively. All their problems had come from Cooley's bad decisions. A quick pat on his coat pocket assured him that the map still rode there. Cooley had wasted what little gold they'd eked out of the Trafalgar Mine and set off a series of killings. Mandy's sister and her customer, and likely a federal lawman.

England Dan's duty was once more clear. Save as many lives as possible rather than rush headlong into a fight he wasn't fit to wage. He mounted Whirlwind and turned the horse's face. Getting through the woods took forever, but the horse strained to return to its owner's side.

"You get the varmint?" Alberto Gonzales fixed England Dan with a fevered gaze.

"Can you sit upright in the saddle, or do I have to sling you over it?"

Gonzales protested weakly as England Dan boosted him up. He damned his savior for not bringing in the outlaw. His biting critique of England Dan's heredity and personal habits became so feeble, they descended into mumbled whispers. Then he passed out.

England Dan rode behind, his arms around the still breathing deputy. He had to save the man or again he would have made the wrong decision like the one that had brought his disgrace in the army.

CHAPTER ELEVEN

LARS JENSEN FELT good about killing the annoying lawman. Alberto Gonzales had become worse than a burr under the saddle blanket. Being forced to watch his back trail while trying to recover the map for his brother had made Jensen a tad anxious. He didn't like the feeling. When he got the map and handed it over to Poke, the last of his collywobbles would be put to rest. It was always good when Poke wasn't on the warpath, and that would only happen if Beeman's map was recovered.

He slowed when he reached the edge of the wooded area. The forest turned dense only a few yards in. The pine and the juniper grew close-packed, making riding more difficult. The occasional game trail gave the best chance for finding the fleeing woman. Her mule wasn't inclined to pioneer a new path through the trees.

Jensen hopped down and walked along, leading his horse. His sharp eyes failed to find any trace of the mule walking along the first game trail. He stopped and considered what a frightened girl would do. A quick left turn took him deeper into the forest. A smile curled his lips. A dead bush had been trampled into dust on the ground by a hoof. Dried branches were broken and scattered a ways along the trail. He was back after the woman.

Hurrying along, he found increasing evidence that someone had come this way. It had to have been the woman riding the mule. Who else was out here? The deputy was dead, and the man who'd been with the whore hadn't been evident anywhere along the trail. Still, Jensen wanted to be ready.

The clearing gave him a quick look as the woman rode her mule into the forest on the far side. He swung into the saddle and urged his horse forward. He grinned as the whore looked back over her shoulder and spotted him. Her best bet was to keep going straight and not let him close the distance between them.

Then he saw her tactic. She darted into the woods. Somehow the trees swallowed the mule with its rider.

"Come on out, girlie. I don't want to hurt you. All I want's the map. Give me the map and you can ride that mule to Santa Fe for all I care." He doubted she was dumb enough to believe him, but trying wasn't going to cost him anything. One thing he was always good at was gulling people into believing him.

He felt a surge of accomplishment. Calling out as he did flushed her like a dove from a bush. She wove in and out between the closely spaced trees. The low-hanging limbs didn't bother her as they would him, seated on a taller horse. Jensen bent low to avoid a tree limb, then stopped and sat upright. Something felt wrong. He turned and looked around. Seeing nothing, he walked his horse back into the clearing.

A bullet tore through the air above his head. Jensen whipped out his six-shooter, then hesitated. Sniffing at the air as if he could locate the shooter that way, he swung about to where he saw a silhouette across the clearing. A quick shot forced the would-be back shooter to retreat. Jensen fired a couple times to get rid of the annoyance, but he had lost his target. Wasting his ammo left him vulnerable. Sitting stock-still, he waited to see if the sniper would come after him again. A full minute passed, but no one showed himself.

Jensen wondered if he had gotten in a lucky hit. He preferred to get close to the men he gunned down, to make sure. Like he had with the deputy. But riding across the clearing to find a body, either dead or sorely wounded, took time away from chasing down the fugitive woman. While he hadn't seen if she carried a weapon, the notion that preserving his limited store of ammunition seemed a good idea. There was no telling what new trouble he might find.

He ejected the spent cartridges and reloaded, all too aware how few rounds he had in reserve. Jensen slipped the six-gun into his holster and plunged into the woods to catch his quarry. She couldn't have gotten too far, not on a mule.

And he was right. Less than ten minutes later, he overtook her.

"Missy, you stop right now, and I won't hurt you none."

The fear on her face as she looked over her shoulder

at him made him feel good. She tried to dodge, duck-
ing down into a ravine and hurrying to reach a large
creek.

"You ride in water to hide your tracks. It's no good
now. I see you. Sloshing around like that only slows
you down."

She bent forward and tried to turn the mule into a
racehorse. Jensen thought she recognized him as the
man who had shot up the house of ill repute back in
Oasis.

"You and the other one, are you sisters? Is that the
way it is?" He shook his head as the only answer that
made a speck of sense came to him. Poke had always
said he was a slow thinker, but *slow* didn't mean he
wasn't thorough with figuring everything out. "You
look exactly like her. You won't end up dead if you give
me the map."

The girl let out a squeal and tried to get her mule up
an embankment near the creek. The ground looked
solid. It was mostly muddy. The surefooted mule slipped
and slid and then began slewing back down the slope to
where Jensen waited.

She looked up, fear etched on her face. "You killed
Mindy. You killed my sister."

"You look exactly like her. Twins, eh? I'm real sorry
about shooting her and the john with her. The galoot
wasn't who I wanted."

Mandy jumped off the mule and tried to escape on
foot. Jensen considered taking a shot or two at her. If
he winged her, that'd stop her dead in her tracks. Then
a better idea came to him. A quick grab brought his
lariat to hand. Hemp slid on hemp and made a loop.

He whirled it above his head and cast. The summer he'd spent with Poke rustling cattle came in handy now. The loop dropped over her. A yank on the rope tightened around her legs and sent her falling flat on her face.

Jensen leaned back in the saddle. His horse remembered all it had been taught when he had worked at running brands on the West Texas herd. It dug in its front hooves, then began backing away to keep the rope taut. He pulled her along in the mud until she stopped fighting.

"You going to behave, or do I have to hog-tie you?"

"Don't kill me, mister. I got no quarrel with you."

"And I don't have a problem with you—if you hand over the map. You have it on your person?"

Mandy sat up and kicked free of the rope. She made no effort to stand or get away. Jensen decided to see if she'd give him the map. She wasn't bad looking. Maybe she was smart, too, and saw how futile it was to fight the inevitable.

"Mister, you know what I did back in town. Me and my sister. Don't kill me and I can make life a whole lot better for you."

"More enjoyable, you mean?"

"Yes." She batted her emerald green eyes. They took on a cunning he had seen many times before. Women always thought they could hoodwink him. Sometimes it was diverting to let them think they had, but mostly he enjoyed watching their expressions change to fear when they recognized what they really faced.

"Me and you can have a high old time," Jensen said, "after you hand over the map."

"Map, map, what are you talking about? I don't have any map." Her coquettish mask dropped for a moment. Then fright replaced it.

He pointed his pistol straight at her. Shaking his head as if she had been naughty, he cocked the six-gun.

"I'm a real good shot. At this range there's no way I can miss." He fired.

Mandy jumped a foot. The bullet had kicked up a small tower of mud directly between her knees. She scooted back, not caring that her dress rode up or that she was wallowing in the mud.

"Where do you want the next bullet to hit? It'd be a shame to scar up your face. That's a hard shot, anyway. If I miss, it can shatter your cheekbone or take out an eye. Now, some gents get excited over a one-eyed whore. But they're few and far between." He leveled his gun again and sighted along the barrel.

"I'm telling you, I don't know anything about any map. It . . . it must be something Cooley has."

"The man with you back at the whorehouse?"

"Him, yes. We skedaddled and thought to hide out at his mine."

"The Trafalgar Mine?"

"Yes, that's the name. He said he was going to get rich. I thought he meant at that mine, but it looked all played out. I don't know about such things, but he was dead certain sure of himself."

"Where is he?"

"He ran out on me when you rode up. I took his mule to get away. I never saw him after you showed your face."

Jensen heard truth through her fear. His mind raced. She knew where to meet him, but getting that from her was going to take a fair amount of time. If it hadn't been for Poke getting sprung from Yuma so soon, taking a week or two getting the girl to talk would have been a lot of fun. Considering that she worked as a soiled dove, she might even have shown him a few things. He was certain he would have taught her some, too.

But time was short. And he tapped his trigger finger against the guard on his six-shooter. He needed ammo, he needed supplies and he needed the map.

"Take off your clothes."

"What?" Her eyes went wide.

"All of it. Every stitch. You can stand up so I can see that you don't have the map." Even if he didn't have a lot of time, there wasn't any reason not to enjoy himself as much as possible in the time he did have.

Mandy stood and stared daggers at him. Then she began unfastening all the ties and bows that plastered filthy clothing to her trim body. Jensen wasn't blind. He saw that she wasn't hiding a map anywhere, but he had a scheme to find Cooley and the map. He showed real appreciation as more and more naked skin showed.

"Wash your clothes in that stream yonder." He gestured with his pistol.

He enjoyed the sight of her on her knees beating her clothing clean on a rock.

"Go on. Get dressed."

"Everything's still wet."

He grinned. This made her furious—and even prettier. She pulled on the clothes and ran her hands over the skirt to squeeze out as much of the water as possible. A quick gesture with his six-gun got her over to the mule. It had found a juicy patch of grass and contentedly chomped on it. One large brown eye turned up to glare at him for disturbing a perfectly fine meal.

"You got saddlebags or anything like that?"

"You can see that I don't. There's the saddle and nothing else."

He poked around, although he knew she was right. What came next had to be done just so or she wouldn't believe it.

"I'm going to tie you up. You wait here." He backed toward his horse, gathered his lariat and fumbled about some to step into the lasso. A quick twist made it look as if the horse had backed up while the rope tangled around his feet. He fell heavily and yelled to the horse. Obediently, it began backing away, as if he had roped a calf again.

Jensen had to wiggle and thrash about on his own since the rope didn't actually pull him along. A quick glance showed the woman took the chance and jumped onto the mule. Her heels raked at the mule's flanks and got the animal running in nothing flat. When she got out of sight, Jensen stood and wiped off the mud. Taking a bath appealed to him, but letting the girl get too much of a head start wasn't in the cards. He wanted her to find Cooley. Taking the two of them together would be as easy as pie.

Jensen considered tying up Cooley and making him watch what he did to the girl. But only after he had the map safely tucked away. He stepped up and snapped the reins to get his horse walking slowly on the trail left by the fugitive.

Letting her keep far enough ahead so she wouldn't spot him was something of a chore since she rode so erratically. It was as if she thought that zigzagging through the forest confused her trail, but she had taken one thing he'd said to heart. When she found a creek, she splashed into it and headed away. Jensen got his bearings. The creek led back, more or less, to the direction of the cabin. That made him wonder if Cooley wasn't waiting there. He decided to keep on this trail, if the whore and the miner had some prearranged rendezvous other than the cabin.

They knew the mountains in these parts better than he did. Taking a risk that lost him the trail—and the map—wasn't in the cards. For once, he played it close to the vest.

He rode along the bank, keeping a sharp eye out for when Mandy left the creek to cut across the countryside. She kept the mule's feet wet longer than he expected. Jensen thought on whether this was clever or if she rode like that because she was scared of him. He hoped it was building fear that drove her.

Seeing that fright in a woman's eyes excited him. Thinking that she still dreaded him was thrilling.

Thinking on this and becoming inattentive almost cost him his carefully laid plans. He rode into the large meadow, on the side opposite where he had left Alberto Gonzales dead, and would have exposed himself to the fleeing girl. She rode the mule hard to a tight stand of trees a half mile off.

If Cooley was going to meet up with her, that was the sort of place he'd have chosen. That was where Jensen would have picked. It gave shelter from prying eyes and was back in the direction of the cabin. He judged how long it'd take him to cross the meadow. Deciding he had a few minutes to spare, he dismounted and let his horse crop at the juicy grass while he built himself a smoke. Tying off the pouch of tobacco and sticking it back into his pocket gave him a sense of satisfaction. He expertly rolled the cigarette and lit it. The smoke billowed into his lungs and relaxed him. When he caught up with her and Cooley, that would be the time to let excitement build. Chasing after the two wore down his patience.

He finished his cigarette and mounted. Before he trotted his horse across the meadow, he reared back. His six-shooter came into his fist, but he slid it back into the holster, cursing softly. Coming from the distant copse was the mule, but the soiled dove wasn't riding it. Or any white man.

Seated astride the mule was a wildly gesturing Indian. Flanking the mule were a half-dozen Indians on foot. Another came from the woods on a sturdy pony. From their dress, it wasn't a war party.

"Hunters," Jensen whispered as he soothed his horse, patting its neck. "They got lucky and caught the whore."

Four more Indians followed the one on the mule. Shooting it out with so many was out of the question, especially when they hadn't taken the girl captive. Somehow, they had stolen her mule. Her body might lie in the woods, or she might have escaped. That was unlikely, but her luck had been favorable so far.

Lars Jensen frowned as he considered what trail to ride now. The girl didn't have the map. Cooley had it, but she wasn't meeting up with him. The Indians looked as if they had just played the winning card. And they had. They'd keep a mule, which was both useful and considered part of a brave's status in the tribe.

He watched the hunting party disappear into a different section of the forest. When they were out of sight, he turned toward the far side of the meadow, riding in the direction of the miner's shack. The only place he was likely to find Cooley now was back at the mine. Somebody's luck had to change—and Jensen intended it to be the miner's.

CHAPTER TWELVE

J OHN COOLEY GASPED for breath. He had run himself
into the ground along the narrow mountain trail.
Mandy had ridden the mule along here, but he wasn't
sure he saw any spoor. But where else could she have
gone? Chest hurting, he stopped, put his hands on his
knees and bent over. Every time he sucked in air, his
lungs filled with fire. He had almost recovered when he
heard someone on the trail behind him.

Mandy was ahead. The only one who'd be between
him and the cabin was the blond killer from town. Lars
Jensen. He looked around, suddenly frantic. Strug-
gling uphill was out of the question. He'd kick loose
rocks and slip and slide and never get out of sight before a man astride a horse trotted up.

Going the other way looked like suicide, but he had
no choice. Peering over the edge, he saw the loose rock
extended only a few feet. Below that, a rocky ledge ran

parallel to the trail he was on. He dug in his boot for the jump. He swallowed hard, closed his eyes and kicked out hard.

He let out a scream as he launched himself into the air. With a frantic twist that hurt his ribs, he turned half around. Fingers clawing frantically, he caught at the rock. The loose rock. He had a double handful of loose stones that did nothing to keep him from plunging downward. He remembered the sheer cliff just beyond the lower ledge. That was his fate, to fall and fall and fall . . .

Cooley slammed hard against the mountainside and somehow dug his toes in far enough to slow his descent. Grabbing wildly, he caught a rock in his left hand. The sudden stop almost yanked his arm from his shoulder joint. He hung with his face pressed into the rock and dirt. And he cried in joy for that. He hadn't plunged to his death. With great deliberation, he moved his toes around until he found purchase. Then he sought handholds. Once he was secure, he inched downward to the rocky ledge.

Unabashedly, he flopped face down and sobbed. Everything he had done in the past day or two had moved him ever closer to death, but this time, he had seen his own demise rushing up. The relief now was more than his overworked emotions could handle.

He shook with emotion but had to stifle it when he heard a horse passing along the trail fifteen feet above. If Lars Jensen looked over the edge, he would see Cooley. Shooting fish in a rain barrel flashed through his head. A man as skilled with a six-shooter as Jensen must be couldn't miss.

The outlaw hadn't missed when he had plugged

Mindy and the man with her. Cooley fought back a new wave of blubbering. Jensen thought he'd killed Mandy and a penniless miner named John Cooley.

It gnawed at Cooley that Jensen was going to catch up with Mandy. He wished there was something he could do about it. Cooley sat up and drew his six-shooter. He was no match for a stone-cold killer like Jensen. The best he could hope for was the outlaw carelessly turning his back. Cooley had six shots, and that was it. He wasn't a sharpshooter, not like his partner. He had watched Rutledge practicing. The man never missed with that Brit pistol he carried. Cooley almost believed the stories about Rutledge graduating from some fancy military school and being in the army. That heavy, faded, red wool cavalry jacket he wore, the one with the epaulets missing and the buttons ripped off, looked like something Cooley had seen in a book once about the British Army.

He'd gladly hand over his six-shooter to his partner if England Dan would kill the outlaw. Cooley had no doubt Rutledge was capable of such slaughter, which was a good thing. Try as he might, Cooley failed to summon the courage ever to shoot anyone else. Even Lars Jensen. Even if it meant saving Mandy.

Maybe even if it meant saving his own life.

He carefully got to his feet. Jensen had ridden past. All Cooley had to do was climb back to the upper trail and return to the cabin. From there he could get back to Oasis in a day and tell somebody that a dangerous killer roamed the hills. As that idea crossed his mind, he almost laughed at its absurdity. Nobody in Oasis cared because there wasn't a marshal there. Bisbee? They had law, but no marshal had jurisdiction out here.

Getting back with his partner was his only hope of worming out of this predicament.

Planning on getting to the cabin and doing it were different things. Nowhere along the narrow ledge offered a way up. He kept walking until the ledge petered out; then he took his life in his hands and slid down to a broader ledge. This led in the direction opposite to where he wanted to go, but Cooley had no choice. Nervous as a long-tailed cat beside a rocking chair, he kept walking when this trail opened onto a slope leading down into a wooded area. From previous scouting around, he knew a large meadow opened beyond the forest.

Warily, since Jensen might pop up like a prairie dog at any turn, Cooley made his way through the trees, angling around to where the trail led back to the cabin. The cool, damp forest calmed him. His mind settled and worry ran away.

That peace was shattered when he heard a loud guffawing from somewhere ahead. Cooley dropped to the ground, flat on his belly, and slithered like a snake to hide behind a fallen log. Heart pounding, he screwed his eyes shut. That had to be Jensen laughing. Who else was he likely to find in the forest but the gunfighter?

The laughter faded to the point at which Cooley strained to hear it. He jumped when the mirth was replaced with chanting. He came up to his knees, gun drawn. That wasn't Jensen. It was an Indian performing some strange ceremony—he could tell by the exuberant chanting.

Stepping over the log, he made his way forward. His gun swung to and fro until he saw the brave through

the trees. Covered in dirt, the Indian danced around a
guttering campfire. Cooley had no idea what ceremony
he was witnessing or why only a single Indian was
dancing. He hunkered down to watch. There had to be
more Indians lurking. Having a pack of them after his
scalp was a blunder to be avoided at all costs.

He trained his sights on the lone Indian, then sank
back when the dance stopped. The Indian dropped to
his knees and looked as if he prayed. Many of them had
been sent back East to parochial schools. Cooley wondered if this one had adopted American ways. Watching the erratic behavior got him nowhere. He skirted
the camp and started through the forest to get to the
path going back to his cabin.

"Who?"

Cooley jerked around, his six-shooter coming up at
the question. The brave stood behind him, hand on a
sheathed knife.

"I don't want any trouble. You get on back to your
dancing or whatever you were doing."

"You have food for No Shadow?"

"No Shadow? That's your name?" Cooley let his
partner deal with the roving bands of Indians throughout the hills. "Do you know England Dan Rutledge?
Him and me are partners back at a mine." He kept the
six-shooter leveled but gestured vaguely with his left
hand.

"England Dan? A good man. He gives me whiskey."

This surprised Cooley. Giving firewater to the braves
got you in big trouble if the law found out. The cavalry
had tossed more than one trader into the hoosegow for
dealing with Indians, swapping whiskey and guns for
fresh meat and buckskin clothes.

"You still have any of the whiskey? I need to wet my whistle something fierce."

No Shadow motioned for Cooley to follow him. He didn't walk back to his camp but instead danced. Cooley found himself mimicking the moves, then cursed himself for such folly. When he got to the campsite, No Shadow crouched beside a large beaded leather pouch. He rummaged about inside it and pulled out a small pint bottle.

"What's in it?" Cooley had expected amber fluid. The bottle held a clear liquid. He took it when No Shadow held it out to him. He pulled out the cork and sniffed. No smell. A quick sampling made him want to spit it out. "That's water. You gave me a bottle of warm water."

"Drank whiskey already," the brave said. He took the bottle and tilted it back. A single long draft emptied it. With a grand gesture, he wiped his lips, then held the empty bottle in both hands over his head as if making an offering of it.

"What're you doing? Making an offering to the Great Spirit?"

"Not Great Spirit. Big Owl. Stay away, Big Owl!"

Cooley looked around, but the trees were empty of birds, owls or any other kind.

"Owls don't fly around hunting in the daylight. We had a pygmy owl roosting in our mine for a spell. But they aren't big. Not like a great horned owl. Is that what you mean by a big owl? They are big birds." Cooley frowned.

The brave glared at him as if he had said something dumb. "Big Owl screeches death. You will hear him."

"I don't believe in omens, especially one caused by a varmint-eating bird."

"You will die!" No Shadow jumped to his feet and brandished his knife. The blade flashed silver as it swung in wide circles. No Shadow came toward Cooley.

Cooley didn't even realize he had his six-gun out again. When the brave raised the knife high over his head, Cooley fired. The bullet tore through the attacking man's chest. Rather than stop him, it infuriated No Shadow. He lunged. The blade slashed down, barely missing Cooley's shoulder. A second bullet fired at close range hit the Indian in the chest. This slug killed him outright.

The man's weight forced Cooley back. He fell with No Shadow stretched on top of him, the knife driven into the ground next to his ear. Panic set in. He cried out and shoved. The brave refused to budge. Scrambling harder, Cooley rolled No Shadow off him and got to his feet, six-gun pointed at the motionless body.

"You tried to kill me. You . . . you . . ." Cooley's gun hand shook so hard, he had to grab his right wrist with his left hand to control himself. He stared at the body and then the gun. He seldom fired his gun. He had never shot at another man. Now he had gone and killed an Indian.

Nobody would care. This was just a wandering Indian. Cooley couldn't even figure out what tribe claimed No Shadow from the paint on his face and body.

Keeping his left hand on his wrist, he pulled back and shoved his pistol into his holster. He nudged No Shadow with his toe, hoping to see some signs of life. The full weight of what he had done finally hit him. Cooley stepped back and sat heavily on the ground, staring at the body. Conflicting thoughts crowded into his head. He ought to bury the man, but was saying a prayer over the grave wrong? No Shadow looked as if he had been praying to a god, but which one? Cooley wasn't much on churchgoing, but he knew he had committed a sin shooting a man.

"Wasn't a crime. Not a sin," he muttered. "He came for me with that knife." The hilt poked up from where it had been sheathed in the earth. That was proof he had only defended himself. It wasn't like he'd shot the Indian in the back. "I tried to avoid him. That counts for something. It has to."

Even if he had wanted to report the death, there wasn't anybody who'd care. Oasis didn't have a marshal. The sheriff had his office over in Bisbee. But there was Alberto Gonzales. He was a deputy marshal, but there wasn't any reason for him to care about a single death when he was busy chasing down Lars Jensen. This was a ways from his office, if he had one over in Mesilla.

The sound of horses caused Cooley to snap out of his funk. He jumped to his feet and looked around in fright. Movement showed several riders coming slowly through the forest from the direction of the meadow.

Cut off from where he had been headed, Cooley retreated the way he had come. He dived headlong and skidded on his belly as the riders came fully into sight. Twisting around, he saw four mounted Indians. All had the same color paint on their face as the one he had shot down.

"Self-defense. I killed him because he came at me with the knife." He drew up his knees and circled them with his arms. Shakes racked him again as he watched the Indians ride about the campsite before dismounting and approaching No Shadow's body.

When one of them pointed in the direction where Cooley had been headed, he breathed a sigh of relief. Then he tensed. Two others found his trail back into the woods. From the way they stood almost chin to chin and argued, he knew they had found how he had escaped after shooting No Shadow. The entire band looked in his direction, but the one he focused on wore fancier buckskins. The beads shimmered in the sunlight, with some silver worked among the colored beads. That had to be the chief, and what he said carried weight.

He stared straight at Cooley. It was doubtful his gaze penetrated the brush between Cooley and the hunters, but it caused new shakes to torment the hiding man. He clutched his pistol and knew he was a goner if the Indians came for him. He had four shots left. Or perhaps it was three. He hadn't counted the rounds already in the cylinder when he grabbed the six-shooter back at the cabin.

Edging away slowly, trying not to rustle the leaves, he put more distance between himself and what was likely his death. The Indians wouldn't understand why he'd had to kill No Shadow. All they knew was that one of their tribe had been shot. Cooley kept moving like a crab until he got to his feet, found the game trail and lit out running. He gasped for breath before he got too far, but fear kept him stumbling along longer than his endurance would have otherwise permitted. Finally close to collapse, he threw his arms around a tree and supported himself.

Legs wobbly and his lungs filled with liquid fire, he tried to listen for pursuit. His hammering pulse turned his ears into kettledrums. If he kept to the trail, the Indians would overtake him in jig time. They rode their ponies. He depended on shank's mare.

Cooley pushed away from the tree and left the trail, hopping and jumping along like he had been given a hotfoot. This added distance between his boot prints. He began choosing rocks to land on, green carpets of pine needles that wouldn't betray his actual course, anything to hide his tracks. He jumped, grabbed an oak tree limb and began inching along until he leaped across to another. Leaves fluttered to the ground, but the Indians wouldn't follow such a trail. Leaves fell all the time on their own.

He hoped they weren't good enough trackers.

Panting from exertion, he clung to a limb to rest. His heart dropped when he heard the steady pace of a horse coming toward him once again. They had traced him in spite of his best efforts. Cooley closed his eyes and fought to keep from sobbing.

CHAPTER THIRTEEN

ALBERTO GONZALES JERKED, moaned and almost escaped the circle of England Dan Rutledge's arms. The miner tensed and leaned back hard to keep the deputy from falling off the horse. The stallion tried to balk at the uneven weight, forcing England Dan to stop until the load was once more even. He looked past the lawman and let out a sigh of relief. It seemed he had been riding forever and getting nowhere. At last he saw the final bend in the trail before reaching his cabin.

"We're almost there. Don't up and die on me."

"Won't. Need to get Jensen. Get Jensen," the deputy whispered hoarsely.

"That's right," England Dan said, giving the man a reason to keep breathing. "You'll catch him for sure. Just think on that."

The black stallion rounded the bend and headed straight for the shed, where the mule had been stabled.

England Dan let the horse have its head. He ducked as
Whirlwind went inside, then kicked free and let the
deputy fall into his arms. The weight staggered him,
but he kept from dropping the injured man. He swung
Gonzales around to sit on a hay bale. When he was
sure the man wouldn't topple, he tended to the horse.
By the time he finished, Alberto Gonzales fought to
climb to his feet.

"Come on. We'll get you bedded down, then see
about the bullet in you."

The deputy marshal muttered something incoher-
ent. This spurred England Dan on to greater speed.
He kicked open the door and heaved to get Gonzales
onto the nearest bed. As exhausted as he was, England
Dan had no time to rest. He started a fire and got a pan
of water boiling. The few rags scattered around the
cabin went into the water. Sterilizing them wasn't going to be perfect, but the deputy wasn't going to complain. From his drawn look, pinched expression and
labored breathing, he wasn't going to live much longer.

England Dan sterilized his knife blade in the Franklin stove, got his boiled rags and set to work cleaning
the wound. After he wiped away the blood, he began
digging around in the man's chest to pry out the bullet.
Gonzales turned paler, and England Dan sweat buck-
ets, but the hunk of lead finally popped free. The ex-
cess blood was mopped up with the hot rags. Then
England Dan wiped away the blood on the other man's
face.

As dangerous as that wound looked, it was minor.
The bullet had creased the deputy's forehead and left
a shallow if bloody gash. England Dan had thought
Alberto Gonzales was dead when he saw the head

wound. Lars Jensen probably thought the same, or he would have finished him off with a final bullet.

"Take some water." England Dan poured a little over the deputy's lips.

Gonzales stirred. His eyelids fluttered, and then he focused with surprising strength. "You got it out?"

"Rest. You need to get to town, where someone can look after you."

"Stop Jensen. Kill him for me. I'll see you get a reward." It seemed that was all Alberto Gonzales could focus on. He winced, then subsided, but he didn't pass out.

England Dan marveled at how strong and determined the lawman was. He had been dancing on the edge of his grave and turned away. Business left unfinished had to be completed. The miner had to wonder if Gonzales would have shown so much fortitude if Jensen had been killed or caught. Job done, life over?

Somehow, he doubted it. There was always another owlhoot to bring to justice for a man like this.

Having the deputy's stallion made the trip back to Oasis easier. If they both stayed upright in the saddle, it was a long day's ride. England Dan was anxious to be rid of the responsibility so he could get to other things. He stood in the doorway and looked along the trail where Mabel had carried Mandy and Cooley. Or at least the woman. England Dan worried that his partner had lit out for parts unknown, but he wanted to be sure he wasn't lying dead at the bottom of a ravine. John Cooley was his partner, and that meant something to him.

Noise from Gonzales' bed made him look back. The lawman held a tin cup with both hands and drank a bit.

Against all odds, he was strong enough to tend to himself. A little. This changed England Dan's plans. Getting the lawman to Oasis was important, but finding Cooley ranked higher.

"If I leave food and water where you can reach it, will you be all right?" Asking a man wounded as severely as Alberto Gonzales had been if he could take care of himself was foolish. England Dan knew the answer before Gonzales grated it out.

"Get on his trail. Go on. Leave more water, and I'll ride with you—and him—back to town."

"I need to find my partner first." He saw how this upset Gonzales. The man was focused on one thing and one thing only: catching Lars Jensen. Anything else was blasphemy.

"Jensen. Him." The deputy sank back and closed his eyes. His lips kept moving. *Jensen. Jensen.*

England Dan placed water and what food he thought was palatable for a wounded man on the table; then he slid it close to the bed. Gonzales had either fallen into a coma or a deep sleep. It was hard to tell which it was. Leaving him was a risk in either case.

"Cooley," England Dan finally said. Other than sitting and holding the lawman's hand, there wasn't much more he could do. The bullet had been plucked out of Gonzales' chest, so it wouldn't poison him. He needed to rest and recover his strength. "I have to find if you're still alive."

He cleaned his Webley and made sure it carried a full load. Sorting through the larder for trail rations, he came to a decision. The Trafalgar Mine wasn't much, but it belonged to the pair of them. Trying to claim all of it for himself without proof that Cooley

had died would raise the hackles of the townspeople.
Not that they admired or respected Cooley. It was a
matter of law. Any number of citizens would send word
to Bisbee to investigate.

Walking away from the Trafalgar was a possibility
since there wasn't much gold left in its veins. He patted
his coat pocket where the map to the Irish Lord Mine
rested. If that hidden mine was abandoned, he could
claim it for his own. But who left a mine known for the
richest strike along the Mogollon Rim? The map must
be something else. He looked at Alberto Gonzales. The
federal deputy marshal knew things like this for certain.

England Dan wished he had some, a few, even one
solid fact to operate on. He sighed. Cooley might know.

He checked Gonzales one last time and stepped
outside. Barely had he started toward the shed before
he heard footfalls pounding along the trail. A glance
to his left showed a decent place to lay down an ambush. He scrambled behind the rocks and drew a bead
on a notch in the trail. Anyone coming through the
narrow passage would be a sitting duck.

The running sounds came closer. He tensed. His
finger drew back on the trigger; then he sagged and put
his head against the warm rock. England Dan sat up
quickly and called, "I almost shot you!"

John Cooley spun around, eyes wide. His hand
rested on the butt of his six-shooter. In his headlong
rush, he had been oblivious to the ambush.

"Dan! There you are."

England Dan slipped and slid back to the trail. He
stuffed his Webley back into his holster and studied
his partner. Cooley looked a fright. His clothing was

ripped, and mud and dirt caked him so heavily that he left behind a small cloud of dust as he moved. Hardly realizing he did it, he glanced down at the trail. The boot imprint with the worn heel and hole in the sole was a perfect match for the boot print he had found what seemed an eternity ago. His tracking skills proved better than he had ever hoped, for all the good they had done him. He'd not found his partner; his partner had returned on his own.

"Where have you been? What happened to Mandy and our mule? Did she steal Mabel?"

"She rode out on Mabel, yeah." Cooley nervously looked over his shoulder. "Let's get into the cabin."

"Who's after you? Jensen?"

"Not him. I . . . I had a run-in with some Indians, and, well, there was some shooting."

"Big Ear and a few braves are hunting east of here. You mixed it up with them?" England Dan went cold inside. Big Ear had never taken well to reservation life, and he often slipped away to hunt and more often to raid. Every time the cavalry ran him down caused a little more animosity.

"Is he kinda crazy? This Big Ear fellow?"

They walked back to the cabin. England Dan stopped Cooley from rushing inside. "Don't make any noise inside. The deputy's asleep."

"Alberto Gonzales?" Cooley hopped from foot to foot. "That's good. He can talk to the Indians and tell them it was all a mistake."

"What have you done?"

Bit by bit England Dan wormed the story out of Cooley. If his partner had wanted to start a new fight between the white men in the mountains and the Mogollons, he couldn't have planned it better. No Shadow might have been loco, but he was still valued by the tribe. Truth to tell, England Dan was a bit fond of No Shadow himself. Mostly, even if he had been touched in the head, he wasn't dangerous.

Cooley never got out enough to find out where the real dangers lay in the mountains. Now he had lit a fuse that would burn down to months or even years of killing.

"I didn't know. He tried to kill me. It was self-defense."

England Dan wasn't buying it, but calling his partner a liar would only make matters worse.

"Look, Dan, we'll tell the deputy and let him take care of this. That's his job, isn't it?"

"Gonzales is too single-minded about catching Lars Jensen to bother parleying with Big Ear."

"If these Indians are so riled up and want to scalp any white man, maybe they'll catch up with Jensen and kill him. That'll satisfy their bloodlust and remove a dangerous outlaw."

"That's something out of a penny dreadful. It's never going to happen. And the deputy's not in any condition to negotiate with Big Ear or anybody. Jensen shot him up pretty bad and left him for dead."

"He's dead? You put a dead man in our cabin!"

"He's not dead, but he's in a bad way. I want to get him into Oasis, where somebody can look after him. It's not my job—our job—to nurse anybody back to health. He'll want to send a telegram to his boss, too. This might bring the federal marshal himself in to arrest Jensen."

"More law coming in," Cooley mused. He stroked his

stubbled chin, then shook his head. "I don't like that. Having the mine overrun with lawmen's not a good idea, but what else can we do? Jensen. The Indians. Everybody out there's got one thing on their mind."

"To kill you," England Dan finished for him. "And Mandy is roaming around the hills, too. What about her?"

"She's a big girl. She can take care of herself. I never told her she could take the mule. She up and stole Mabel, she did."

England Dan held down a rising disgust at such careless sentiments. Mandy's sister had been murdered, and if she wasn't lucky, she'd end up being shot by Jensen or, worse, taken as a slave by Big Ear. If that happened and the cavalry got wind of it, a new Indian war was guaranteed. Cooley had not only set the explosive; he had lit the fuse.

"You still got the map?" Cooley asked. "I say we leave the deputy and go get rich. The Irish Lord is waitin' for us out there."

"It's a map to a mine, but it more likely shows something else. Since Jensen is so eager to get the map, he must know there are riches held there. With a criminal like him, it must be where loot from some robbery was hidden."

"If he stole it, why wouldn't he know where it was without the map?"

England Dan replied. "If he doesn't know, then maybe somebody else from his gang of robbers hid the loot and made the map, for whatever reason. Now Jensen is after it."

"That makes sense," Cooley said. "That means, if we get on the trail right now, Jensen won't know where we're goin'. We get the loot or find the mine or what-ever the map leads us to. Then we're rich!"

"We should be so lucky. First, we get Gonzales to town. Then we figure out what to do. Go fetch his horse."

"The one in the shed? I saw it and wondered whose it was. I considered takin' it, but then you jumped out from behind the rock and scared me something fierce."

"The horse. Get it saddled and ready for the trail. I'll see to the deputy."

Cooley went off, talking to himself about following the map and getting rich. England Dan was glad he hadn't told his partner that he knew where to start looking—and that No Shadow had been the one to put him on the right path. The landmarks from the west side of Coronado Pass were all wrong. Approaching from the east and using Mule Springs as a starting point made sense of the markers on the map.

He was glad Gonzales was asleep. Or maybe he had passed out. He hardly roused when heaved out of the bed and half walked, half dragged to the door. By the time England Dan got outside, Cooley was leading Whirlwind to where they could hoist the deputy into the saddle.

"We can't all ride. Let's leave the deputy and go find the mine." Cooley stared hard at his partner. "You still have the map, don't you?"

"It's safe. Once we get him to town, I'll show you."

"I'll ride behind him," Cooley said. With a quick move, he climbed into the saddle behind Alberto Gon-zales. "Watch out. I can't hold him!"

"Oh, my God!" England Dan reacted quickly when the deputy tumbled from the saddle. He caught the heavy load, but it drove him back. He collapsed under the weight and sat heavily, the man weighing him down.

He twisted and protected Gonzales as the stallion reared. Cooley fought to keep control. The horse whirled about, pawing the air, then kicking out with its back legs.

The next thing England Dan knew, Whirlwind bolted and ran back toward the shed, with Cooley clinging to it and trying not to be bucked off.

England Dan rolled a moaning Gonzales onto his side, climbed to his feet and hurried down the path after his partner. Cooley was nowhere to be seen. The runaway horse was carrying him back toward Big Ear and, for all England Dan knew, Lars Jensen. Anybody Cooley ran into along that path was likely to be gunning for him.

It was a dilemma without a good solution. England Dan heaved the lawman to his feet and got him back into the cabin. The bed creaked as Gonzales' weight pressed down. At least it wasn't deadweight. Not yet. England Dan stared at the unconscious man. There was little more he could do to help.

But Cooley? His feckless partner needed all the help he could get. Reluctantly leaving Alberto Gonzales, he set off along the path to track down Cooley before he got into more trouble than he could handle.

CHAPTER FOURTEEN

THE BLACK STALLION reared and began pawing at the air. John Cooley fought to stay in the saddle. As he reached out to grab the saddle horn, Alberto Gonzales melted in front of him and tumbled to the ground. All Cooley thought of was keeping the horse from trampling its owner. Explaining how the deputy died wasn't anything he wanted to deal with. The federal marshal would never believe that his deputy had been shot up and then stomped to death by his own horse.

Cooley had spent a fair amount of time in the saddle but never on such a spirited horse. He yelped as he was jerked around. Clinging to the reins and the saddle horn kept him astride Whirlwind, but it sunfished, landed hard enough to jolt him, then lit out like somebody had set fire to its tail.

"No, not that way. No!" Cooley's protests meant nothing to the frightened horse. It put its head down and ran full out along the narrow trail. From horse-back he stared down the precipice on his right. That scared Cooley, but the horse insisted on running back in the direction of the distant meadow, the very spot where England Dan told him Alberto Gonzales had been gunned down. Worse, he knew he was riding toward Big Ear and his hunters.

If they figured out he was responsible for killing the crazy Indian, he was a goner. Cooley bent low and clung to the horse for dear life. It was a powerful animal, but it had to tire sooner or later. Cooley hoped his wild ride didn't end with Whirlwind stumbling and sending them both over the cliff.

When Whirlwind began flagging, Cooley gently tugged on the reins. At first this spooked the horse again. It had a new rider who wasn't able to control it. But the long run had tired it enough, so more tugging on the reins began to work. Lathered and flanks heaving, the horse came to a halt.

Cooley started to jump down, then realized he might never get back on. The horse had a mind of its own. He patted Whirlwind's neck and did what he could to soothe the animal. He preferred riding Mabel. It wasn't as noble an animal, but the mule wasn't inclined to run off at a breakneck speed.

He tried to turn the stallion around, but the horse wasn't having any of it. Cooley surrendered to the inevitable and gave the deputy's horse its head. It began walking along the trail leading to the meadow. Worry made Cooley reach down and touch his six-shooter. Too many dangers lay ahead. By the time they exited the forest and entered the meadow, both horse and rider had calmed down.

Cooley tentatively turned the horse about, but again it took control and headed for a stream. He let it drink, still not dismounting. He ached all over from being pounded and bounced about, but if he wanted to return to the cabin, he dared not let the horse go. Walking on such sore legs would take him forever.

"Come on, don't bloat," he said, pulling on the reins to draw the horse away from the stream. As he succeeded in steering the horse in a new direction, he spotted Mandy upstream. The woman drank her fill and started away without noticing him.

The horse decided to go to the woman, so Cooley let it. He fought conflicting emotions. Mandy only made his life more complicated, but he was attracted to her. But not returning straightaway to the cabin posed a danger. The Indian hunters prowled around. So did Lars Jensen. But Mandy was out here, as well. She had moved from the spot along the stream to sit under a piñon pine, and there she softly cried. This was enough to make him forget his determination to stay in the saddle. He swung off the horse and clutched the reins to prevent the horse from rearing.

"Mandy? Are you all right?"

The blonde looked up, startled, and swiped at the tears welling in her eyes. She sniffed, wiped away the tears and glared at him. "What do you want?"

"I . . . I came hunting for you." The words came easily, even if they weren't true. Not exactly. "Why'd you run off?"

"The tall gunman came. I wasn't going to sit there and let him kill me like he did Mindy."

"I'll protect you," Cooley said. He sat beside her. She jerked away when he tried to hold her hand.

"Your mule ran off," she said. "It stranded me when I tried to rest."

Cooley looked around as if Mabel would show up. The mule was nowhere to be seen. "What are you going to do? There's more trouble than Jensen out here."

"I know. Indians. They stole the mule. It ran off, and I went after it, and they grabbed it. I hid so they wouldn't find me, but they took the mule."

She cried more now. This time she buried her face in his shoulder. That made Cooley a tad uncomfortable, but he wasn't going to push her away, even if she had let the Indians steal the mule.

"Let's get away from here." Cooley tried to disengage and get her to her feet. Both of them riding the stallion posed a problem. He wasn't sure the horse would allow a solitary rider on its back, but he had to try. The entire area was a giant trap waiting to be sprung. He wanted to be far from the steel jaws, if that happened.

She wasn't getting to her feet. Cooley started to get mad, but then he saw the tail end of his mule vanish through the heavy woods.

"Mabel!" he called, and then whistled. The mule had sometimes come when he called it like a dog. He laughed in delight when it began weaving through the trees, coming toward him.

He felt as if he had stepped off a cliff when he saw the Mogollon hunter riding the mule. Alongside the brave came another, this one on horseback. Flitting like shadows, a half dozen more Indians appeared, all on foot. He rested his hand on his six-gun, but he had sense enough not to throw down on the hunters. They all carried rifles.

And the grim, determined expressions on their faces showed they weren't likely to think kindly of him if he drew the gun.

"No!" Mandy saw the Indians and recognized her fate. She grabbed Cooley's arm. "Don't let them take me. You said you'd protect me, John. John!"

He pulled free. He tried to think of a way out of this. Putting himself in England Dan's boots failed to give him a clever plan. His partner thought fast on his feet, and if he were here, they'd be safe.

Cooley wondered if they read the guilt on his face. He had killed one of their band.

Rather than babble incoherently, he kept his mouth shut. The Indian on the horse rode up and stared at him. The hunter's expression was unreadable. Cooley tried to figure out if this was the chief or just another of the band. The idea that the others were on foot—or riding his stolen mule—and one rode a horse told him what the pecking order had to be.

"Hello." Cooley hoped his voice didn't crack with strain. Using every ounce of his willpower, he took his hand off the butt of his six-shooter.

"Yours?" The one he thought was the chief pointed to the stallion with his rifle.

"Yes." Trying to explain how he had borrowed the horse from the deputy was too complicated. Letting the chief know Whirlwind had run off with him when he failed to control it was even worse.

The Indians argued among themselves for a moment; then the chief made a chopping motion with his hand, cutting off further discussion. "You kill one of our warriors?"

Cooley didn't have to feign shock at the accusation. How could the Indian possibly have known?

"I'd never do such a thing. I was riding around, looking for her." He pointed to Mandy, who shied away from him. She hugged herself and looked at him, frightened. He knew what she felt.

"You not on foot?"

Cooley remembered seeing the Indians looking for his boot prints and how he had done everything possible to hide his trail. They sought a man on foot, without a horse. "That's my horse. I've been riding it."

One brave spoke up and began pointing to his own moccasin-clad foot. Cooley knew the chief would ask to see his boot soles. The hole would be all it took to convict him since it proved he had been where No Shadow had been killed.

"You're a big, powerful chief. Here. Take my horse. My gift to you." The stallion seemed to understand and wasn't any happier with the new change of ownership than it had been about letting Cooley ride it.

The chief hopped down and went to the black horse. It tried to shy away, but the chief handled it better than Cooley ever could have. In a few seconds, it was nuzzling him. The chief grunted and handed the reins over to one of his braves on foot. He turned and grinned. Cooley didn't like the way that looked.

"Her."

"What?" Mandy exploded. She tried to run. Another brave caught her in a steely grip. Struggle as she might, there wasn't any way to get free.

Cooley's hand twitched just above his holstered pistol. He looked from Mandy to the other Indians. They all

had their rifles resting in the crooks of their arms, but he
saw how alert they looked. The smallest mistake on his
part would bring those fearsome weapons around.
They'd fill him with lead in a split second.

"G-go on. Take her."

"You coward!" Mandy clawed her way free. Her cap-
tor let her get to Cooley. She tried to rake out his eyes.

He stepped back. "It's for the best. Don't worry. I—"

"You low-down, no-account, belly-crawling snake
in the grass!"

He stepped away as the Indian who had grabbed her
bent, got his arm around her waist and hoisted her kicking and screaming off the ground. The best Cooley
could muster was a weak smile to match the broad grin
on the chief's face.

With a quick jump, the chief mounted the stallion.
The brave imprisoning Mandy heaved her over the
back of the chief's other horse, then mounted and held
the woman in place. The entire band left, even taking
Mabel. All Cooley could do was watch them vanish.

He dropped to his knees, shaking at his brush with
death. If he'd put up any fight, they would have killed
him. He knew it. Losing the deputy's horse was bad,
but they'd already stolen Mabel. Taking Mandy only
added to his humiliation.

He used a tree for support as he got to his feet. On
rubbery legs, he began retracing his path through the
woods. Getting back to the cabin became his only
goal. England Dan would know what to do. He always
did, damn him.

It was past sundown when he reached the trail leading from the meadow. Taking the rocky path in the
dark posed a problem. A misstep and he'd tumble

down the steep cliffs. But if he didn't risk his neck on the trail, he had to spend the night out in the open without any gear. All he had was his pistol, and there wasn't enough ammunition to even go hunting. The gunfire might draw Jensen. And he was a poor marksman. He was more likely to miss and end up with an empty gun.

"Where's Gonzales' horse? Did it throw you?"

"What? Who's there?" Panicked, Cooley drew his six-gun and waved it around.

"Put that away before you hurt yourself."

Coming from the gloom of the forest, England Dan looked ten feet tall. Cooley dropped to his knees, relieved. The feeling was brief, however, when he realized what he had to tell Dan, and shame took over.

"They took the horse. They have Mabel, too. And Mandy. They stole her away. What are we going to do, Dan? What can we do?"

His partner dropped to the ground and sat cross-legged. Cooley could barely make out his face in the dark, but what he caught of his expression wasn't pretty. Rutledge was furious with him.

"There wasn't anything I could do, Dan. Nothing! They outnumbered me. There must have been twenty of them."

"The Mogollon hunting party?"

"The Indians! They got the drop on me. They ambushed me and—"

"Shut up, Cooley. If that was Big Ear's band, there were a half dozen. One less since you killed No Shadow." A long pause. "You got lucky. If they suspected you'd killed him, they'd still be torturing you."

"They took Mandy."

"They kidnapped the girl and let you go? Even if they had no reason to suspect you of killing one of their tribe, why'd they spare you unless they thought you were dickering for your own life? You traded the horse and the girl for your own stinking hide."

"No, I fought them, but there were too many of them. You have to believe me."

"Quiet!"

"Dan, I—"

"*Quiet!* Listen." England Dan got to his feet and turned slowly, then began sniffing the air. "That way. Their camp's over yonder, not too far, either. I hear them chanting, and the smoke from their fire's blowing this way."

Cooley saw him take a deep breath and hold it before letting it go with an explosive gasp. He took a couple steps in the direction of the smoke.

"Wait, Dan. Where are you going?"

"Big Ear's camp is over there. Not far. We're going to save the girl."

"How? There're too many of them. I don't have many bullets. Not enough."

"I don't, either. That means we have to be smart. Smart and sneaky."

"You'll get us killed!"

England Dan laughed harshly. He came back and grabbed the front of Cooley's shirt and lifted him to his feet. With his face only inches away, he spat out, "You should be so lucky. You wouldn't have to live with knowing what you've done today."

"You're the big hero," Cooley shot back. "What do you know about saving anyone?"

"We'll sneak to the camp, decoy them away, then

get Mandy and the horse. How many other horses were there?"

"Only the chief's. And the mule. My mule!"

"I did this once before in an Indian village—East Indian."

"We'll be killed if we try."

"That's exactly what my commanding officer said. I disobeyed him and saved half a village." England Dan made a small choking sound. "The other half was slaughtered by sepoy deserters, but I saved some of them. A few. Not enough."

"We can't shoot it out with the Indians. If we go to Oasis and get—"

"Come on." England Dan shoved him in the direction of the Mogollon camp. Cooley stumbled along, hanging onto his six-shooter even though he knew it was almost empty.

Cooley tried to veer away, but his partner herded him better than a sheepdog did its flock. They crossed the meadow to the edge of the forest. A solitary sentry guarded the two horses and mule. The rest of the hunting party was wrapped in blankets around the dying campfires. Cooley duckwalked beside his partner. He almost cried out when he saw Mandy trussed up and roped to a tree.

"I see her," England Dan whispered. "I'll take care of the sentry. You free the girl."

"But the horses!"

"I'll sneak them out from under their noses. Wait and see."

Cooley knew they were going to get caught.

"I don't have a knife. How can I get her free if the knots are tied real tight?" He recoiled when a blade was pressed into his hand. The last excuse for not going through with his partner's harebrained scheme was gone.

England Dan pointed. He waited until Cooley slipped around the campsite before going off to deal with the sentry. Cooley closed his eyes for a moment, tried not to panic, then moved as silently as possible to free Mandy.

She slumped forward, chin on her chest. He almost wished she were dead. Then he wouldn't have to risk making any noise that'd alert the hunters. But she sneezed and strained against the ropes holding her securely to the tree.

"Shush," he said. "Don't make a sound."

"John? Is that you, you son of a—"

He clamped his hand over her mouth to stifle the outburst. Only when she subsided did he release her. Sawing away at the bonds proved harder than he had expected. The knife was dull and the hemp rope tough. Once she let out a squawk when he nicked her, but she didn't curse him anymore. He finally sawed through the rope. She sagged forward. He supported her, then helped her to her feet. She took a step and fell heavily. The Indians had hobbled her.

Cooley made quick work of those ropes. He rubbed circulation back into her ankles and started working up, but she shoved him away.

"How do we get away from them?" Her soft voice carried in the still night.

He pressed his finger against her lips, then pointed. England Dan came up with the two horses and mule.

"Get on," his partner urged.

Cooley started to mount the chief's horse since

England Dan already rode the black stallion, almost invisible in the shadows. Mandy pushed him out of the way and jumped up, leaving him to ride the mule.

"This is better," he said. "I can't ride bareback too well."

"I noticed," Mandy said. "I never rode any other way when I was growing up."

England Dan shushed them again. Walking the mounts slowly got them a hundred yards distant before an outcry came from the Indian camp. They kicked their horses and mule to top speed. Cooley called out for the two on horseback to wait for him. He kept looking over his shoulder, sure the Indians were pounding closer, in spite of being afoot. He bent low and whispered to Mabel. The mule knew what had to be done. It might not have been as fleet as the horses, but it wanted to get back to its stable as much as Cooley did.

CHAPTER FIFTEEN

"HE'S IN REAL bad shape." Mandy placed her hand on Alberto Gonzales' forehead. "He's got a fever. Not much, but he's so pale. He's not in good shape."

"He lost a lot of blood before I got him back here," England Dan said. He sat on the far side of the table in the only other chair. Mandy had pulled the second chair close to the bed to tend to the deputy. She seemed to know what she was doing, which was a relief. England Dan was tuckered out from trying to take care of the wounded lawman.

"How much longer do you think we can stay here?" She soaked a rag in water, rung it out and draped it over Gonzales' brow to help bring down the fever. Pale rays of sunlight sneaked past the broken limbs of a tall pine tree to fall on the man's drawn face.

"Yeah, what do you think?" Cooley perked up and looked around as if the Indians were hiding inside the small cabin. "We should get on the trail. Get back to Oasis."

"You're right," England Dan said, resigned to the trip. It made sense, even if it would push the deputy even closer to dying. They shouldn't have left him alone before, but how else could they have saved Mandy from Big Ear? Life felt like a giant scale. Too much weight in one pan caused the other side to soar upward. Take weight off the heavy pan and the balance was restored. Only it seemed like his life and everything around him bounced up and down faster than he could tolerate.

"Jensen is still roaming around, unless him trying to kill the deputy was all it took for him to hightail it," Cooley said. "You think he returned to Mesilla?"

England Dan touched the coat pocket where he carried the map. That piece of paper had set off a fire that burned up everyone around it. "He's still out there," England Dan said, "unless Big Owl got him."

"What's that?" Mandy looked up from tending the deputy. "Is he one of the Indians?"

"It's nothing. No one," Cooley said uneasily. He got up and went outside.

"What's spooked him? Who *is* Big Owl?"

England Dan tilted back in the chair and laced his fingers behind his head. He felt like spinning a yarn. Mandy was the kind of woman likely to appreciate a tall tale.

"One of the Indians, No Shadow, was half loco. He told me about a giant ogre that prowls the forests, howling and carrying on. Big Owl only screeches when someone's about to die."

"So if we don't hear the howls, we're all safe?" Mandy chuckled at that. She clapped her hands over her ears and danced about, pretending to be scared.

England Dan felt a cold knot form in his belly. He had laughed at No Shadow, too, but had the brave heard Big Owl? If he had, the prophecy had proven true. No Shadow was dead. The Irish stories about banshees had been good for scaring the dickens out of new recruits to the British Army, but as far as England Dan knew, none of them had ever heard a wailing banshee. Big Owl might be real.

The possibility made him all the more eager to get back to town.

"We're going to try to get the deputy to Oasis again. I'm not sure we're safe here, not with Big Ear and Jensen out there."

"When he figures out we've returned here, he'll come after us, won't he?" Cooley referred to Jensen, but England Dan was more worried about the Indians.

Worse than one of their tribe being murdered, their pride had been punctured. The Mogollons cared almost nothing for personal possessions, but horses were the way they rated social status. Big Ear had lost not only his horse, but another horse and mule had been taken as prizes by enemy raiders. His standing with his braves had to have taken a knock. The only way to recover was victory in battle. That meant going on a rampage against miners—and specifically the ones who owned the Trafalgar Mine—rated high on how to recover their wounded pride.

"I don't care if he's strong enough. Let's get on the trail. We can be in town in ten hours. Less. We have mounts now."

"What about me?" Mandy looked hard at Cooley. England Dan knew what she meant. Return to town, then what? That was between her and his partner, but he suspected the girl was in for a disappointment. Cooley wasn't the man to marry, much less look after her the way she expected. She should have known that after everything that had happened thus far.

"You're going with us, of course," Cooley said. His eyes darted about. "Dan, help me get Gonzales up. He's more than I can handle by myself."

"He's not the only one you can't handle," Mandy said sourly. She gathered a few things, stuffed them all into a blanket and slung it over her shoulder. "Well, let's go. I don't want to stay here anymore."

England Dan shared her feelings, but for different reasons. Although Cooley looked as if he was helping, Gonzales' full weight bore down on only one set of shoulders. Stumbling along, the deputy making feeble effort to walk, England Dan got him outside the cabin.

"Fetch the horses and the mule," he ordered Cooley. His voice carried the snap of command. His partner hurried off to do as he was told.

"All I've gotten out of this is a dead sister," Mandy said, voice shaking with both exhaustion and anger.

"He's not the right man for you."

"Are you?" Her emerald eyes boldly challenged England Dan. He shook his head. "Too bad. You're more of a man than he is."

He didn't have to answer. Cooley led the two horses and mule up. Without asking, Mandy jumped onto Big Ear's stolen horse and waited impatiently. Hoisting Alberto Gonzales onto his horse took longer than England Dan liked. The lack of cooperation from the deputy showed his worsening condition. He stepped up behind Gonzales and reached around to take the reins.

"I don't want to ride Mabel," Cooley complained. He grumbled even more when both Mandy and England Dan ignored him and started on the trail for town.

England Dan would have enjoyed his partner's consternation if Big Ear and Jensen hadn't been hunting them. The Indians and the outlaw had to come back here eventually, once they realized there wasn't any other place to hole up. He tightened his grip on the lawman as they rode. Every yard seemed to take more out of the deputy.

By time they rode into Oasis, it was close to midnight, and which of them was in the worst condition was a matter of dispute. Alberto Gonzales barely stirred. Mandy had tumbled off her horse more than once when she fell asleep. Cooley complained endlessly, and England Dan ached all over. Not a bone in his body remained untouched by the constant pounding. His exhaustion matched that of the others, but he had to keep going. He was in charge.

"We need to find someone to look after Gonzales," he said. "You know anybody, Mandy?"

"Madam Morgan took care of folks who came down with typhus a year or two back. She might take him in, but not without getting paid. Nobody gets a free ride at her brothel."

"We don't have any money," Cooley whined. "It's all gone."

"Would she take Big Ear's horse as payment?" England Dan saw Mandy oppose that right away, and he knew why.

"I'm not giving up my only gain on this sorry misadventure," she said. "This is *my* horse now."

"Keep it," England Dan said, drowning out Cooley's protest. If they got caught, no amount of argument with the chief would save their scalps. Better to put as much distance between them and the hunting party as possible.

"We don't have a lot of choices other than the cathouse," England Dan said. "She must owe you something for working there."

"The way she keeps books, I doubt there'd be much."

"But you're so persuasive," Dan said. "You must know the right thing to say to her?"

"I may be able to wheedle Madam Morgan into taking care of him. If she thinks she's doing something out of the goodness of her heart, she might give in, just a little. You sure you don't have any money, just to make her charity a bit easier?" Mandy looked hard at him, then shrugged. He doubted anything he gave her would ever reach the madam's purse.

They rode to the brothel. After England Dan handed down the deputy, Mandy and Cooley worked together to drag the unconscious man to the front porch. Cooley almost ran back to climb up on Mabel. He waved halfheartedly and then called out as he got the mule trotting away, "I'll see how he's doing later."

"I wonder if he's hitched," Mandy said almost to herself, her hand checking the deputy's feverish brow. She shook her head. "Doesn't matter. He's not going to make it."

"He's hung on this long. He's a tough hombre," England Dan said.

Mandy looked away when Madam Morgan came bustling from the brothel, arms waving about to chase off her wayward employee. Mandy stepped up and began a heated dialogue that slowly went her way. The madam snorted and spat but finally started pointing in a way that showed she was being swayed by Mandy's words and would let her and the deputy stay. England Dan tipped his bowler in her direction, then rode off. Keeping the deputy's horse felt like theft. If he sold the animal, there'd be money to help Alberto Gonzales recuperate, but riding like the wind astride a noble steed again called to England Dan more than he cared to admit. He thought of keeping Whirlwind more as tending it for the deputy than stealing it.

He'd promised Mandy he'd see how the lawman was faring later. A decision about the horse's ownership could be made then. Later. Maybe much later. He had a lot of miles to travel.

He caught up with Cooley, who stared longingly at the Thirsty Camel Saloon's entrance. Laughter and music echoed from the dim interior.

"You spent the last of our money on Mandy," he said.

"It wasn't worth it," Cooley said sadly. "Look at the trouble I got into. She even thought I'd take care of her."

"She thought you were going to marry her after her sister was murdered. I wonder how she got that idea." England Dan saw his partner's eyes dart about as if he had found himself trapped in a cave with a hungry bear at the entrance.

"I never outright said I'd do a thing like that. Marriage isn't something a fellow ought to jump into, all blinded by a purty filly batting her eyelashes at him."

"That's so."

"You don't have a nickel to spare? I've got a powerful thirst." Cooley looked hard at the saloon and licked his chapped lips.

England Dan ignored him. "Going back to the mine's not a good idea." He reached into his coat pocket and pulled out the map.

"True," Cooley said. "With the Indians after us, and Jensen prowling about, and Deputy Gonzales all shot up, we . . ." His voice trailed off when he saw the map. "You've had it with you all this time?"

"I know how to find the starting point. No Shadow told me this spot here is Mule Springs. From there, finding the peaks all lined up shouldn't be too hard."

"Mule Springs is on the other side of the mountains," Cooley said in a voice crackling with excitement.

England Dan put his heels to Whirlwind's flanks and rocketed away, letting Cooley astride Mabel follow at a slower pace. Riding alone for a few minutes suited him and gave him a chance to think. The Trafalgar Mine wasn't yielding the gold it once had. With all that had happened, it was more likely to be his grave than his salvation. There might be nothing to be found where the X on the map promised, but before the map showed up, life had been dull. It was time for some excitement.

It was time for a wagonload of excitement. He put his head down and let the wind cut past his face. For the first time in months, he came alive.

CHAPTER SIXTEEN

"THERE'S NO DOUBT. Big Ear and his hunters passed here within the last day." England Dan traced the moccasin outline in the dirt. He scooted along the ground on his knees and picked up a broken twig that one of the Mogollons had stepped on. Then he pointed to a bush with a limb torn off. "See how it's still oozing sap? They might have passed through here within a few hours."

"Hours?" Cooley swallowed hard. His heart began pounding faster as he looked around. He rested his hand on his pistol, even if that wouldn't get him too far. He had checked the load several times since leaving Oasis. Every time he had come up with three good rounds, three spent cartridges. Praying for the live rounds to multiply hadn't worked for him.

"Don't worry. They're heading north, and we're going east. They're back to hunting. If they bag a deer or two, they'll dress it out and return to their tribe, wherever they're camped."

"It might be in that direction," Cooley said uneasily. He stared into the thick woods where England Dan had been leading them. The trees had been so dense in some places, they'd had to dismount. Cooley was tired of banging his head on low limbs and blundering through thickets rife with thorns. Mabel got feisty when he did, and it took a goodly while to pull the stickers from the mule's legs.

That was still better than having the stickers on his legs, but not much. He stared at his hands. If he hadn't spent so many hours mining, moving ore and lugging heavy loads, his hands wouldn't have been callused. That made plucking the thorns from Mabel's forelegs less painful. He lifted his left hand and bit down on a buried thorn, caught the tip in his teeth and pulled. He spat the offending spine out.

"Then we'd better stay ahead of them. We can travel faster."

Cooley touched his holster again. Leaving Big Ear's horse with Mandy back in town had been a good idea, though he hadn't thought so at the time. The chief might come on them and steal their animals again, but he wouldn't get mad that they had his horse. England Dan had snuck out without being seen when he stole the mounts.

It was a good thing England Dan had the map. Cooley had tried to orient it and failed every time. He didn't doubt Rutledge told the truth about being in the British Army and getting all that military training, including map reading and the like, but most men lied about their past. He had no reason to think his partner did, but stretching the truth was a time-honored duty. Who wanted to sit around a campfire at night, bored and without any liquor, and hear the same stories over and over? Embellishing them with every telling kept the entire audience amused.

He looked at his partner and wondered if he really had served with the Brits in a place he called India but where the natives weren't like the Mogollons or the Tonto Apaches but instead wore towels around their heads and brandished knives all rippled like waves on a lake. Or was that another story he told about traveling from island to island to reach Australia? It all jumbled together. Cooley knew how to keep his own tall tales straight. Doing that with anyone else was too much a chore. Besides, every new telling entertained that much better if he didn't try to make sense of it.

Sometimes he wished he had gone to school. Not being able to read made him feel England Dan took advantage of him. It was hard to know if he was being gullible or hardheaded about what he believed. Having to make his mark on documents like the deed to their mine added to his feeling of being taken advantage of. He had to believe whatever Dan told him. That map didn't have any writing on it, but he still had a hard time figuring out how to use it.

His partner mounted and slowly rode toward the denser part of the forest. He made such slow progress that Cooley walked alongside Mabel to give the mule a rest. It felt good stretching his legs and working the cramped muscles in his butt, too. How cavalry troopers rode fifty miles a day was something of a mystery to him, but he knew they did. A black trooper from the Ninth over in Fort Bayard had told him about how chasing down the Warm Springs Apaches required them to make that distance day after day. And they'd done it riding on McClellan saddles.

Cooley rubbed his hindquarters, thinking about having to sit on two planks of wood for twelve hours a day.

"John." England Dan held up his hand to signal they ought to halt.

"What's wrong?"

"Hush." England Dan jumped to the ground and drew his Webley. He didn't carry many more rounds in that old gun than Cooley did in his six-shooter.

On cat's feet, he walked over to his partner. England Dan pointed through the trees. Cooley caught his breath. An Indian.

"Are they Mogollons?"

His partner nodded. They watched for several minutes as a brave stalked through the trees, an arrow nocked and ready to fire. Cooley caught his breath when the hunter drew the string back and loosed the arrow. Smooth as silk, the Indian pulled another arrow from his quiver, got it ready and fired faster than most men could fire a Winchester. He disappeared through the trees.

"He hit something. If we're lucky, it's a deer. That'll keep him busy for a spell." England Dan dropped into a low crouch and turned his head slowly, listening for any hint of other hunters. He came to a decision to get closer and see what the hunter was doing.

Cooley started to stop England Dan from scouting ahead, but he ended up with the stallion's reins in one hand and Mabel's in the other. Long anxious minutes passed before England Dan returned.

"He got a feral pig. Almost as good as a deer."

"What do we do?"

England Dan stroked his stubbled chin, then pointed toward the southeast. Without a word, they made their way on foot in that direction for close to an hour, then mounted and rode at a quicker gait until sundown.

"There's a stream. We camp here."

"I'm hungry. What are we going to do for food?" Cooley's belly rumbled to prove his point. England Dan rubbed his own to quell its equally noisy response.

"Find some berries or roots. I'll see if there's a fish or two that's never seen a fisherman with a spear." He dropped to the ground and used his knife to hack at a small sapling. He sharpened the point, then looked up from his work.

The moon had edged high above the treetops by the time they fixed their meal of trout and dandelion greens. Cooley finished the last piece of fish and stretched out, staring at the moon, hands under his head.

"This reminds me of an ancestor. You knew Davy Crockett was my great-uncle, didn't you?"

"You never mentioned it." England Dan worked to hone his knife. When it was satisfactorily sharp, he hacked at some small twigs and added them to the fire. It burned with little smoke. He kept it low and somehow added only twigs that didn't send a curl of smoke into the air to betray them. Now and then he warmed his hands.

Cooley slid closer to get his hands warm, too. The fire was too low to put out much heat, but he knew better than to build it up with Big Ear and his band roving the hills.

"Yes, sir, he was. Not the most famous of my relatives, mind you, but you being a foreigner and all, he's the one you most likely have heard about."

"Killed down in Texas?"

"That's what he wanted them Mexicans to think. He got out of the Alamo, settled down in San Angelo. Raised a family, he did. They—"

"I studied about your Civil War. San Angelo wasn't settled until after the war."

"Davy wasn't in San Angelo after escaping Santa Anna's army. There was a mission there. He stayed with the friars until it became San Angelo."

"Why'd the priests go against Santa Anna?"

"Oh, Davy was a silver-tongued fox, he was. He talked his way into their mission and proved he was worth keepin' around. That man was the best shot that ever lived."

Cooley continued to spin his tale until the fire died to embers. When the sound of his own voice started putting him to sleep, he watched wisps of clouds light up as they crossed the face of the moon. His eyelids began to drop.

Then he came awake, his six-shooter out and cocked, and he looked around, wild-eyed.

"What was that?"

"I never heard anything like it," England Dan said. He had his pistol out, too. The screech came again, shrill and nerve jangling. "No Shadow said he'd heard Big Owl."

"A banshee? An Indian banshee?" Cooley swallowed and gripped his pistol so hard, the muscles in his forearms began to knot. He swung around and raised his pistol as the howl ripped through the night.

He let out a startled yelp when his partner yanked the gun from his hand.

"If you shoot, Big Ear will hear and know we're out here."

"If I don't, that thing—Big Owl—will come and kill us." Cooley took his gun back but made no effort to fire it. There wasn't a decent target. Wasting ammo shooting blindly into the dark would make the ogre thing all the bolder. He swallowed hard and settled down, vainly trying to make out a shape or a movement in the forest. As far as he could tell, there was nothing out there that hadn't been there before sunset.

"Banshees don't kill anybody. They just warn of your death." England Dan got to his feet. "No Shadow made it out to be an ogre, and I doubt he'd ever heard of a real banshee, but it sounded the same."

"Where are you going? You can't go out there!" Cooley panicked when his partner homed in on another screech and took a step in that direction.

"If it's a banshee, one of us is doomed. It won't matter if I face it down or just listen from here. I want to see what's making the ruckus." England Dan laughed without humor. "If I find it, maybe I can dicker with it."

"Dicker?"

"If only one of us is supposed to die, there's no reason it has to be me."

"I'm coming with you!" Cooley shot to his feet. Rutledge's sense of humor was odd, and he couldn't tell if he was joking now. If not, and arguing changed the banshee's mind, he wanted to get his two cents in. England Dan talked better, but he couldn't spin a tale for love nor money. Cooley knew influencing a banshee took more than a silver tongue. It had to, if he wanted to keep on living.

"It might be different with an Indian banshee," England Dan said, speaking over his shoulder.

Cooley sped up to pull even with him. "What do you mean?"

"Big Owl might not speak English. I'm not sure a regular banshee speaks English, either, since I never talked to one."

Cooley frowned as he worked through what his partner said. "You never talked with one, but you've heard one before?"

Nothing but silence came as they hiked deeper into the trees. Then England Dan said, "Once. I thought it was an Indian sepoy trying to rattle my command. If it was, he succeeded. Half my men pissed themselves."

"There! Over there!" Cooley reached for his six-shooter again. Shadows moved. Then the howl came.

"I don't see anything. And the sound's getting farther away. We ran it off coming out here."

"Does that make one whit of sense? Two men chasing off a banshee? Even an Indian one? What's it got to be scared of? We're flesh and blood, and it's . . . something." Cooley stared hard at the shadow where he knew Big Owl had been hiding. As his eyes adapted to the darker forest, he saw a tree limb swinging to and fro. It had been broken halfway through, and a small breeze set it to swaying about.

Cooley ran his finger over the break in the limb. The ragged edge showed something had passed by under the limb, caught it and tugged hard enough to break the wood. He wished it had been cut with a knife. That'd show a man had sawed through it, even if the only ones out here other than him and England Dan were the Indians and Lars Jensen.

"It's gone now. I don't hear anything but the normal night forest sounds." England Dan made a dismissive wave with his hand.

"The animals and bugs and things wouldn't have anything to fear from a banshee, would they?" Cooley felt a shiver up and down his spine. "That'd make Big Owl fit right in with the rest. It's us thrashing about out here that's not natural."

"We're not, but the sounds are back to normal, so everything in the forest has decided we aren't a threat."

Cooley jumped a foot when England Dan took his shoulder and gently pushed him back toward camp. Reluctantly following, he wondered why he'd ever come out in the first place. It was safer in camp, especially if a fire kept the night at bay. The night and Big Owl. Out here, Cooley was exposed and vulnerable.

"It's only a few hours until dawn. We need to be on the trail by then. If the sounds came from some sort of animal we're not familiar with, I want to get away from its territory as fast as we can." England Dan settled down by the fire and warmed his hands.

"You think it's not a banshee?" Hope flared. Cooley knew he was grasping at straws, but that was fine with him. Any chance that what they heard wasn't a banshee soothed his ruffled feathers.

"Whether banshees exist is a matter of faith. I don't know if they do, but something made those sounds. Anything that nasty sounding's likely to have sharp teeth and long claws. If it gets hungry, I want to be far, far away."

"Banshees exist," Cooley said with conviction. "That map shows the Irish Lord Mine. After tonight, we need to change the name of the mine."

"How about we find the mine first before getting all high and mighty about its name?"

Cooley ignored his partner. "I'm renaming it the Lost Banshee Mine." He cocked his head to one side, expecting Big Owl to chime in with another howl.

Crickets chirping were the only sounds. Not even the wind stirred the trees. He wasn't sure if that wasn't scarier than hearing the ogre crying out for their flesh and blood.

He left for town before England Dan woke up the next morning.

CHAPTER SEVENTEEN

H<small>E WANTED TO</small> kill somebody. Anybody. Waiting a couple days with nothing to do got on his nerves. Lars Jensen rocked back in the chair and looked around the Thirsty Camel Saloon. Five customers this late afternoon. Not a one of them carried iron on his hip. Two of them had knives sheathed, but shooting down a man armed only with a knife was a bit cowardly, he thought. Years back he had seen a man, a real killer, who didn't like guns and wore a pair of knives sheathed at either hip.

Jensen had seen him face down a young cowboy who thought he was better than he actually was. Out in the street, squared off and to the death. The cowboy had gone for his smoke wagon and cleared leather. Then his finger triggered a round that dug into the street at his feet. The knife man had whipped out his blade and tossed it with deadly accuracy. The tip had cut through the cowboy's vest and shirt, slid between his ribs and snaked its way into his heart. Jensen had released his breath then, not even knowing he'd been holding it.

Men with knives were deadly, but not these two. He was faster than either of them. One was old and gray. The other was still wet behind the ears and could be goaded into making mistakes. Gunning them down wouldn't satisfy his bloodlust.

Jensen scowled and stared into the foam dancing about on the top of his half-drunk beer. There had to be someone else in Oasis to kill, but he was feeling listless. Stirring from the chair took too much energy. Roaming around the hills hunting for Cooley and the girl had tuckered him out. Avoiding the band of Indians had caused him to get impatient and that drained his energy, too. Worst of all was catching the girl and having her get away from him.

He wished he had the deputy to kill again. That had perked him up for a while until the girl got caught by the Indians.

"He's not gonna be happy," he said into his beer.

"How's that, mister? You ready for another?" The barkeep looked at him from halfway down the long wood plank. Ray Hendrix recognized how prickly his customer was and avoided Jensen the best he could. The need to keep peddling his weak beer collided with his good sense telling him to hightail it from the saloon.

"What time is it?" Lars Jensen had a watch, but it was too much trouble to fish it out, open the lid and read the face.

"Going on five o'clock. Are you ready to switch over to whiskey for some serious drinking?"

Jensen had to laugh at the blatant attempt to sell more expensive booze. Or maybe the bartender wanted him to drink so much he passed out. That'd solve a lot of problems.

"Another beer," he ordered. "And bring a shot of that popskull you have behind the bar. The whiskey with the black label."

"That's the best I've got," the barkeep declared. "Coming right up."

Hendrix brought the beer and set it directly in front of Jensen, with the shot beside it.

"That's not for me. There. Put it there." He pointed to the chair across the table from him.

The barkeep silently did as he was told, then hurried away. Some men preferred not to drink alone, but those who made up their drinking companions were mostly loco. Jensen didn't care what anyone else thought. It was close to time.

He looked up and saw the tall blond man push through the swinging doors. A quick look around sized up everyone at the bar. Then he came over, threw a leg high over the back of the chair and settled down. With a quick move, he downed the whiskey.

"Another," the man said.

"Coming right up, Poke." Lars Jensen signaled for a bottle this time. He almost laughed at how the barkeep scuttled about like a crab, wanting to make a sale but not daring to disturb either of the men at the table. Lars read in his face that greed kept him in the saloon when he wanted nothing more than to skedaddle out the door and never stop till he got to Bisbee.

Lars Jensen had the aspect of a killer. Poke Jensen looked like a man who killed killers.

"You have any trouble getting here?" Jensen watched his brother's reaction closely. Poke had a hair-trigger temper. Asking the wrong question could set him off.

"Getting out of the prison was harder than I thought. The vaquero was supposed to leave me two horses and plenty of water. One horse died within an hour of me riding it, and there wasn't anywhere near enough water." Poke knocked back another shot, wiped his lips and settled down for serious drinking. Lars Jensen made no effort to corral the bottle his brother had commandeered.

"I thought you were being paroled. It sounds like you had to escape."

"They decided they liked me so much that they were going to keep me another six months. I couldn't let them do that since I'd already told you I'd be here today. I never break my promise."

"No, sir, you never do," Lars Jensen agreed. "You might be many things, but a promise breaker's not one of them."

Poke fixed his brother with eyes like stilettos. "You promised me you'd have the map. Give it to me."

Lars Jensen tried not to show how uneasy this made him. "There's been a lot of men dying for that map," he said. "Do you really need it to find the loot?"

"The cavalry payroll's buried up in the Superstition Mountains, and I don't know where. Beeman hid it and made the map to pass along to me since I decoyed the soldiers away after he took a couple bullets."

"You weren't tried for the robbery. All they charged you with was that arson up in Prescott last year."

"Beeman died with a bullet in him but passed the map to Rivera before he succumbed, but then Rivera upped and died out in the desert. I got a description of the drifter who found him from another prisoner who was locked up after me."

Lars Jensen saw the chance to lie, but his brother had an instinct that made him decide that wasn't a good idea. Since they'd been little children, Poke had seen right through his lies. Better to fess up.

"I shot the drifter outside this very saloon, but he didn't have the map. Wait!" He held up his hand. "I figured out that a miner had it. He bought it for a few dollars because the drifter had no notion what the map showed. From what I gather, he—and the miner—thought it was a map to what the local folks call the Irish Lord Mine."

"How'd they come by that idea?" Poke Jensen stopped drinking and leaned forward, his elbows on the table. The way he thrust out his chin and a tiny tic under his left eye warned Lars Jensen that he was running out of time to explain. His brother exploded like a case of old dynamite when he got hot enough under the collar.

After Poke had struggled with a dead horse and not enough water to get through the Sonoran Desert south of Yuma Penitentiary, the short fuse would burn fast.

"I never saw the map, but Beeman must have hid the payroll in a mine shaft. It has to be an abandoned mine, right? Rumors have it the owner of the Irish Lord up and died and nobody works the mine. They don't even know exactly where it is."

"It could be any mine. You don't know that Beeman hid anything in this Irish Lord hole in the ground."

"What I'm saying, Poke, is that we don't rightly need the map if that's where he stashed the money.

There has to be a deed filed somewhere telling the location of the mine."

"Where's the map?" Ice water dripped from Poke's every word.

"This miner, Cooley by name, must still have it, but tracking him down's proved real hard. I shot a whore and her john, thinking it was him. Turned out to be Cooley's whore's twin I shot. It was a natural mistake."

"Natural. Lars, you're telling me you've been chasing around, trying to find this Cooley fellow, and he's sidestepped you so many times you lost track of him?"

"There've been other problems. Indians. And a federal deputy marshal from over in Mesilla. Don't worry your head none about that, Poke. It was me he was after, not you. I took care of him. But all this gave Cooley the time to get away. He knows the country here better'n I ever could."

"You don't have the map. You've concocted some cock-and-bull story about an abandoned mine, then tried to gussy it up with a dead lawman and Indians. Is all that about right?"

Lars Jensen shifted uneasily in his chair. He moved so his hand came closer to his six-shooter. If his brother even twitched, he'd throw down on him. Poke was fast, but he'd been in a hellhole of a prison for six months. That might give enough time to clear leather and shoot him. Ever since they'd been teenagers, he'd wondered when the showdown would happen and the cause. If he'd asked, his brother would have dealt him into the cavalry-payroll theft, but avoiding robberies with Poke was the safest thing to do. Getting blamed—and shot—because a theft went wrong had always seemed inevitable.

Poke wasn't too good at taking the blame when things went south.

"That's a good telling of it. What I'm saying is that we probably don't need the map. Mule Springs has to be the spot where Beeman drew the map. It's where he got shot up by the soldiers on his tail."

"The Superstition Mountains are as big from the other side as they are on this side. You could hunt for the rest of your life and not find more than a stone in your boot." Poke leaned back and fixed a deadly stare on his younger brother. Lars forced himself to meet that gaze without flinching. To show any fear now would set off a reaction in his brother that wouldn't end until people—lots of them—died.

"I've got some ideas about finding the map."

"Where's Cooley's mine? I know the hard-rock men. If there's a flake of gold left, he'll go back there. He can't help himself."

"He's got a partner," Lars said, nodding. "Chances are good one or the other of them will be there. Let me ask around town about Cooley and meet you at that mine when I know more."

"Meet me there when you have the map." Poke pushed to his feet, a little tipsy from drinking so much whiskey, one shot after another. "I've got other business to take care of."

Lars watched his brother carefully to be sure he didn't go for his iron. Instead, he left. When Poke was at the door, Lars called out, "See you up in the hills. It's the Trafalgar Mine you want."

The barkeep gasped at that. Lars Jensen shut him up with a hiss like a stepped-on rattler's. It was almost enough to make him laugh when Hendrix found a stack of clean shot glasses that needed special polishing and he stared hard at every imagined speck. The satisfaction he felt at cowing the man faded. His brother had done the same thing with him. He touched the butt of his six-shooter, then left the saloon. Poke had already disappeared, whether on his way to Cooley's mine or somewhere else didn't matter. He had his own job, and it wasn't going to be easy. Finding the map in a few hours when he had been hunting for weeks put pressure on him that rankled.

Getting into any kind of pickle with Poke was wrong. And dangerous.

He tugged his hat brim down to shield his eyes from the sun and set off for the brothel at the edge of town. The only thread he could tug on ran into the cathouse. Jensen started walking slowly, but his stride lengthened as he worried more about his brother's patience running out. Poke meant what he said. Jensen considered how to approach the matter. The decision was made for him. The madam sat on the front porch, rocking and sipping at a glass filled with amber fluid. He doubted she drank the rotgut served at the Thirsty Camel. She had the money to buy good swill.

"Come on up and set yourself down, mister." Madam Morgan motioned to him. He settled into a chair beside her, wary of the vitriolic woman. If she was going to be halfway civil, he intended to take advantage of it. She was irked when he poured himself a drink without her offering first.

He knocked it back. The whiskey was as good as he thought it would be. He sampled another couple fingers of the rye. "I'm looking for the cute blonde."

"We got plenty of those to choose from." She eyed

him over the rim of her glass. Her rheumy eyes worked to focus better.

"The one I want's the one whose sister was killed." He shifted a little in the chair and glanced at his pistol.

"This ain't your first time here, then, is it?" Madam Morgan squinted harder at him. Recognition began to dawn on her.

"I wasted my time before. Doing that a second time would make me mad. Real mad." He considered another drink and decided against it. Keeping a clear head if shooting started was important. He had to remember finding the map mattered more than leaving bodies in his wake.

"You're interested in a certain lawman, I reckon. What's it worth to you if I told you where he was?" Madam Morgan looked cagey.

He snorted in disgust. "Absolutely nothing. I want the girl. What's her name?"

"Mandy."

"And the miner who hires her. Cooley."

"John Cooley."

"John? That's actually his name?" Jensen chuckled. "That's about the most apt name I've come across in a month of Sundays."

"I never thought on that before. But you don't care about the deputy?"

"Not a whit." He wondered why she had dangled that in front of him. She must not have known he had left Alberto Gonzales dead in a field somewhere in the hills. "Mandy. Where is she? And where's Cooley?"

"I can pass along a way to find them. For a price." Madam Morgan looked downright canny now.

"I'll pay the price," he said, standing. "The price is

a single bullet in your head." He cleared leather fast and pointed his six-gun at her. She had enough whiskey in her not to flinch, but he saw the flash of fear. He only had to nudge her a little more to find what he wanted to know. He cocked the gun and made a show of aiming.

"You kill me, you'll never find them." The words sounded lame. They both knew it.

"I'll find them sooner or later, and until then I'll have the warm memory of killing you." He waited. He had to give her credit for not begging or crying. There was enough gumption for her to face him down. "She's inside, isn't she? That saves me shooting you."

Jensen edged around her, wary that she might draw a hideout pistol and shoot him in the back. He remembered how she had waved around the straight razor the last time she tried to stop him. Madam Morgan made no move this time. He ducked inside. A pair of half-dressed women lounged in the parlor. They started to come to him, then saw he wasn't here for the kind of service they offered.

"Mandy. Where is she?" One of them, a mousy brunette, rolled her eyes toward the stairs leading to the second floor. That was good enough for him. He started up the stairs, then slowed and stopped halfway up.

Voices filtered down from above. He strained to make out the muffled sounds.

"She wouldn't dare touch you, not with me here."

"She'd dare anything since I'm running out on her after she agreed to take me back. That's something she'll never forgive, me breaking my word."

". . . missed you so much, I had to come back."

"You're a liar, John Cooley. What really brought you back here? You wanted to see if he could get you a reward? Is that it?"

Jensen wondered whom the woman meant. The nearest lawman was in Bisbee. He had seen to that. Nobody else passed out rewards. Jensen reached for his gun, only to feel his feet pulled out from under. He crashed facedown onto the steps. The edge of a riser caught him in the middle of his forehead. His neck cracked and blood spurted from the head cut. He was dragged down the steps, hitting one after another.

Dazed, he grabbed for his six-shooter, but it was on the top step. Every passing second he was yanked farther away. When he reached the bottom of the stairs, he shook his head. It felt as if something had come loose inside.

"Get rid of him, Gus. Permanently."

Lars Jensen grunted as a boot crashed into the middle of his back. The brothel's bouncer kicked him again. Jensen appreciated the attack. Always kick a man when he was down.

Because he might get up if you didn't finish him off.

He rolled left and then jerked right, coming over to lie on his back. He grabbed the bouncer's foot as he tried to kick him again. A powerful twist sent Gus stumbling and gave Jensen a few seconds to recover. Sitting up made him dizzy. He fought through it. Madam Morgan had defined the fight. If Gus came back, it'd be a fight to the death.

The bouncer growled like a mad dog and lumbered over. Jensen reached down, found his sheathed knife and pulled it free. A quick stab as Gus tried to land on top of him ended the man's life. Jensen lay pinned under his deadweight. When he regained enough strength, he heaved and got the body off him. Blood soaked his shirt—and very little of it was his. Gus bled out like a slaughtered pig.

Madam Morgan gasped, rushed to the door and ran. Catching her would have been easy enough, but his brother's words burned into his brain. He wiped off his blade on the bouncer's pants. By the time he made his way to the top of the stairs and retrieved his gun, the door to the first room stood open.

A quick look inside showed it was empty. Jensen swore, then stumbled down the hallway to the back stairs. He fell more than walked down the steps and threw open the back door.

All he saw was a dust cloud slowly settling in the direction of town. He'd come close to catching Cooley. But the miner didn't have that much of a head start. Lars Jensen pushed his hat up so the cut on his forehead wouldn't stain the band, and he ran as fast as he could to reach the livery stables. He had a miner to chase and a map to retrieve.

CHAPTER EIGHTEEN

COOLEY SHIVERED AS he snapped the reins and kept Mabel plodding through the chilly dawn. More than once he had looked over his shoulder to see if anyone was catching up. The wind whistled through the treetops, but no sound matching that of the night before added to his fright.

"Big Owl," he whispered. "That's who it was coming for me. Damn you, Dan, taking me into the hills where an ogre is all set to eat my flesh." He jumped again as a mourning dove spoke and another answered. He urged the mule to a quicker gait. Mabel responded, as if fearing what lay behind them, too.

He drifted off to an uneasy sleep, letting Mabel move along without guidance. The rising sun touched his face and caused him to sneeze. This shook him awake. An instant of panic passed. Cooley had no idea where he was. This was brand-new terrain for him, but the direction told him he was still headed back toward Oasis. An hour later he came across a road and knew where he was. If he turned left and headed uphill, he'd arrive at the Trafalgar Mine eventually.

That wasn't in the cards. He'd run out on England Dan, and one man working the mine couldn't produce enough gold to live on. Being alone at the mine after what he'd experienced sent a new shiver up his spine. Big Owl. Big Owl and the Lost Banshee Mine. As much as he wanted to cash in on the vast wealth in the hidden mine, the banshee had shrieked and he'd heard it, and so had No Shadow, who had died. The sooner he got out of the Superstition Mountains, the better. He felt a mite guilty about leaving his partner without so much as a fare-thee-well, but England Dan was welcome to the mine.

A bad taste came into his mouth. He was welcome to their played-out mine, only he'd heard the banshee scream, too. That meant he was a goner if he lingered in the mountains.

Cooley took the fork in the road leading into Oasis. Returning before he was rich was wrong, but Mandy had learned to accept his failures. Not that he was that much of a failure. He owned half the Trafalgar Mine, and if Dan actually found the Lost Banshee Mine, it stood to reason he was entitled to half. They were partners and had never formally dissolved their union.

As he rode, the rising sun warm on his back, he stared at the road ahead. Emptiness stretched all the way down into the foothills. Cooley appreciated that. He had no desire to fight off a banshee, if such a thing was possible. He wished Dan had told him more about the ghosts or whatever banshees were. All he really knew was that they howled before somebody died.

And one had sung its death song for him to hear.

"Maybe it doesn't count. Big Owl is an Indian banshee. No Shadow died, and he was one of the Mogollon tribe." The memory of how the half-loco brave had died worried him some. He'd had more than a little part in the death. "I must have been forced by the banshee to kill him. I never wanted to shoot him." Cooley swallowed hard. "It was a curse. A spell. The banshee cast its spell on me so I'd do its bidding."

As he rode more, this seemed plausible. Not only were Indians the only ones likely to die when Big Owl screeched, but the curse made someone else perform the deadly deed.

By the time he rode into Oasis, he was positive this was what had happened. He hadn't been responsible for the Indian's death, and hearing Big Owl meant someone else—one of the Mogollon hunters, perhaps— was slated to die.

Cooley rode around to the back of the brothel, not wanting to face Madam Morgan. He had seen her sitting on the front porch, swilling her liquor. Sneaking in to see Mandy without dickering over a fee with the madam was the only way he'd get inside. He doubted Madam Morgan would even let him see Alberto Gonzales and find out how the deputy marshal was faring. She had a habit for charging for everything, and he didn't have two nickels to rub together. The only reason she would have taken the deputy in was to get a favor from him later. Having a deputy marshal beholden to you gave leverage to do all kinds of illicit things.

He left the mule in the shed behind the cathouse.

The horse that had been the Mogollon chief's reared
when he put Mabel in the stall next to it.

"You remember me, don't you, you miserable hunk
of horseflesh?" He tried to soothe the animal, but it
bucked and kicked. It remembered him with no fond-
ness. "Mandy deserves you, the way she stayed behind
and let me go into the hills."

Memories of the banshee's cry made him hurry
back to the house. He gingerly tried the side door.
Locked. A bit of rattling loosened the latch enough so
he could slip in. He heard two of the girls talking in the
parlor, but looking into the back room was his goal.
The door creaked as he opened it and peered inside.

Alberto Gonzales thrashed about on the narrow
bed. Cooley tried to decide if the lawman was in a
coma or asleep and enduring a nightmare.

"Maybe he's hearing a banshee." He meant the
words as a joke. Instead Cooley scared himself.

He decided the deputy was doing just fine. His color
was good, a full plate of food sat on a side table and,
from the look of the half-filled glass, he had drunk
enough water to revive a man dying of thirst out in the
Sonoran Desert. Gonzales was on the mend.

Closing the door gently, he heaved a sigh. If the
deputy had died, the US marshal over in New Mexico
would have sent a small army to investigate. Although
he wasn't wanted for anything in particular, Cooley
had run afoul of the law a few times as he made his way
through Texas on his way to Arizona. A diligent law
enforcement officer could find a wanted poster or two
down in San Angelo and a couple other places.

There wasn't any chance that Davy Crockett's descendants would bail him out, either. If there were any others.

Carefully climbing the stairs to avoid the loose steps that would squeak and betray him, he got to the second floor. At this time of day, none of the cribs was occupied. He made his way to the room at the head of the stairs. The door was ajar. He peeked in and smiled broadly.

"Now, that's the way I like to see you," he said. A quick twist spun him into the room to close the door behind him.

Mandy let out a squeal of surprise. She sat on the bed clad only in her undergarments. Sweat plastered the thin muslin to her body, perfectly outlining her fine form.

"What are you doing here, John?" Mandy made no effort to hide her partially clothed body. He had seen her with far less on. "You lit out like somebody had set your tail feathers on fire."

"I missed you so much, I had to come back." He sat on the edge of the bed and reached out for her. She swatted his hand away.

"What? Did your partner finally give you the boot and you came running back to me?"

"Mandy, dear heart, Dan wouldn't do a thing like that. We set out to find that mine, but he was more dedicated to the hunt than I was. I came back for you."

"For me?" Her emerald eyes glowed. "What's that mean? You have a ring for me?"

The banshee's curse must have taken a different form. He'd heard its lament and hadn't died, but Mandy expected him to be enslaved by marrying her. Cooley wasn't sure if dying outright wasn't a better fate.

"Better," he said, warming to his diversion. "A golden pile in the biggest, best, most productive mine in all of Arizona." He saw the flash of greed in her eyes. Plowing on, he said, "All we have to do is follow a map and claim it."

"Map, map, that's all I hear. Let's see it." Mandy began dressing.

A momentary pang passed through Cooley. He shouldn't have dangled the lure of riches until after they'd enjoyed a reunion.

"Dan has it." At mention of his partner, he cringed. The banshee cry might have been for Rutledge. Abandoning him out there in the mountains might have meant his death by now. "But I can take it from him." What use did a banshee have for a map? England Dan's death need not be in vain if it made his partner and his partner's best girl rich.

"I'm tired of working for Madam Morgan. That's why I left before, but with you gone, there's not a whole lot else I can do. She's getting her revenge on me for cutting and running, and I don't like it. I'm as close to being a slave as you can get without shackles on your ankles." Mandy stroked his arm and looked coy. "Are you sure this mine's worth wandering around in the mountains? There're so many dangers up there. The Indians. That horrible Lars Jensen. And the deputy got himself shot up real bad."

"I looked in on Gonzales, and he's recovering." Cooley saw her reaction. She hadn't expected him to see to the deputy's condition. "It must have been your expert nursing that brought him back from the brink of death." That got Mandy thinking again about something other than getting shot.

"Come, on, John." She threw her clothing into a carpetbag and herded him out the door. At the head of the stairs, she paused.

"What's wrong, my dearest?" Even as he asked, he heard voices below. Madam Morgan was talking with someone out on the porch.

"The back way. Explaining why I'm leaving to Madam Morgan when she's doing business is dangerous. She's been known to have girls whipped for interrupting her."

"She wouldn't dare touch you, not with me here."

"She'd dare anything since I'm running out on her after she agreed to take me back. That's something she'll never forgive, me breaking my word."

". . . missed you so much I had to come back." Cooley tried to look sincere as he reached out to take her in his arms.

"You're a liar, John Cooley. What really brought you back here? You wanted to see if he could get you a reward? Is that it?" Mandy pushed free of him.

Cooley let her rush him down the corridor. He paused in an effort to kiss her, but Mandy was in a hurry. She shot down the back stairs. A quick glance back showed a tall-brimmed hat thrusting up into sight as a man came up the stairs from the parlor. Cooley took the steps down two at a time, got outside and ran to catch up with Mandy as she went to the shed where her horse and his mule were stabled.

She rode bareback. As he got into his saddle, she tossed him her carpetbag. He leaned back and fastened it to the saddlebags bouncing on Mabel's hindquarters. By the time he finished, Mandy was halfway to the middle of town. The mule was fleet of foot—for a mule.

Mandy kept up her breakneck pace through town and onto the road leading back into the Superstition Mountains.

He caught up with her when she reached a fork in the road and needed his direction on which way to travel.

Cooley swallowed hard when he pointed to the road that'd take them back to where he'd left England Dan. He strained to hear any hint of the banshee's cry. All that came to him were sounds from town and the promise of more quiet deeper in the hills.

"That way," he said, drawing even with her. "I left Dan up there."

She responded by snapping the reins. Cooley wasn't sure if her single-minded determination to find the Lost Banshee Mine and all the gold locked in it was a good thing. Right now he wanted to run off at the mouth so all memory of Big Owl disappeared. As it was, he stewed and muttered to himself most of the day. It came as a relief when Mandy led her horse to a stream to drink.

"We're deep in the mountains now," he said. "Sunset comes quick up here. All the peaks." He motioned vaguely at the tall mountains already blocking the sun. The real reason he gestured was to turn around in the saddle and get the lay of the land. This was a decent spot to camp. Trees dotted the area, but no banshee could creep up on them as they slept without being seen. Thicker forested areas lay a ways off, giving a chance to react if Big Owl tried to come after him.

"How far ahead of us is your partner?" Mandy bustled about, taking airtights from her carpetbag. She motioned for him to lay a fire and get coffee brewing.

Cooley talked as he worked. "He's a couple days higher in the mountains by now. It doesn't matter if we spot him. He's going to Mule Springs since the landmarks are all visible from there."

"I was over in New Mexico for a spell," Mandy said, shoving an open airtight toward the fire to heat the contents. Cooley wasn't too interested in what was inside. His belly grumbled, and anything would sit well with him. "There was some trouble around Gila. I don't think anyone in Mule Springs knows or remembers me."

"Trouble with the law?"

"Not exactly. I worked in a saloon, and one of the drunks got frisky. When he refused to let me be, I took his gun from him and shot him. His brothers took offense, so I left town in a hurry."

"Beautiful and deadly," Cooley said with some admiration. "That's about the perfect combination in a lady."

Mandy beamed at the compliment. They sat close to the fire, eating slowly to make the skimpy food last. By the time they finished, the sun had vanished and a chilly wind kicked up, sighing softly through the pines and drowning out the rush of water in the nearby stream. The combination of riding like a fool, having a belly with enough food and feeling the warmth of a fire at his feet caused Cooley to stretch back. He stared up at the stars. Rutledge had told him the British navy had conquered the world by knowing which stars to follow. All he knew was the Big Dipper. Finding north was good enough for any traveling he did.

He started to point out the distinctive constellation to impress Mandy when a twig snapped a few feet away.

Cooley rolled around and stared up at a tall, dark figure. Starlight glinted off the blued barrel of the six-gun.

"You folks surely don't make it hard to follow you. A blind man on your trail'd have no problem finding you."

"Jensen!" Cooley sat up and reached for his six-shooter. For his effort a gun barrel laid up alongside his head. His pistol went flying.

"I am tired of chasing you all around. Give me the map, and you can walk away from here without any lead in your gut."

"Give it to him, John!" Mandy came to her knees.

"I don't have it. My partner's got it. I don't know where he is. Not here."

Lars Jensen gritted his teeth. He stepped forward and landed a kick that caught Cooley on the shoulder. Pain rattled through him. He moaned and clutched his injured arm, then rubbed the spot on his temple where he'd been buffaloed.

"Take her and let me go. I don't know anything. Just don't hurt me!" Cooley screamed when Jensen landed another kick, this time between his legs. White pain shot into Cooley's groin and seared nerves throughout his midsection.

"I've got no reason to take her. Your partner's not likely to swap a whore for the map. Now, you . . . you know how to get the map, and that makes you valuable. I could torture you and find what I need, but you might up and die on me, so I'm taking you to my brother. I'll let him do whatever he wants to get you to talk." Jensen chuckled. "That way, if you die, it's on him, and he can't blame me."

Jensen pulled Cooley to his feet. Wobbling about,

Cooley clutched at the outlaw and turned him around. The little dance won Cooley another blow to the head. His neck snapped, and he saw stars, only none was in the overhead constellations.

Dazed, he sprawled on the ground. Jensen towered over him, a dark and menacing figure. When the gunshot rang out, Cooley jerked and sank back, more dead than alive.

CHAPTER NINETEEN

D AN RUTLEDGE ROLLED over and tried to keep the thin blanket over his shoulder. It was partially pinned under his body and wouldn't stretch. Grumbling, he sat up and freed it, then pulled it up to his chin as he lay flat on his back and stared at the dawn working its way across the sky. High clouds caught the earliest light and worked themselves into fish-bone patterns.

"Looks like a good day to ride," he said loud enough to wake his partner. When he got no reply, he sat up. A surge of panic hit him. Cooley was gone. His gear wasn't where he had laid it out the night before. Twisting around, he saw where Whirlwind was tied to a tree limb. Mabel was gone.

England Dan came to his feet, sleep still fogging his brain. The howling the night before came back to his memory. Big Owl. Banshee. Or what Cooley had been certain was the banshee. He patted his coat pocket. The crinkle of paper assured him that his partner hadn't stolen the map and gone off on his own to get rich. England Dan smiled ruefully at the idea. Cooley got lost going from their mine to the cabin. Of all the skills he might possess, reading a map wasn't one of them.

Thinking on it, England Dan realized that his partner lacked skill in most things. That made them a good partnership. His expertise was appreciated by the man who got drunk and spent their last few dollars in gold flakes on a treasure map.

To be sure that there hadn't been some violence that had spirited Cooley away, he studied the ground. He finished his tracking near the stallion. Disgust filled him. Cooley had left on his own, probably scared off by the banshee.

"What could it be?" he wondered aloud. A complete search of the area failed to turn up any sign of whatever had made the hideous wailing the night before, but he was certain the mule tracks going toward town were Cooley's. Nobody else had disturbed the ground for fifty yards in any direction.

He started a fire and boiled a cup of coffee. Food was scarce, but he found a moldy, rock-hard hunk of hardtack and buffalo jerky so stale he thought his teeth would fall out trying to rip off a piece. Even soaking it in the fierce coffee did little to soften it. When he finally finished his breakfast, it sat in his belly like mining dross. That came as much from the quality of his meal as from his mounting anger at Cooley for running off. Partners didn't do that.

Even ones frightened away by Big Owl.

"You idiot," he growled. "You're the one who renamed it the Lost Banshee Mine. You scared yourself for no reason."

But there was some reason. Whatever had made the sounds the night before had to be fierce. Bears roamed the mountains, but that hadn't been a bear. Nor had it been a mountain lion. Those were the top predators. Imagining some little toad hardly the size of his hand making such a savage hunting cry made him laugh. He sobered when he pulled his six-shooter and checked the cylinder. Three rounds. That was all he had to defend himself from whatever filled the night with such a haunting cry.

A banshee's hunting cry warning him he was going to die.

His food became even less digestible when he thought that No Shadow's tall tale carried some truth. Cooley had run off. Had he also died? The banshee had wailed to warn of impending death. England Dan ran his hands over his dusty clothing. It hadn't been him who died. That left his partner.

"Serves you right, if you did."

Cooley should never have gone off into the night on his own like he did. While his partner wasn't the bravest man in the world, he at least could have said goodbye. Leaving a note was out of the question since he didn't know how to read or write, but something other than skulking away would have been the honorable thing to do.

He took out the map and turned it around, finding the speck that marked Mule Springs. That was the starting point to the Irish Lord.

"The Lost Banshee Mine," he corrected himself. "That's what Cooley called it, and that's what I'll find."

He folded the map and thrust it back into the volumi-
nous coat pocket. If the partnership had been dissolved, everything he found was all his. Big Owl or not,
banshee or not, he was going to be rich.

With newfound determination, he packed his sparse
gear and swung into the saddle. The stallion gamboled
about, ready to run. Keeping Whirlwind from tearing
off took some skill, but he was gaining experience riding the spirited horse. He headed across the stream and
deeper into the mountains, hunting for a pass through
the Superstition Mountains that led to New Mexico
Territory and his starting point at Mule Springs.

By midday he had to admit how turned around he
was. Storm clouds slipped in from the south and hid the
sun, further robbing him of direction. Not for the first
time, he wished he had a compass. Even that wasn't a
guarantee to keeping on a trail leading to Mule Springs.
More than one miner had complained that the iron in
the rocks tugged at a compass needle and gave false
readings.

Waiting for night so he could read the stars wasn't
that good an idea, either. The heavy clouds warned of
a torrential downpour. Finding the tail of the scorpion
or the pointer stars in the Big Dipper had to wait for
clearer skies.

Reinforcing this, a heavy wet raindrop splattered
against the crown of his bowler. He looked up and
caught another drop in his eye. Wiping it out so he saw
clearly again, he hunted around for a place to ride out
the storm. A canyon mouth beckoned, offering a few
shallow caves for refuge. He rode to the first one and
saw it was hardly five feet deep. Rain pelted down with
increasing fury, but he kept hunting until he came to a

cave higher on the canyon wall that extended into the hillside.

England Dan led the stallion in out of the cold, wet rain; then he settled down in the cave mouth to stare at the gray curtain. Dust turned to mud, and the wind made him shiver. After a few minutes of it, he came around to Cooley's way of thinking. From the first time he'd heard of the map, he thought it was a nobbler. So many things kept him from getting Cooley's— *their*—money back. Finding the cowboy with a couple bullet holes in him had only been the start to changing his mind.

Everybody wanted the map enough to kill. He considered giving it to Lars Jensen since the outlaw Gonzales wanted so badly had to be the primary culprit.

He took it out and ran his fingers around the increasingly tattered edges.

"Is this for real? Why would a criminal like Jensen who likely never worked a day in his life want to find the mine? Not to work it, no matter how rich the ore." He returned the map to his pocket. Hunting for the Lost Banshee Mine felt more and more like a wild-goose chase. Cooley might have been the smart one, not in getting conned into buying the map but in knowing when to fold and leave the game.

The rain continued to drive downward in sheets. Whirlwind neighed occasionally to show disdain for being trapped in a cave when there were wide-open spaces to gallop along and hills to climb. Letting the rain lull him, England Dan drifted off to a half sleep. Cooley had cut and run for the wrong reason. The right reason might have been the impossibility of finding the lost mine, if the map was legitimate. England Dan had no notion of where he was. There was a good reason these had been named the Superstition Mountains. Too many prospectors had gone missing over the years. With every disappearance, a new story popped up.

"Banshees," he muttered. How absurd that was. Stories told around the campfire entertained and amused and were never intended to be the gospel truth. Cooley had left the quest because of the howling, but a better reason to give up and go back to Oasis was the distinct possibility of finding nothing.

His chin dipped and rested on his chest. England Dan came instantly awake when the banshee cry came rolling up the canyon between claps of thunder. His hand moved away from the Webley. There wasn't anything to shoot. Nothing he saw, at least. The rain was slowing, and a large stream now made its way along the canyon floor. No animal hunted in such foul conditions.

He stood and tried to see through the downpour. Nothing moved that wasn't driven by water. A flash of lighting striking a distant peak got him to counting. Ten seconds. A British naval officer had once told him every second equaled a mile of distance. Ten miles.

Barely had the thunder died when he heard Big Owl crying again. If he let his imagination run wild, the Indian banshee called out his name.

Dan. Dan. Dan.

Whatever—whoever—made the eerie sounds was in for a world of trouble. If there hadn't been another outcry, he would have been on the trail heading back to town. The Trafalgar Mine wasn't the richest in the hills, but it still had a few good months left, at least for a single miner. As far as he was concerned, Cooley had given up his share when he left.

But the banshee call set his spine and firmed his resolve. Nobody scared him away. And if it was an animal, its skin would sell for a fortune back East. There had never been anything like it before.

He led the stallion out. The horse balked at the now slow rainfall, but by the time they made their way to the canyon floor with its broad, shallow, fast-running stream, the rain had faded into a drizzle. Riding back to the mouth of the canyon set off the banshee. It positively cackled in triumph at running him off. Without hesitation England Dan wheeled the horse about and retraced his course, going deeper into the canyon. He had gotten lost, so it hardly mattered if he became even more turned around if he found the cause of the spooky cooee.

Riding slowly, he scouted both walls of the canyon. On his left the rock rose at a steep angle to a mesa. Here and there abandoned mines showed gaping black mouths. Tailings dribbled down the side of the hill like tongues sticking out. England Dan had seen this too often to find any of it as an ill omen. The far side of the canyon soared almost vertically. Getting to the ridge running along that wall required either clever rock climbing or finding a trail wide enough to accommodate a horse. Riding to the rim would have been out of the question. The thought of hiking up such a trail, coaxing Whirlwind to keep moving and not panicking, made England Dan discard the idea of scaling the wall. He kept riding. The only way out had to be ahead.

The mines became fewer, but the tailings spewed out in longer falls, showing their ore had been more profitable. From the look, they had been abandoned within the last year. He wished his map had led here.

Any of these mines was accessible and capable of being restarted—if any gold remained.

He jerked upright when the banshee cry sounded again. The horse tried to buck. Rather than fight Whirlwind, he dropped to the ground and clung to the reins. The mocking shrieks came from a mine uphill from where he listened. The way the horse's ears twitched proved he wasn't being deceived about the direction.

It took some coaxing to get the stallion onto an old double-rutted road leading to the mine almost at the top of the sloping side. England Dan fastened the reins to a signpost with a weather-beaten sign declaring this to be the Top Hat Mine. The horse tugged and tried to get away, but the post proved strong enough to hold him. When he saw the horse wasn't going to pull free, he drew his six-shooter and began trudging up the hundred yards of trail to the mine.

"Who's in there?" he shouted at the mouth of the mine. It was time to put the banshee claim to the test. Finding out what had caused the wailing drove away any fear that Big Owl might actually exist. All he heard was his question echoing away. A quick search of the area revealed nothing of note. The heavy rain wiped out any chance of finding footprints around the mine.

Footprints or hoofprints?

"What's Big Owl's track look like?" he said aloud. He mentally kicked himself for thinking the Indian ogre was real. Something had made the hideous screeches, but the supernatural wasn't possible. Ghosts and leprechauns and fairies didn't exist, no matter what his upbringing said. His mother had gone into the garden every morning to watch for fairies. When he was younger, he had accompanied her, but what she saw was always just beyond his sight.

His disbelief in such things continued to bring woe onto him during his years at Sandhurst, where dogma tended toward belief in the divine right of kings more than the wee folk. For him, the two beliefs were the same.

Six-shooter out, he pointed it into the mine. If he had enough ammo, a few shots into the dark shaft might produce answers. If whoever was trying to spook him dodged the bullets, he'd find out the truth fast. Only three rounds left made him hunt for other ways of flushing out anyone in the mine. If they were even in the mine.

A more thorough search around the mine convinced him that whoever—whatever—made the noise had taken refuge inside rather than hiding outside. No trace of boot prints on either side of the mine opening was apparent, but scuff marks just inside hinted at someone entering. He reared back and looked to the top of the slope. From the way the rocks curled about, a mesa stretched out of sight. With enough time Big Owl could have scrambled all the way to the top, but England Dan felt he would have spotted him—it.

He shook himself. Keeping his thoughts fixed on finding the *man* crying, he stepped into the mine. Instinct took over. He reached up to a ledge just inside the mine and found a mostly melted miner's candle and a tin of lucifers. With practiced ease, he lit the candle and held it in front of him to cast dancing shadows along the walls and floor. He stuffed the tin of lucifers into his pocket.

"I'm coming in. Give up and you won't get hurt. I'm

sick of you trying to scare me." England Dan edged forward, half bent over. The ceiling hadn't been cut out for a man his height. Only gnomes would have been comfortable in here. The walls were rough-hewn, but what he noticed was the lack of rails on the floor. Getting ore out from the depths of the mine was always a chore, but rolling it out sped up recovery of gold. Whoever had dug this mine relied on dragging bags of ore out rather than rolling them.

He looked harder at the floor. A mule pulling a sledge made sense. If so, he wanted to avoid stepping in any piles left by an animal.

Every few yards he stopped and listened closely. Sometimes a mine creaked. This one was solid. He pressed his ear against a wall, not sure what he expected to hear. Another of the legends miners told was of tommy-knockers, the ghosts of dead men warning the living of impending doom. He felt nothing but contempt for such a notion. Anyone foolish enough to work in a mine should know the danger.

The candle dripped wax around his fingers. He slid his six-shooter back into the holster and switched hands. As he held the candle stub in his right hand, he felt the ground shake. A sudden gust of fetid air snuffed out the candle. He shied back in surprise, landed flat on his butt and slid fast into a dark pit. As he fell, the banshee wailed again.

Then he hit the bottom of the abyss.

CHAPTER TWENTY

HE HAD ALWAYS wondered if being hanged was painful. Lars Jensen considered that to be his fate. In spite of all the gunfights he had been in, he never thought a bullet in the gut was the way he'd check out. The law hunted him all the time. But they wanted him to stand trial for a few crimes. His brother, Poke, was a constant threat. Fast with his gun and faster to anger, though, Poke was as likely to pistol-whip him as shoot him.

"Shot from behind. Figgers." He coughed and spat blood. Jensen took in a slow breath and choked again. If the bullet had gone through a lung he was a goner. Forcing himself to sit up, he probed his wound.

The hole in his chest showed the bullet had entered his back and sailed on through his body. That was good. He had no way of digging around to get the bullet out if it had stayed inside. But his lung. Jensen pressed down on the oozing hole until his fingers were coated with his own blood. Then he examined his bloody fingers only an inch or two from his eyes. The world didn't focus right, but after careful study, he saw that only bright red stained his hand.

"No pink. No foam." He sank back to the ground. The bullet hadn't punctured his lung. For all the pain hammering away at his brain, he was in pretty good shape. Other things inside had been torn up, but nothing serious enough that he'd just lie back and let death take him.

Jensen worked to open his vest and shirt. He used his knife to cut off a long strip of his shirt and pressed down hard over the exit wound. The pain hit him like a sledgehammer. Only iron will kept him from passing out. Working to doctor himself took longer than he expected, but the front wound was stanched. The back wound proved harder because of the way he had to twist himself around. Eventually he had a bandage secured around his body and both wounds sealed off.

Whether he slept or passed out hardly mattered. When he came to his senses, it was well past sundown. The exact time wasn't important, but from the stars, he guessed it was midnight. Crawling to the stream, he drank what he could. When he woke up again, he thanked his lucky stars that he hadn't drowned. His face rested on a rock inches away from the running water. He pushed away and found a grassy area where he slept until sunset. He awoke feeling better. Movement hurt like fire in his veins, and where once he could whip his weight in wildcats, a kitten or two would have had no trouble beating him now.

He worked out what had happened, and it galled

him. Anger built and he propped himself against a tree, plotting his revenge.

"You're a dead man, Cooley. As if I hadn't planned to kill you, anyway, but now? Dead. And the girl. I'll string you both up and let the wolves rip the flesh from your living bodies. I'll watch every minute and to hell with the map."

When those words escaped his lips, a lance of cold drove into his heart. Poke wanted the map as bad as he'd ever wanted anything. Giving himself up and being caged in the Yuma Penitentiary had been bad, but he and Barton Beeman had ridden together for close to a year. That was as long as any partnership had lasted. Lars was family, and Poke expected the blood tie to be forever—or until he ended it. But having a partner to rely on was different for him, more than blood, more than something religious. Lars wondered if his brother knew who'd killed Beeman. If he did, there was a man who would know the frightful meaning of torture that would turn an Apache's stomach.

He drifted off as rain began to fall. The downpour stopped eventually, and he woke up, soaked to the skin but feeling better. Weak but steady on his feet, he went to his horse and dragged himself into the saddle. There wasn't any reason to see if Cooley had left a trail. Time, wind and rain worked to erase it. Barely hanging on, he turned his horse toward Oasis. The miner returned there over and over. If Lars had a chance of finding him and the map, the town gave the best odds. More than that, there must be a doctor who could be sure he got patched up right.

Jensen fell from the horse once on his way back to Oasis. It shook him up but enough strength remained for him to get to his feet. Resolve hardened. Coming this far as hurt as he was counted for something. He stood on a rock and flopped into the saddle. This time he tied himself on and somehow got back to town.

Everyone who saw him avoided him like he was a leper. That suited Jensen just fine. Taking care of himself mattered. It took longer than he thought to find the doctor's office. He cut the rope around his waist and tumbled to the ground, staring up into the sky.

"Mister, you look like you're in a bad way. You want some help?"

"You the sawbones?" The world swam around. The man had a kindly look, as if he fixed up wounded men.

"He left town. Went to Bisbee. Everybody's going there because of the copper strike." The man shook his head sadly. "They're swapping one yellow metal for another, and if you ask me, gold's the better one to hunt. You ever see how they pull copper ore from the ground? They dig a huge pit and—"

"I've been shot. There's no way I can get to Bisbee. Who's able to tend me? A midwife? You must have one around."

"Well, sir, I'm the vet. Been rummaging through the doctor's surgery to see if he left behind anything I can use. Horses and cattle aren't much different than people, you know."

"Fix me up." Jensen reached for his six-shooter but left the iron in its holster. Killing this fool now doomed him if the gunshot was as bad as it felt inside. There was plenty of time to shoot him after he worked on Lars.

With that comforting thought, Jensen hardly groaned as the veterinarian got an arm around him and heaved him upright.

"Let's get you inside. I never used that operating table. Looked inconvenient for big animals. Working on horses is my specialty, and getting one to lay down on a table's silly, don't you think?"

Jensen restrained himself and let the vet ramble on as he worked. He passed out once or twice but finally focused on the man as he washed blood off his hands.

"You've got an iron constitution, mister. That, I'll give you. I went into the wound and closed off a couple arteries leaking to beat the band. Drained the fluid inside so you won't puff up and—"

"Shut up." Jensen tested the limits of motion in his arm. It'd be a while before he was back to speed in clearing leather. Holding his hand out and seeing how it shook told him he had better wait on using his six-shooter at all.

"The shakes'll go away soon enough. They did with that other fellow. Maybe I ought to hang out my shingle. Cows and cowboys. Work on both people and animals. That's the way to make a better living since everyone's so eager to leave for Bisbee."

"You stitched up somebody else? Here?" Jensen looked around. The vet had cleaned up the place if there'd been another patient here.

"Naw, went over to Madam Morgan's. She had a fellow in a back room recuperating."

"One of the whores shoot him?"

"He didn't look the sort to cavort with the likes of Madam Morgan's ladies of the night. This fellow was a lawman."

A lawman? There was no lawman in Oasis anymore, thanks to him. But . . . could it be? "A deputy marshal?" Dizziness hit him like an ax handle between the eyes. "Alberto Gonzales by name?"

"Might have been. Madam Morgan never told me what to call him, but he had a badge. A badge and a couple holes in his chest."

"And a head wound?"

"Only a scratch. Head wounds bleed like the devil. Whoever took him to Madam Morgan had cleaned him up a mite, and he still looked a fright. Why, when I first saw him, I thought he was a goner. Just like you."

"But both of us are alive and kicking."

"Kicking like a newborn colt, yes, sir. Now, I have to get out to the Lamont spread. Jake's got one sick heifer. From the sound of it, he might have a case of Texas fever on his hands."

"Splenic fever," Jensen said. "They call it splenic fever down Texas way."

"I'm sure their drovers do that very thing. Sounds bad having a disease named after your home state. You can stay here, I reckon. The table's not too comfortable, but it's better than sleeping in the livery. You want me to check on you when I get back to town? It'd be tomorrow."

Jensen waved him away and sagged onto the operating table. His run of bad luck refused to stop. Getting back-shot was one thing, but finding that the deputy from over in Mesilla was still alive almost did him in. He had been absolutely certain he'd killed him. He played it back over and over again in his head. Sighting down the rifle barrel, the squeeze and report, the way the deputy jerked and flopped about. Riding up and putting another round in him before going after the girl on the mule. It was all so vivid and yet had turned into a dream. Gonzales was still alive.

"If the vet is to be believed," Jensen grunted. Moaning from pain, he got off the table and made certain his six-gun was loaded. The way his hands shook warned him that even shooting the deputy in the back was risky.

Never before had he felt so awkward. Even the first man he'd killed had not made him so apprehensive.

Jensen left the doctor's surgery and pulled himself onto the patiently waiting horse. Walking any distance still lay beyond his strength.

Poke had gone off somewhere, but when they finally met up he'd expect to see the map. Crazy ideas flashed through Jensen's head. His brother had no idea what the map looked like. A fake map would serve the same purpose—if that purpose was to keep breathing. Poke couldn't expect him to accompany him to find the cavalry payroll, not all shot up like he was. That gave him a decent head start when the map proved to be a forgery.

Jensen shook all over when he realized he was in no condition to make the forgery. Worse, his brother need only stare into his eyes to know it was fake. Poke had been like that with him since they were children. He'd never been able to lie and, after a while, had given up even trying. Telling the truth and taking the consequences had been easier.

Up till now. Poke had spent time in the penitentiary and had lost the stolen payroll and his partner. Speaking the truth now would make the vet's efforts to patch him up go for nothing.

He had no idea where Cooley and the girl had gone after he'd been shot in the back. That girl was a feisty one, but he had ignored any threat she posed. Making that mistake a second time wasn't in the cards.

"The whorehouse," he muttered. "Where else would she go?"

The trail was cold except for Madam Morgan's house of ill repute. Riding slowly, trying not to let the occasional dizziness compromise his seat astride the horse, he made his way down Oasis' main street. He kept as sharp a lookout as he could for the deputy but got to his destination without running into him.

He had bulled his way into the cathouse before. A john and the girl who looked exactly like Mandy had died the first time. The second time it had been necessary to kill the bouncer. Gus, the madam had called him. Neither time had he caught Cooley.

"The side door," he said softly. "He comes and goes that way so he can use the back stairs."

Jensen rode to the small stable behind the house, dismounted and found a decent place to sit in the shade and watch the comings and goings. He pulled the Winchester from its sheath and laid it across his knees. If he got into a gunfight, he wanted as much firepower as possible.

The warmth wrapped itself around him like a blanket. He began drifting off to sleep, only to come awake with a jerk when he heard voices. The rifle pressed into his shoulder, but he saw only the madam's arm poking around the side of the building. He lowered the rifle, then hoisted it again when a man came to the end of the porch and leaned against the railing.

Alberto Gonzales!

Jensen's hands shook so hard, his sight picture bobbed around. He had to make the first shot count and couldn't do it. Lowering his rifle, he got to his feet and drew his six-shooter. On cat's feet, he went to the side of the house, then edged closer to the front porch. A quick look around between the railing supports gave him the entire picture. Madam Morgan sat between him and the deputy. Gonzales presented only a booted foot as a target, his legs stretched out in front of him.

"I walked around, but nobody's seen them." Gonzales coughed, then pulled his feet up so Jensen had no direct look at the deputy.

"You described the girl? Blonde, green eyes, a favorite?"

"I did. And her john. It's like killing two birds with one stone. Get your girl back and find the owlhoot I'm after since he seems to want the girl and Cooley dead." Gonzales coughed again, a rumble from deep in his chest, and then spat over the railing.

"I'll pay plenty to get Mandy working here again." Madam Morgan sounded smug. "And you owe me for taking such good care of you when you needed it most."

The deputy laughed harshly. "You want human flesh. I want horseflesh. They stole my horse. I'm sure it had to be them." He paused and said in a lower voice, "I can't be bought, but I owe you a favor or two for what help you've offered. You sure you don't know where they might be holed up?"

Jensen perked up. He listened harder. The deputy was doing his work for him. Although Gonzales sought Cooley and Mandy because he thought they'd lead him to that fierce desperado Lars Jensen, he could stay out of sight long enough to grab the map. The deputy wanted him, but the lawman never mentioned the map. If he had no idea the map even existed, Poke would have no trouble finding the payroll since the lawman never expected his brother to show up.

Jensen crouched down and rested the six-shooter on the edge of the porch, waiting to take a shot. Then he drew back. The deputy was on foot. The safe thing was to kill Gonzales, but he was hunting Cooley. Too many possible outcomes collided in his dazed mind. Jensen sank down. If the lawman hadn't found his fugitives by now, he wasn't likely to. So shoot him down. Now. But Gonzales posed no real threat all shot up and recovering and lacking a horse.

Jensen sat at the end of the porch, thinking hard. If Cooley hadn't come back to Oasis, the only other place he might be found was the Trafalgar Mine up in the hills. He had no reason to hightail it out of the county since he thought his worst nightmare—Jensen smiled, liking the notion he lived in Cooley's mind, chipping away at his courage—had been killed.

He made his way back to the stable and his horse. Leaving the deputy alive galled him, but killing him could wait for another day. Finding Cooley and the map for Poke was his foremost duty. He swayed about in the saddle but hit the trail for the mine. It was his last, best hope to find Cooley.

CHAPTER TWENTY-ONE

D ON'T KILL ME. Take her, take her!" John Cooley gagged when Lars Jensen grabbed him around the neck and started strangling the life from him.

He thought he was a goner when the outlaw jerked. Falling away, he dropped to hands and knees. Blood pounded in his ears, but he thought he'd heard a gunshot. A quick check showed he was still in one piece. Cooley got to shaky feet and frantically hunted for the best direction to run away. Then, from a long ways off, he heard someone calling his name.

"John! Snap out of it. Come *on*!"

He jerked away from the hand grabbing his arm. Off-balance, he stumbled, caught his heel on a rock and sat heavily. Still dazed, he threw up his arms to protect his face.

"John!"

He lowered his arms and saw Mandy standing over

him. The last puff of gun smoke slipped from the barrel of a gun.

"Mine?" He pointed at the six-gun she clung to so fiercely.

"Yes. Now, come on. We've got to get out of here."

"You killed him?" He hardly believed it was possible. Mandy a murderer? But the first time he fired a gun at another he'd killed No Shadow. That scared him as much as anything ever had, and yet Mandy seemed to know what to do now.

"We have to get out of here. Didn't you hear what he said?"

"I . . . What do you mean?"

"He said he was taking you to his brother. There's another one like *him* roaming around hunting for us."

"We need to go," Cooley said, finally seeing through the veil of shock that had clouded his mind. "Now!"

He grabbed what little they had in camp and stuffed it into a sack. By the time he'd finished, Mandy came with the mule and her horse.

"Where do we go?" He was thinking clearer now. "Not back to town. There's nobody there who can help us."

"That deputy is in Madam Morgan's backroom, but he was still in a bad way. And returning to your mine's no good. There's nothing for us there."

"I don't know where England Dan is. Off looking for the Lost Banshee Mine."

"What? Oh, the mine on your map. I thought you called it the Irish Lord." She put her heels to her horse's flanks and splashed around in the water a few seconds before heading upstream. He trailed her, realizing this was the best way to distance themselves from

the body lying on the ground. There wouldn't be hoofprints to give them away if Jensen's brother came hunting for them.

They had ridden for a few minutes when a thought
hit Cooley.

"His gun! I should have taken his gun." He started
to turn Mabel around to head back the way they came.
Mandy held up his gun and waved it around.

"We've got this one. Don't go back. The shot may
have alerted his brother. I heard Madam Morgan gos-
siping about a man who got out of Yuma Penitentiary.
That must be his brother. Anybody sent to Yuma's one
bad hombre. Real bad."

"I'm not afraid of crossing him," Cooley said. "I
shot an Indian. And I would have taken care of Jensen
if you hadn't."

Mandy let him come even with her in the stream. She
handed him the six-shooter. "You take it. I'm tired of
lugging around this heavy iron, and you've got a holster."

"Don't you fret none. If I see trouble coming, I'll
keep you safe."

"Seeing it coming is the hard part," she said. Mandy
urged her horse to keep splashing along in the cold
water until it began shivering. She looked left and
right, then cut to her left up a canyon.

Cooley started to ask why she'd picked this direction;
then he realized there wasn't a difference. One way was
as good as the other, as long as it was away from where
Lars Jensen lay dead. He settled down and began to
enjoy the ride, watching Mandy bounce along on the
horse. Without any fuss, she began choosing the direction they traveled. His attention was on the woman, and
a fine sight for sore eyes she was, too. Because of that,

when sundown cast long shadows across the canyon floor they rode, he had no idea how they had gotten here.

"Time to camp," he said. "Over there looks like a good place."

"We need to keep riding, John. There. See it?" Mandy pointed to the ground.

"It's getting dark. What are you looking at?" He hopped down from astride Mabel and then dropped to his knees. Mandy had been far more attentive than he to see the scuffed moccasin tracks.

Cooley began counting and thought he made out at the tracks of at least four Indians.

"Big Ear," he whispered.

"They went deeper into the canyon. We should retrace our path."

"Blundering around in the dark is dangerous," he said. "Who knows what's out there hunting? Big Ear's moving deeper into the canyon, ahead of us. Unless he doubles back, he'll never see us." Cooley laughed. "It's like we're hunting him."

"What if this is a box canyon? The hunters won't find any game and will come back."

"Or they might be herding a lot ahead of them to kill in the box. That'd mean they have a lot of dressing to do and meat to pack for the rest of their tribe. That takes time."

"If there's that much game, they'd send a runner back to the tribe to get help carrying it out. The runner'd come right on past us."

Cooley's mouth turned to cotton. The Mogollons hunted the man who had killed No Shadow. It might not matter much to them what white man they found.

They'd blame anyone they came across. That he was in their way and actually had shot the loco No Shadow was a twist of fate he wanted to avoid.

He knew any of the Indians would immediately recognize the horse Mandy rode as having belonged to their chief. Revenge for No Shadow or not, the theft spelled trouble for anyone caught with the pony.

"It would be best for us to backtrack," he said. Cooley stepped up onto the mule, but Mabel wouldn't budge. Her long ears swiveled back and forth, and the way she snorted warned him she heard someone else along the canyon floor. From the evidence he'd found, four Indian hunters were the most likely to be coming.

"Ride!" Cooley sawed at Mabel's bit. The mule bucked once, then broke out in a rapid walk. He tried to encourage the mule to a quicker gait, but the travel that day had been long and tiring. Mabel wasn't going to be pushed faster than she wanted.

Mandy passed him in the dark. He started to call out to her, but the echoes in the canyon deterred him. Big Ear might not know he had them on the run. If they reached the mouth of the canyon and escaped down another, they could elude the hunters entirely. He touched his almost empty six-shooter. If the Mogollon chief caught wind of them, even though he was on foot, he'd run them into the ground.

Worse, the Indians would consider Mandy to be an escaped slave. Cooley would end up scalped and left for dead, but the girl's fate would be sealed for years to come. He bent low over the mule's neck and whispered words of encouragement. Mabel might not know what he said, but she responded. From what he said so urgently, he'd certainly scared himself.

"See how the stars are blocked on either side but clear in the sky directly ahead?" Mandy pointed. Cooley wasn't interested in what was in the sky as much as he was in the Indians catching up with them. He had seen how they ran faster than a horse. With the mounts picking their way gingerly in the dark, a brave on foot traveled lots faster.

"Keep riding."

"We're almost at the mouth of the canyon, John. The open space shows the sky. The canyon walls aren't blocking the view."

"Go to the left. I remember another canyon branching off in that direction."

They exited the canyon. He felt as if he had been freed from chains. The high canyon walls held in heat and piped sound. Here, the air was cooler and nocturnal forest sounds greeted him. Not allowing Mabel to slow, he veered to the left into the canyon he remembered. They should have come this way earlier, but Mandy had insisted on the one filled with a hunting party.

These canyon walls were farther apart, but sounds still echoed. When he felt the mule faltering, he came even with the girl and said, "Slow down. Not so much sound."

"My horse needs to rest, too," she said. She hopped off the horse and led it along. Cooley followed her example, though his legs turned shaky within a few minutes. He was getting close to the end of his rope and needed to catch his breath.

"You think we outfoxed them?" Mandy sat beside him and took his arm. She laid her head on his shoulder.

"They never knew we were behind them. If Lady

Luck's smiling on us, they kept going up the canyon and can leave at the far end. There's nothing to say that was a box canyon."

He went over everything he had thought. It was all wild guesswork. Big Ear knew the Superstition Mountains and had no reason to blunder down a box canyon. While the chief hunted the man who had killed No Shadow—and possibly even sought his escaped slave— the band went after food to feed the rest of the tribe.

"John," Mandy said softly, "somebody's out there. To your left."

He jerked around in time to see a dark figure rise from behind a tree stump and sprint away. Without thinking, he shoved Mandy away, got his pistol out and fired. The report deafened him as surely as the foot-long tongue of yellow-orange flame blinded him.

"What're you doing, you fool!" Mandy got to her feet and took a step in the direction of the spy. "Even if you killed him, the rest heard the shot and will come running."

Cooley closed his eyes. He wasn't sure if the pounding he heard was his heart hammering away or the moccasined feet of the retreating Indian.

Or was the sound from a half dozen sets of moccasin-sheathed feet rushing toward them?

He stared dumbly at the gun in his hand. There weren't many bullets left. Working up the courage to count how many rested in the cylinder lay beyond his nerve. "What are we going to do?"

"Try to lose them," Mandy said. "Lead your mule. Come on, John, come on!" She tugged at his arm and got him moving.

Mabel balked, having been frightened by the gunshot. Cooley threw his arms around the mule's neck and pushed with all his strength. The animal had turned . . . mulish.

"Come on, or I leave you behind," he said. "The Indians will eat you!"

The threat got the mule moving. Whether the mule understood or not was of no concern. Cooley was making tracks toward the branching canyon. He never slowed when he reached the wall and careened around it. With a jump, he landed astride Mabel and forced the mule to an even faster pace. Mandy kept up with him, the stolen Indian pony she rode barely straining.

"We did it. We got away," he said after a few minutes.

"John. Wait. Listen." Mandy cupped her ear with her hand.

Cooley took in a dozen things all at once. Both the mule and the horse twisted their ears around toward the back trail. Then he heard deep gasping as if someone had run miles and miles but kept slogging away. His imagination added the pounding of Indian feet on the hard, rocky ground. Big Ear had found their tracks and come for them.

"We can outrun them. Come on." He tried to get more speed from the mule and failed. He glanced over and wondered if Mandy's horse could take two on its back and make faster time. Abandoning Mabel rankled Cooley, but she had been taken by Big Ear earlier and rescued with no ill effects. He could do it again.

Facing the hunting party was another way out. He touched his gun. He had one or two bullets left, if that. If he got in a good shot and hit one Indian, the rest might take cover or turn and run away. Or they might rush him. He'd be dead in a heartbeat if that happened. There was no way he was skilled enough to tackle even one Indian armed with a knife or a war club. And the entire band had arrows. He ran his hands over his chest. He was only seconds away from looking like a pincushion.

"What are we going to do?" asked Mandy.

Cooley stared at the woman. She expected him to get them out of this fix. For a moment, pride filled him. Then fear took over. If he took her horse and left her behind, he could get away.

Two quick steps took him to her side. The horse tried to rear, but she held it down. Somehow, the animal's fright calmed his.

"What would Dan do?"

"Well, what's the answer?" Mandy sounded peeved rather than scared. This buoyed him up.

He drew his six-gun and faced the darkness where Big Ear and his braves advanced on them. The decision came to him. It scared him as much as it puffed him up with pride that he had made it.

"Go on, vamoose. I'll hold them back as long as I can."

"You'd do that for me, John?" She gave him a kiss, the first one he'd ever gotten from her that carried real passion. She broke off, panting. "We'll stand them off together."

He lifted his six-shooter and fired when the first of the Indians loomed in the darkness. The second time he pulled the trigger proved a dud. The hammer fell on a spent cartridge. He hefted the gun to use as a club. Then all his courage disappeared. From behind, from deeper in the canyon, came the banshee's howl.

"Big Owl! It's Big Owl!"

He wondered who shouted the warning, then realized his throat was sore from the effort.

"They're running away, John! They're turning tail and leaving us alone!"

He turned from the hunting party and faced into the canyon. The echo from the banshee's shriek rolled on and on and on until his blood froze in his arteries. One of them was doomed to die.

CHAPTER TWENTY-TWO

ENGLAND DAN SLID and slid and . . . crashed into a solid rock wall. Lying stunned, he tried to figure out if his eyes were open or not. He blinked. There wasn't any difference between closed and open. Groaning, he moved. He ached all over. Carefully checking himself, he found only strained muscles. No broken bones. Nothing but a few bloody scrapes. Not even a headache. For that, he was glad. A concussion meant he'd die down here.

"Where's here?" He began feeling around in the pitch black until he judged that the pit was about six feet wide. The walls matched those of the mine shaft above. But one side sloped drastically. The other was more gradual. "Which side did I come down?"

He failed to figure that out. He had turned around and flopped and gotten banged up so much that he was disoriented. He felt around for the candle he had carried. It had been extinguished when he fell into the pit and was nowhere to be found.

Trying to think through his dilemma got him nowhere until he remembered the lucifers he'd found with the candle. He drew one out and lit it. The eye-dazzling flare showed him how bad off he was. One side of the pit was steeper than the other. The more gradual slope still presented quite a climb. He used the last match to position himself for his escape. Rocks slid under his boots as he scrambled. Faster and faster, he worked and kept sliding back to the bottom of the pit. Out of breath, he sat in the dark and worked out a plan. When he regained his breath, he found one wall and felt around for rock outjuts. He edged up the slope, using the solid wall for support. Gradually inching his way up, he finally slipped and slid and flopped onto the solid mine floor.

He rolled over and sat up. Sulfurous curses escaped his lips when he saw the faint outline of the mine opening—on the other side of the pit. If he wanted to leave the mine the way he'd come in, he'd have to make one prodigious leap. In the dark, missing the other side was a distinct possibility. A second plunge back into the pit might cripple him. Or worse. It would be his grave.

"I'm not dying like that," he said. Working the Trafalgar Mine had taught him the dangers of hard-rock mining. The more chances a miner took, the shorter his life was destined to be. England Dan judged the risk of jumping to the other side to be as close to suicide as he'd ever likely come.

Putting the mine entrance to his back, he began edging along. He dragged one hand along the wall and stepped gently to be sure he didn't fall into a second invisible pit. Why the first one had been dug was a mystery he would never solve. Miners worked lonely shifts. If they didn't have a partner, many turned downright loco. The solitude and the constant danger slid dark fingers into their sanity, and the hard physical exertion and the occasional blasting with dynamite shook up the brains.

Then again, England Dan had seen sinkholes open up and swallow half a town. There seemed no good reason for it to happen. It just did.

He stopped and caught his breath when he heard a whispery sound.

"Who's there? Tell me!" He made no effort to keep the fright from his voice. Then he screamed.

The banshee's howl filled the narrow mine shaft. It started low and built until he clapped his hands over his ears to shut it out. After a few seconds, the screeching withered to a hiss. Then even that vanished. He dropped to his knees and shook.

"I'm not Cooley," he said to himself. "I don't believe in banshees. There's no Big Owl like No Shadow claimed. There's nothing supernatural in this mine. There's not." England Dan tried to convince himself and did a halfway-good job. Whatever he had heard had nothing to do with supernatural spirits foretelling his death.

Getting back to his feet, he continued deeper into the Stygian gloom. No new cries sounded, but he heard a shrill whistling from ahead. Continuing his cautious advance, he came to a glowing spot on the floor. Curious, he tried to nudge it with his boot. The spot appeared on top of his boot. His head snapped upward, and he let out a joyful cry. An air vent opened above him. A tiny patch of blue sky appeared, then went away.

"Clouds. Rain clouds. But that's the sky!" He shoved his face up and inhaled deeply. Fresh, cool, damp air smacked him in the face.

He had found a way out—if he could fit into the shaft leading upward. The rock chimney was narrow. If he got stuck in it, he was a goner. At least he saw his destination. Unlike in the pit, he'd have fresh air as he shinnied out.

Reaching up, he felt around for handholds. The ragged interior a foot above his head gave him a way to get into the chimney, but as he went up, the rock turned treacherously slick. The shear planes were like glass, and the width began to decrease. Within a few feet after a twenty-foot climb, he felt as if his body had been pressed into a vice. Every inch he went up caused the sides to crush down twice as much. Tamping down panic, he sucked in a small breath rather than try to get a lungful of air. Sweat ran down his body and got into his eyes when his eyebrows failed to dam the flow off his forehead. Straining to reach, he got his fingers over the exterior edge. The rock had a sharp edge that cut into his flesh.

He cried out and used the pain and rising fear to surge upward. He grabbed a handhold on a chamisa growing at the edge of the rock chimney. Muscles screaming in pain, he jerked as hard as he could. If he failed to get free now, he'd never escape the vertical stone coffin.

His shoulders pulled above the ground level, letting him look around. One elbow slammed down hard enough to raise his body another couple inches. A sec-

ond elbow gave even more leverage. England Dan
sucked in his breath and finally got half his body out of
the rocky trap.

Gasping for breath and knowing he was almost safe
added to his strength. The next time he scooted up so
he sat on the edge of the vent. Twisting this way and
that got his feet out. He flopped onto his back and
stared up into the sky. The storm had blown out, but
clouds still veiled the nighttime stars. Eyes closed, he
rested from his exertion; then he woke with a start
when the banshee cry sounded once more.

He sat up and grabbed his bowler to keep it from
being blown off his head by the gusty winds. The darkness hid the mesa beyond a few yards, but the sound
emanated from the rock chimney he'd just climbed.

On impulse, he fell over the vent, blocking it with
his body. The howling immediately stopped. Rolling
onto his side let the wind find the vent again. The banshee cry returned, but pitched differently. England
Dan played with the vent, blocking parts and letting
the wind surge down in different patterns. The whistle
had come from the wind in the vent this whole time,
not from Big Owl. Not from the banshee.

To be sure, he began a careful study of the mesa top.
He found faint traces of animal tracks not entirely
washed away by the rain. Everywhere he looked showed
only signs expected on an Arizona mesa. No ogre. No
banshee. No Big Owl.

Muscles protesting from the exertions in the mine
and getting to the mesa, he stretched and walked
around until he felt halfway normal. He went to the
edge of the mesa above the mine and looked down. The
mine mouth was about ten yards below him. Getting

down to where he'd tethered his horse required him to explore for a descent giving him adequate handholds.

Caution told him waiting until morning was the smart thing to do. He pushed his bowler back, wiped his dusty forehead and looked out over the valley. A flash of light caught his eye. At the canyon mouth someone carried a torch. Two. Three.

Whoever hunted down there using torches worked their way into the canyon. If they came far enough, his horse would make a fuss. England Dan wasn't going to be left on foot after all he'd been through. He paced along the drop-off until he found a slope that, while dangerous-looking, wasn't treacherous. He took a deep breath and began the descent. Rocks kicked loose under his boots. Handholds betrayed him. He skidded and slid halfway down before stopping himself.

Face pressed against the hillside, he cautiously looked down. The next possible step lay five feet lower. As he worked up the courage to make the drop, his boots lost purchase. He fell that last five feet. He caught himself in the nick of time. Panting from exertion, he skidded lower until he dropped to the ground.

The mouth of the mine gaped only a few yards away, looking as if a giant yawned. Darker rocks above on either side turned the mine into a face with open eyes. He shuddered at the sight. The light of day made the mine look . . . ordinary. At night it turned into a monster waiting to swallow whole any fool entering.

England Dan ignored his misgivings about the mine and took the trail down to where his horse was tethered. A few minutes calming Whirlwind worked wonders. England Dan swung into the saddle and rode to the canyon floor. His choices were limited. If he rode to the mouth of the canyon, he had to pass several men carrying torches. Other than Big Ear and his hunters, he had no idea who roamed the hills.

Not having any desire to cross the Indians, especially with his six-shooter almost empty, he considered going to ground and hoping they passed him. That the Indians ventured out in the night with torches told him they trailed something—someone—important. The Mogollons, like most of the Apache tribes, stayed close to camp and their protecting fires through the night.

Riding at a steady pace into the canyon kept him away from them since they were all afoot. Or they had been when Mandy stole Big Ear's horse and Cooley recovered their mule. He ran the risk of getting trapped in a cul-de-sac. That gave the best chance he saw for avoiding Big Ear.

As he crossed a rocky patch, he slowed to keep his horse's hooves from clacking. Sound carried along the canyon, trapped by the walls. He couldn't help but look up, trying to see the mine where the air vent had caused the banshee whines. The darkness hid the mine. But something else caught his attention.

He whirled about.

"Cooley!" His partner's voice carried from behind him. Cooley was sandwiched between him and the Indians. Adding to the danger, Mandy answered Cooley's outcry. The two of them were in peril from the hunters. He tried to make out what they said. Their voices were too muffled, but the tone convinced him they knew they were being pursued.

His hand drifted to his six-shooter, then moved away. Adding his gun to whatever Cooley and Mandy carried wasn't too useful. He knew Cooley. His partner would never have thought to bring extra ammo. He wasn't big on planning.

The trees dotting the canyon floor made it difficult to determine their exact position behind him. If he rode past them, he'd find himself facing Big Ear and his band. And what if he did find Cooley and Mandy? They knew they were being pursued.

Again he touched his six-gun. His weapon was useless. Then he settled down and knew violence wasn't the answer to saving his partner and Mandy—and himself. He cupped his mouth and let out a bloodcurdling shriek. He tried to duplicate the shrieks he had heard earlier, the one coming from the mine and fed by the wind down the air vent.

His throat tensed as he let loose an even louder screech. England Dan had no idea what it sounded like as it rattled throughout the canyon, but it chilled him.

It might have been his imagination, but he thought he heard the stomping of feet getting farther and farther. Then he quit before he lost his voice entirely.

And heard Big Owl's answer to his screech.

CHAPTER TWENTY-THREE

W E'RE CURSED!" JOHN Cooley sank to the ground
and brought his knees up to hug them. He shook
his head. "Nobody escapes their fate when the banshee cries out."

Mandy had blanched at the sound, but now color returned to her cheeks. She walked around and pointed
toward the mouth of the canyon.

"They're leaving. It scared off the Indians. We can
get out of here if we hurry." With a tug on her horse's
reins, she brought it around to jump up. When she saw
Cooley hadn't budged, she went to him and shook his
shoulder. "Snap out of it. We've got to go. There's no
telling how long the Indians will run. If they get their
courage back, they might come for us again."

"It doesn't matter, I tell you. We're cursed. We heard
the banshee. Big Owl has chosen us to die!"

"You are loco, John. I don't know what made the noise, but it's not a banshee."

"It could be his partner that howled like the very devil," came a voice Cooley recognized. He perked up and looked around. Peering into the dark, he called, "Dan? Is that you?"

"None other than." England Dan rode slowly to a spot between Cooley and Mandy. "I wasn't expecting to see you again."

"We were hunting for you," Cooley said. "I had to go fetch Mandy in town. Then I came back, and those Indians got on our trail."

"Mandy," England Dan said carefully, as if trying to believe such a wild claim. "You had to get her to join the search? Why didn't you tell me?"

"I know what you think about her being a whore and all. This way there's no way you can tell her to leave."

"You don't like me?" Mandy went over to England Dan and stared up at him. "He never said anything about that. Neither did you."

"I've got nothing against you," England Dan said peevishly. "Cooley lit out before because the banshee scared him."

"I don't reckon you claim to have made those sounds, too." Cooley clambered to his feet and crossed his arms. He thrust out his chin. "You were as scared as I was."

"Don't bet good money on that," England Dan said. "What happened in town that changed your mind about bearding the banshee in its den?"

"The deputy's storming all around Oasis, hunting for Lars Jensen. He's not sure but thinks the outlaw stole his black stallion." Mandy looked at England Dan's horse. "He won't find him," she said proudly. "I shot him dead." A smile crept to her lips. "Finding the horse thief is another matter."

"She did that very thing, gunning down Jensen, and there's no reason not to take another look at the map since he's dead." Cooley's head spun trying to keep everything straight. England Dan wasn't convinced there'd been a word of truth in anything he said. Mandy's explanation carried more weight, but the way he glared made Cooley sure his partner was going to chase him away.

Cooley looked around, trying not to look too fearful. England Dan hadn't cried out like a banshee before. He wasn't sure he believed him now, even if it was too much of a coincidence that his partner happened to be prowling around the canyon in the direction of the banshee's cry.

"My horse is fresh. I spent the day trapped in a mine," England Dan said. "How're your mounts? They looked all lathered."

"If it means getting away from the hunting party, we can ride them into the ground," Cooley said. He patted Mabel. "It'll take more'n a few hours riding to do this one in."

"And the chief's pony is strong enough," Mandy said. She laughed. "Aren't we a fine bunch of thieves? You've stolen a lawman's horse, and I swiped an Indian chief's horse. John is the only one of us who hasn't stolen anything."

"He never said where he got Mabel," England Dan said, turning his stare on his partner. "I never asked. You steal the mule, Cooley?"

"Let's get out of here. And not toward the banshee," Cooley said. He peered into the night. His fright had passed, but he was still jumpy about being trapped in the canyon.

"Which direction is the mine?" Mandy stood stock-still and fixed England Dan with her emerald eyes. "You came into the valley because the map sent you here."

"Truth is, I got lost. The rain turned me around. I need to get someplace where I can get my bearings. If I do, there's a chance I can find my way to the spot on the map without traipsing all over the Superstition Mountains."

"Town?" Mandy sounded hopeful. "There's nothing to keep me there, not with Madam Morgan likely out for my scalp, but I know folks who can help."

"The madam? Are you sure she wouldn't lend us some aid?" Cooley felt left out. Dan and Mandy were making decisions and expected him to go along with whatever they said.

"No," Mandy said. "Madam Morgan would beat me within an inch of my life for trying. Going to that well again isn't in the cards. She acts like all the girls are her daughters when anyone can overhear. When we're alone, she makes sure we know she owns us. Besides, she thinks I'm a deadbeat."

"You owe her?"

"A ton of money, John. She takes a cut of our earnings and then charges us outrageous amounts for room and board. There's no way we can ever buy our freedom. It's as bad as working a mine and having to buy everything from the company store."

"Stick with us, and we'll be rich from the Lost Banshee Mine."

"You'd cut me in? For how much?"

"Me and Dan'd have to do the actual mining, so we'd take the lion's share." His partner glared at him. "We can dicker over the amount later." That failed to satisfy either Mandy or England Dan, but he felt good enough making the deal. It kept the girl happy, and arguing with his partner always ended up with some sort of compromise, as if Dan wore himself out and agreed to about anything. The Brit had an aversion to such confrontations, and that benefitted Cooley more often than not.

"I see no reason to get on back to town," England Dan said. "If we can find our bearings, going back to the Trafalgar makes sense. We'd have a roof over our head while we try to figure out the map."

"A roof's a good thing right about now," Mandy said. She held out her hand. "It's starting to rain again."

"Time to hit the trail. The rain will wash away any chance Big Ear has of finding us." Cooley settled down on Mabel and waited for his partner to take the lead. This way Dan would ride into an ambush first, but he also had a better sense of direction.

They rode until after midnight. Cooley had no idea what direction they went, but both Dan and Mandy discussed the matter, pointing to stars and taking crazy turns through the dark valleys. As the moon poked through the thin, high clouds, Cooley let out a yelp. He recognized the terrain.

"That there's the road into Oasis. If we go upslope

along it, there's the fork. One trail goes to Arizona Johnston's American Prize Mine, and the other leads to ours."

"He's right," England Dan said. "And not a minute too soon. I'm so tired, I'm about ready to fall off the horse."

"And the horses are stumbling," Mandy said. "We've pushed them as far as we can. It's a good thing we walked them the whole way and didn't gallop any at all."

Cooley saw her look down trail in the direction of town. The pull to return there was still strong for her. An unworthy thought crept into his head. She saw a lot of men at the brothel. Maybe she was sweet on somebody in town. All Cooley offered her was a pig in a poke. Finding the mine was a problem, and no gold would come out until he and Dan worked it. From his days in the Trafalgar Mine, he knew that they might pull nuggets out the size of his fist or toil for a month and get only a few flakes. Gold mining wasn't a dependable way to make money.

Not enough to satisfy a fancy lady like Mandy. He wondered why she hadn't married before now. There had to be ranchers all around willing to take her away from the sporting life. The only reason that made sense was her sister. If she married, that would have left Mindy in Madam Morgan's clutches. Cooley doubted many men would marry Mandy and buy her sister's freedom, too. And if one offered, what he had in mind for the pair of them wasn't anything a respectable wife would tolerate, no matter what they did up north.

With Mindy dead, his hold on Mandy without showing her a pile of gold was shaky.

"There's nothing in town for you," Cooley said. "Your future's got gold in it if you come with me."

The woman looked at him. He caught his breath. Her expression fed his fears about the two of them ever being together.

"Don't worry your head, John. I'm not going to bolt." But she looked at the trail leading to Oasis. "There's nothing for me back there anymore."

Her words said one thing, but she leaned just a tad toward Oasis, as if she intended to gallop away.

"We can make the cabin in an hour if we don't stop." Cooley and Mandy rode side by side, letting England Dan ride ahead.

"Your partner's not too excited about me getting a cut of your new mine." Mandy stared straight ahead. Cooley worried this was only part of her objection to throwing in with him, but what it'd take to bind her wasn't in him. Not yet.

"That's Dan. He's never excited about much of anything. It's got something to do with coming from England. The way he tells it, the air's so thick there, you can cut it with a knife. Everyone coughs up blood, and the whole lot of them go around wheezing like lungers."

"I'd like to see it. London. It's supposed to be so . . . civilized."

"There're places in this country that're better. We'll see them, I promise. You and me, when the mine starts giving up its glitter."

"This map to the Irish Lord—the Lost Banshee Mine," she said thoughtfully. "Why'd the owner abandon it? And why's there a map to it? If he died, there's no call to put it down on paper, and if he didn't kick the bucket, he'd know where his own claim was situated."

"I'm guessing," Cooley said, "that he found himself hurt or real sick. As he was dying, he wanted to let somebody know how to find the mine. Everybody says it's the richest in the entire Superstition Mountains."

"So if the owner drew this map on his deathbed, how'd he get the map to whoever he wanted to work the claim?"

"It's a secret location," Cooley said. "The map's been stolen from whoever was supposed to get it. I bought it off the cowboy back in Oasis. He's the one that took it from the man who was supposed to work the mine."

"What if he shows up? The real owner?"

"Dead," Cooley said, exasperated now. "Don't worry your head none over this, Mandy. I got it all squared away."

"But . . ."

"Hold up!" England Dan held up his hand as if he were the commander of a cavalry patrol. "There's been somebody nosing around since we've been gone."

"How do you know?" Cooley looked up and got a fat, cold raindrop in the eye for his effort. "Any trace ought to have been washed away."

"The rocks. See?" England Dan pointed to a few rocks scattered around on the trail. "I set them up as a marker, and they're knocked over."

"That's not much of a warning," Mandy said. "Or was it set as a trigger for a trap?"

"A marker," Cooley said, beginning to worry. His partner was right, as he usually was. "We used it to leave each other messages. Depending on the stones all stacked up, it told the other one when we'd be back."

"Why not write a message in your cabin?" The girl

looked at him, realization dawning on her. "Oh, you can't read or write, can you?"

Cooley rode ahead to avoid answering. Being illiterate usually wasn't a bother, but admitting it to Mandy felt like a failure. Everything he did and said had to be about perfect, or she'd ride off and he'd never see her again.

"What are we going to do about intruders?" Cooley tried to figure out what marks on the trail weren't supposed to be there. Then it hit him. All the hoofprints were left by whoever had knocked over the stone cairn. "They rode up there within the last few hours." He stared at the sky again, this time putting up a hand to shield his face from the errant raindrops.

"Tracks go up, none back." England Dan touched his six-shooter, then drew his knife. "You stay with the girl. I'll see if they decided to squat in our cabin."

"I can help."

"Stay," England Dan said firmly, as if ordering a dog to heel.

Cooley's anger flared, then settled back to a smolder. Being talked to like that hurt his pride, but he got the mule spun around and headed back down to where Mandy waited impatiently.

"He's going to see if we're in for any trouble. If there is, he'll call me."

"The tracks don't show the rider came back down." Mandy pursed her lips as she considered what this meant. "Dan's riding into trouble, unless whoever left those tracks passed the cabin by and kept riding toward the meadow to the east. That's the only way through the mountains to get over to New Mexico."

"That's the way I read it," Cooley said. When Mandy

sorted it all out, it made sense. England Dan wasn't too likely to find squatters. There hadn't been anything left in the cabin to steal. All they wanted themselves in the cabin was a roof over their head while they studied the map before moving on.

Reinforcing the need for shelter, a few more raindrops splattered on the brim of Cooley's hat. If they waited much longer, they'd be drenched.

"Let's go to the cabin. He's not signaled there's anything to worry over."

"Are you sure, John? If we barge in while Dan's sneaking up on somebody, we might start a fight. And if we don't, it would still rile up your partner because he didn't tell us the coast was clear."

"I don't take orders from him. We're equal partners. Even steven, like he says."

Mandy reluctantly rode a few yards behind Cooley as he kept Mabel moving toward the cabin. Rounding a bend in the trail, he came to a fork. Uphill led to the mine. Farther around the curve of the hill lay their cabin. Cooley reared back and stopped Mabel when he saw that England Dan had dismounted to scout the cabin on foot. Cooley slid from the saddle and drew his gun, knowing its only value lay in bluffing.

His approach was noisy. England Dan popped out from the back of the cabin, brandishing his knife. His disgust was obvious when he saw it was only his clumsy partner. He motioned for Cooley to stay where he was.

Shifting nervously from foot to foot, Cooley waited for Rutledge to go to the door and ease it open. The creaking noise sounded like nails pulled from wood. A quick look inside and then he disappeared through the door. Cooley rushed forward.

"Empty," England Dan said. He sheathed his knife. "The hoofprints go on past the shed."

"The rider went to the meadow." Cooley tried to sound as if he wasn't relieved. He wasn't sure how successful he was.

"We got in just in time. The rain's starting again." England Dan stepped away from a leak in the roof. Water puddled on the dirt floor, turning it to mud.

Cooley hurried to grab a pot and put it under the leak. If the floor turned into a swamp, there would be hardly any difference between standing outside in the rain and being indoors. He put their frying pan under a second leak, then said, "I'll get Mandy."

He ducked back out and went around the trail in time to see her riding away. Cooley started to call to her, but she was leaving of her own accord. If she didn't see how good she had it with him, to hell with her, but her silent departure still festered inside him. Cooley squared his shoulders and returned to the cabin.

England Dan looked up from where he sat across the table. The map was spread out in front of him. "Well? Where is she?"

Cooley cleared his throat, lifted his chin and said, "I sent her back to town. Hunting for the mine's going to get real dangerous, and I didn't want to risk her life."

"Get *more* dangerous?" England Dan snorted. "I must have missed folks getting shot and killed and Indians trying to fill us full of arrows."

"The banshee," Cooley said. "The banshee howled. One of us is going to die. I didn't want it to be Mandy."

"I keep telling you, it was me making the howling noises to scare away Big Ear."

Cooley saw a cloud pass behind his partner's eyes. Another worry had come to him, but he didn't put it into words. As far as he was concerned, the banshee was trouble enough to give up the search and get back to working the Trafalgar Mine. But if he did that, he'd lose Mandy for sure. Whatever promise he made to her had to be golden.

"You have any idea where to start hunting for the Lost Banshee Mine?" Cooley took pleasure in how he had renamed the mine they sought. It irked his partner, and that made him feel a little satisfaction.

He had to feel like he'd won somewhere. The memory of Mandy riding away was going to haunt him for a long time, unless he got a pile of gold and lured her back.

"Let's turn in. I'm dead tired, and we've got a long way to ride ahead." Cooley yawned widely, then rubbed his eyes.

Cooley stretched out on his bunk, listening to the drip-drip-drip of rain coming through the roof and splattering in the pots and pans scattered about. It wasn't long before England Dan's snores drowned out the gentle rain, and Cooley slipped into a fitful sleep, dreaming of Mandy and Mindy and hearing Big Owl.

He slept late the next day; the sun was already up and drying out the cabin. Stretching, he sat up. His partner still sawed wood. Cooley looked from Dan to the map on the table. He had cut and run once. The mistake he'd made then was not taking the map. Now he had a chance to go find the Lost Banshee Mine on his own. After all, he knew the key: Mule Springs.

"We don't have to go to Mule Springs," England

Dan said. He lay on his side. His eyes were wide-open and intent.

Cooley felt a guilty pang for even thinking about taking the map. "What do you mean?"

"I slept on the matter that came to me back in the canyon. Knowing where the mine is from Mule Springs gives me an idea how to approach it from this side. It'd save us a couple days' travel."

"That's a good idea," Cooley said, nodding. "Not blistering my butt astride that mule is worthwhile."

"What we need are some tools from the mine," England Dan said. "That way we'll be ready to do some assay on the spot to make certain we're not wasting our time on the wrong mine."

"We'd better hurry. We done slept until the afternoon. If we don't get on the trail soon, we'll never get there."

"The rain's threatening another downpour," England Dan said. "I say rest up until early tomorrow. The horse and the mule need to be taken care of. Let them rest and then hit the trail all refreshed and ready to whip our weight in wildcats."

Talking Cooley into a few more hours' sleep wasn't hard. It still bothered him when his partner shook him awake. For some reason Dan held a rubber hose.

"What're you doing with that?"

"Mabel ate a burlap bag and is all clogged up. We need to pour mineral oil down her gullet before we get on the trail."

England Dan took another look at the map, stabbed down on the X with his finger, then laughed. "After all we've been through, this had better make us as rich as the queen."

They walked the muddy trail to the shed to take care of Mabel. It was messy, and the mule belched continuously, but two quarts of mineral oil began to work. They hastily left to avoid the stink and returned to the cabin to find the door standing open and the map gone.

CHAPTER TWENTY-FOUR

IT FELT GOOD lazing in the sun. Lars Jensen pulled his hat brim down farther to shield his eyes from the setting sun. It had been rainy most of the day, but the storms had passed, leaving an Arizona sky so intensely brilliant, it hurt the eyes to stare at it. He stirred and moved, so his chest caught the full rays of the sun. It eased the ache he felt from the gunshot. If he faced the other way, the sun might give its healing rays to his back, where the bullet had entered. But in a vague, distant way, Jensen decided that wasn't important. It felt too good this way.

His belly was full, and the sun let him drift toward sleep. A doctor years back had told him to eat a thick beefsteak after getting shot. It would help build his blood, the sawbones had said. It had worked then. Whether it would work now was a matter of conjecture since the meat had been tough and gristly. The best

beef went to Bisbee, along with half the population of
Oasis. No flow of yellow metal, no miners, no reason to
bring in the best fodder for the losers staying on Oasis.

Jensen's mind drifted. He had lost more blood than
he wanted to admit, and it had left him as weak as a
kitten. He had knocked back a shot of the tarantula
juice served at the Thirsty Camel, and it had made him
sick to his stomach. Not being able to hold his liquor
was a flaw Poke would exploit. Best to lounge outside
the livery on the bales of straw and recuperate. His
brother was going to return anytime now from wherever he'd gotten off to and demand to know why his
worthless younger brother hadn't found the map.

"The map. Always the damned map." Jensen drifted
deeper to sleep. A dream began churning about, or was
it a deep thought bubbling to the surface? Why let Poke
boss him around? He'd had nothing to do with robbing
the cavalry payroll. Poke would claim he wasn't deserv-
ing of a cut when he tracked it down since he hadn't
risked his neck to steal it. Beeman had paid the price
already, dying. At least Beeman had handed the map
off to somebody willing to get it to Poke.

None of this was Lars Jensen's concern. He had
troubles of his own.

"I killed him. I shot him dead." He moaned as he
stirred from his half-asleep dream. Alberto Gonzales
had no call being alive. He should be dead and so
should the miners who had the map. "Kill 'em all."

But his wish dream rolled and bucked around him.
He wasn't beholden to his brother. Clear out. Leave
Arizona. California was supposed to be cooler than
the furnace of the Arizona desert. Or Denver. The
Front Range was filthy with gold and silver mines.

That meant wealth to be taken by a clever man. A clever Lars Jensen. Leave here and be done with his brother and his hair-trigger temper.

He had only to wake up, get on his horse and start riding. The sun was soothing. Ride west. To the Colorado and cross at Yuma.

He snapped awake. Yuma. Where Poke had been locked up. Jensen looked around, wild-eyed. It took a few seconds to realize his dream wasn't the cause of this enforced alertness.

"If I'd known it'd be this easy to find her, I'd have staked out the livery stables a long time back." He sat up, using a hay bale as support. Riding slowly toward him, eyes downcast, was none other than the whore who'd been with Cooley.

He slipped his six-shooter from his holster. The way his hand shook bothered him. Pointing it at the girl wasn't going to cow her, especially since she'd had the sand before to shoot him. If anything, she'd laugh at how feeble he seemed. Jensen replaced it and lounged back on the bale. She drew rein a few feet away and dropped off. Looking as if she was as exhausted as he felt, she started into the livery, leading the horse.

"We got good rates for special people like you."

She jumped a foot. She hadn't seen him sprawled out on the hay. A quick yank on the horse's bridle turned its face. Mandy intended to mount and gallop off. Jensen summoned up the strength to stand and lunge forward. His arms wrapped around the horse's neck, keeping it from obeying her.

Mandy dropped the reins and started to run.

"Don't you go make me shoot you in the back. Somebody done that to me, and it hurt like hell. I won-

der who that was." His taunt made her start to shake.
He was glad to see he still intimidated her. "I'm healed
up enough to kill you." Jensen laughed when she skidded to a halt and raised her hands.

"Don't shoot me. There's no call to."

"You're telling me you don't have the map. That
may be true, but you know where it is."

"You'll kill me if I tell you."

"That's not too farfetched a notion," Jensen said.
"But I might not kill you since I've taken a shine to
you. If you don't say anything, you know you'll be
drawing flies out there in the sun before you can take
another breath."

"How do you know I won't lie?"

Jensen considered this for a moment. His legs turned
to jelly under him. If he carried on much longer, he'd
likely pass out.

"If you lie, you know I'll track you down to the ends
of the earth and make you pay. Me collecting that
debt's not anything you want to experience."

Jensen saw her begin to shake even harder. Her
hands lowered a little, then rose once more. A smile
came to his lips. He knew what this meant.

"I don't owe them anything. They almost got me
killed. And . . . and they're both running from Big Owl.
That map's not going to do them a bit of good."

"Big Owl? That Injun stalking around up there?"

"That's Big Ear. This is the banshee."

Jensen had no idea what she was talking about, but
from the quaver in her voice, he didn't have to. It
scared her just enough to be useful.

"Maybe me and Big Owl are in cahoots. That'd
make it all the more certain that I'll find you if you lie."

"He's not the man I thought he was."

"Big Owl?" Jensen saw that he'd guessed wrong. She half turned toward him. He caught the expression on her face. "Or that worthless snake you took up with? Cooley."

"Cooley and his partner are at their cabin. The Trafalgar Mine. It's up at—"

"I know where it is. Why're they there?"

"We were almost ambushed by Big Ear. And England Dan spun a yarn about imitating the banshee. Riding through the storm, not having enough food, it was more'n I could take. They went to their cabin to rest up before following the map."

"They know what's buried?"

"Gold. They think there's a mountain of gold in the mine. The Lost Banshee Mine, Cooley calls it."

"Banshee, banshee, what's this bee in your bonnet about banshees?"

"Look, I'm not lying. They have the map. I saw it," she said, then hastily added, "But I don't know what it meant."

"I'll pretend to believe you're not lying. Don't go gallivanting off. You stay here in Oasis till I find out if they have the map." Jensen edged toward the livery and went inside. It took him longer to saddle up than usual. His arms were as rubbery as his legs, but new energy flowed through him to keep him going. He believed her that Cooley and his partner had the map and they were upslope.

He rode out and wasn't the least bit surprised the girl had hightailed it. Telling her to stay in Oasis meant she'd do the exact opposite. From what he knew about the territory, the only place she was likely to head, thinking to hide there, was Bisbee. If she had lied to him, finding her would be easy enough in a town like that.

Weak and wobbly as he was, he started on a well-worn trail back to the Trafalgar Mine. Although he stopped several times to rest, Jensen still got there just before sunrise. He left his horse beyond the first fork in the road and trudged to the cabin, wary of being seen. With only two of them, they'd have to swap off acting as sentry. They were miners, though, and not inclined to think like army soldiers. He made his way to the cabin wall and found a sizable hole to peer through.

It took a few seconds for him to figure out the layout of the room. Beds on either side with a table between. That was obvious. Part of the back wall was only leaning up from where he'd knocked it in before. But the lump in one bed had a blanket pulled over it. Try as he might, the other bed was just out of his field of vision. Bursting in and shooting the one sleeping man and expecting to get the other before he reacted lay beyond his skill at the moment. All day he had noticed his reflexes were slow, and he had fumbled as he rode. More than once the reins had slipped through his fingers. Killing the one man he saw was easy enough, but expecting the second to fall to his six-gun would push his luck.

And luck it was, not skill. Not until he recovered. He cursed Mandy for shooting him in the back. They deserved his swift leaden justice, only it wasn't going to be swift.

He started to move around to find a second hole to check the position of the men when he heard a sound behind him coming from the path leading up to the mine. Not daring to move, he remained as still as a fawn stalked by a mountain lion. He held his breath so long, he began to get giddy from lack of air.

Whoever was behind him came closer, whistling tunelessly. Jensen knew he hadn't been spotted. Nobody tried to sneak up while whistling. He had played poker once with a tinhorn gambler who whistled as he played, not knowing he did it. If he'd had a better ear or an appreciation of music, he'd have been able to take the gambler for every dime on the table. As it was, he'd just shot him.

Jensen moved like molasses, his hand dropping to his six-shooter. The dark figure on the path passed within ten feet and never saw him. When he heard the door creaking open, he pressed his eye to the hole once more. The man entered and lit a lantern. The pale yellow light showed both miners, the one sleeping and the one who'd just entered holding a length of hose.

"Cooley, wake up. I've the hose from the mine."

Jensen kept from letting out a whoop of glee. He'd been right about the sleeping man. John Cooley. That meant the one who had passed by in the dark was England Dan.

"So what?"

"The mule. Mabel. She swallowed that entire burlap bag. We need to pour mineral oil down her gullet, or she's sure to die."

"You do it. I'm too tired."

England Dan shook his partner. Jensen considered busting in, six-shooter firing. The pair of them were close enough together that missing one hardly mattered. He'd wing the other one. He slid his pistol from the holster and dropped it. His fingers were nerveless. He ducked down and picked up his gun. A few quick swipes got most of the mud off. He flexed his fingers and knew his chances of shooting both men had swirled away. His shoulder ached, his chest hurt and his gun hand was numb.

"Get your bones out of bed. If we get the bag to pass, we can ride out right away."

"That mule'd eat anything."

"Mabel did. Now, get up."

"There's a funnel in the shed. It'll fit into one end of the hose. You can cram the hose down Mabel's throat so I can pour in the mineral oil."

"That's the idea." England Dan stepped back and picked up the kerosene lamp.

Jensen smiled. The light revealed the map spread out on the table. England Dan went to the map and pressed his finger down onto it. He said something to his partner about what was there.

The two miners exited the cabin and hiked away toward the shed, where they stabled the complaining mule and a horse. Jensen stepped away from the cabin into the path and lifted his gun. His hand shook so hard, he braced it with his left hand. The muzzle wandered all over. Unless he was firing a Gatling gun, he'd never be sure of hitting either of the men. And their backs presented wide targets.

Even as that thought entered his mind, the opportunity passed; they rounded the bend in the path and vanished from sight. Jensen slid past the half-open door into the cabin. They had taken the lamp with them, but he remembered the layout well enough to get around the small room in the dark. Two steps in took him to the table. He picked up the map with both hands.

There wasn't anything worth stealing, and he had the map. He ducked back out and held up the map to reflect some starlight. His smirk became a wide smile. This was the map. He had the map.

"Poke, you're gonna be right proud of your little brother." Lars Jensen folded it and tucked it into his coat pocket. Hurrying as fast as he could in the dark without tripping and falling, he got back to his horse, pulled himself up and rode down the trail to the fork. The left trail returned to Oasis. The right meandered into the mountains. He took that, letting the horse pick its way.

CHAPTER TWENTY-FIVE

THE MULE BELCHED. Mineral oil leaked out around the hose England Dan had crammed down the beast's throat and dribbled down to the straw spread over the shed floor.

"Whew," Cooley said, averting his face and holding his nose. "That smell's enough to gag a maggot."

"It's pretty bad," England Dan agreed, "but the mineral oil ought to lubricate its innards all the way through so the burlap bag will pass by morning."

"If Mabel's breath is that bad, what's the smell going to be like when everything comes gushing out the back end?"

"We don't have to clean it up. We're leaving the Trafalgar for good." England Dan felt uneasy as he spoke. This was his mine. His and Cooley's. They'd found the vein, assayed it and staked their claim in Oasis, when there had been a land office there. There were few enough things in his life he took pride in. His father thought he was a failure, and his brother, Syngin, refused to ever speak his name again. The last time they'd been seated at the same dinner table, Syngin had acted as if he were made of glass. He had stared right through England Dan and never answered a direct question or spoken to him.

England Dan had seen similar behavior in India and hated it there, too. He had become an untouchable, the lowest of low in the caste system—someone so despicable, no one of good breeding would even acknowledge his existence.

The Trafalgar Mine was his shining accomplishment, though the gold taken from it had failed to approach the amount he'd need to return to Britain and show up his brother. He knew the estate's finances. If he placed a hundred thousand pounds' worth of gold in a London bank, his net worth would be greater than the family fortune.

"Why bother?"

"What's that?"

"Nothing," said England Dan. "I was talking to myself."

"There's no need for you to. That's what a partner is for." Cooley stepped out of the shed into the cold, crisp night and sucked in a deep breath. "I was going to puke if I stayed in there another second."

England Dan agreed but had enough breeding not to agree. He checked the stars. It was a few minutes shy of sunrise. The high, thin clouds drifting through the sky were dry, all squeezed out of the rain that had pummeled them. The sky promised sunny days without showers to slow them down as they made their way through the mountains to Mule Springs.

"You think the mule will be all right? I want to get another couple hours of sleep." Cooley yawned widely and stretched.

"We can both use some rest. Everything's all packed. All we need to do is load it on the mule and get on the trail at sunup."

"About that," Cooley said. "I won't be able to ride Mabel with all the equipment weighing her down. If you ride that stallion you stole from Gonzales, that means I'm on foot."

"I didn't steal the horse. I claimed it as a reward for saving his life. He never said as much, but he'd have given me Whirlwind if he'd been able to speak."

"Are we talking about the same Alberto Gonzales? That man would take food from his grandmother's mouth if he thought it got him an inch closer to capturing an outlaw."

England Dan stopped and held out his arm to keep Cooley back. He whispered, "The door's wide open. It wasn't like that when we went to tend the mule."

"The whole cabin's falling apart. So what?" Cooley pushed past and went inside.

England Dan crowded close. He held up the lamp. The first thing he saw was the bare table. "It's gone. Somebody took the map."

"What are you going on about?" Cooley was slower to notice. When he did, he let out an anguished cry. "The map! It's gone!"

England Dan cast the lamplight on his partner and studied his face. He wouldn't have put it past Cooley to hide the map, thinking to find the mine and keep all the gold for himself. He'd as much as said the only way he would ever win Mandy back was to pile a ton of gold at her feet. But England Dan had followed his partner out of the cabin. He, not Cooley, had been the last one inside.

The door was askew. It had been broken after they left. He lowered the lamp and looked at the dirt floor. Distinct new boot prints that didn't match either of their sole prints came in and left. Walking slowly, he followed the trail. Whoever had stolen the map had spied on them and then gone back down the trail.

"Is that the way the varmint went? I'll rip his heart out! I'll gouge out his eyes and torture him until the Apaches will sing songs about it!" Cooley got so het up he turned red in the face.

"Calm down, Cooley. I need to think. Who's likely to have taken the map?"

"Mandy," his partner muttered.

"Those aren't a woman's boots. The foot's bigger than mine." He stepped beside a print. The track was a good inch longer, and he had a long foot.

"Lars Jensen is dead. Mandy shot him down."

"I thought you said you killed him. Never mind. I'll take your word that he's dead. Who else knows we have the map? The cowboy you bought it from is dead. The only one who'd know or care is Gonzales."

"Why would he take it? How does he even know about it? That man had a mind so oriented toward catching Jensen, he was a compass needle never wavering from north." Cooley lengthened his stride, intending to pursue the robber right now. England Dan stopped him.

"We'll fall into an ambush for sure if we go after the thief in the dark. It's not long until daylight. Let Mabel get rid of that burlap bag she ate. We take what little equipment we might need and leave the rest so you can ride. Then we go after him."

England Dan held up the lamp and saw how the boot print circled around the path and disappeared in the distance. The only good thing he saw in this was that Big Ear wasn't the thief, not unless he wore white man's boots. And the chances that Big Owl had swooped in to steal their map were less than drawing to an inside straight.

They returned to the cabin. England Dan tried to sleep but couldn't. Cooley was snoring in a few minutes. England Dan worked over their plans and how everything had changed in the span of a few minutes. If the mule hadn't gotten hungry and swallowed the bag, clogging her intestines, none of this would have happened. Then he considered that whoever took the map would have likely gunned them down as they slept. Their luck was good or bad, depending on how he looked at it.

Right now he had to believe a run of bad luck was plaguing them.

He finally drifted off to fitful, nightmare-racked sleep. When he awoke, it was to the mule braying loudly. Cooley already had left his bunk. England Dan stretched, tapped his boots to be sure nothing had crawled in overnight, then pulled them on.

Cooley bellowed from outside, "It's past sunrise. Get out here. We've got a trail to follow."

He stepped out. Cooley was already mounted on Mabel, and he held the reins to the stallion for his partner. A quick look at the sky showed only a few puffy white clouds. "It's not going to rain anytime soon. Maybe by this afternoon. That'll get us going on the trail."

"I wish we had ammunition." Cooley tapped the butt of his pistol.

England Dan had no reason to check his. He knew better than to get into a gunfight with only a single round. More than ammo, they needed supplies for the trail. It was a two- or three-day ride across the Superstition Mountains into New Mexico Territory. That might drag out if they had to chase the map thief much longer, but he figured they were all headed for the same location. Mule Springs was the starting point for the map.

No Shadow had said so, and from what England Dan remembered of the map, he agreed.

They set out down the trail. As he thought, the thief had mounted and ridden away, taking the fork away from Oasis and into the mountains. He settled in for a ride, but Cooley insisted on yammering away.

"We'll catch him soon enough, won't we, Dan? It looks like the tracks are fresh. Might be he curled up somewhere under the stars to catch some sleep last night. Thieving must be hard work, after all."

England Dan grunted and rode a little faster. To his disgust, Mabel matched the stallion's pace. Eating and excreting a burlap bag sat well with the mule.

"We might pick a different way of going about this whole matter," Cooley rambled on. "Rather than overtake the highwayman and force him to return the map, why not let him go on and do our work for us?"

"What do you mean?" England Dan listened with half an ear. Something about the tracks bothered him, and he couldn't put his finger on what it was.

"We keep trailing him all the way to the mine. He finds it, we take the mine."

"We'd be the claim jumpers then."

"No, no, you got that wrong. The Lost Banshee Mine is ours! We came by the map legitimately. He's the crook. But we let him think it's his and swoop in like an eagle on a running rabbit and take it away. He does the work. It's only fair. That'd be payback for him stealing the map from under our noses."

"How good are you with a lariat?"

"What? What are you going on about, Dan? You know I can't spin a lasso to save my life."

"The thief finds the mine. How do we take it from him? I have a solitary round in my gun. You're as dry as the Sonoran Desert when it comes to ammunition. If we don't rope and hog-tie him, how else are we taking the mine from a man who likely has a belt filled with spare ammo?"

"You don't know how well armed he is. He might have become a sneak thief because he doesn't have any more firepower than we do. He couldn't shoot us in our sleep because he didn't have the bullets, so he crept in while we were gone and took the map. That's possible, isn't it?" Cooley grumbled a bit more and fell silent. He recognized the truth in the argument and hated the way it destroyed his wild harebrained scheme.

A half mile farther down the trail, England Dan came to a halt. He hopped down to the ground and ran his fingers over the tracks in the soft earth.

"You lose him? I thought you were the almighty talented frontiersman, the tracker who couldn't be thrown off the trail? Now, my relative Daniel Boone, he—"

"There's someone else ahead of us," England Dan interrupted.

"Two riders? You mean he has an accomplice?"

Cooley came back and leaned over as far as he could while remaining on mule back to study the prints England Dan found.

"I don't think so. The second rider is an hour or two behind our map thief."

"How far behind are we?"

"Another hour. We'll overtake the sneak thief in a couple hours, but we'll find the other rider before that." England Dan paced alongside the trail. "He's not riding to catch up. He's following the tracks, too."

"We've got competition for the map," Cooley blurted. "We have to speed up, Dan. We can't let somebody else get the map!"

"What's it matter who has it if it's not us?" England Dan paced along a few more yards, measuring the strides of the horses ahead of them. One was barely a pony. The other, ridden by their thief, was a full-grown horse. He kept walking and found evidence alongside the road. A tiny pile of fresh horse dung just now drew flies. It had come from a tiny horse. Or one needing a dose of mineral oil.

"I bought that map fair and square. It's not right if somebody—two somebodies—steal what's mine."

England Dan mounted and kept a sharp eye on the trail. A half hour later, he drew rein and shook his head.

"What's wrong now?" Cooley turned belligerent. "You're finding new reasons not to keep going?"

"I want to find the mine," he said. "But you're right about a new complication entering the picture. See that?" He pointed to a section of cut-up sod.

"One of the horses went dancing around there. So?"

"So it's a third horse. The rider came in from the

west." England Dan closed his eyes and tried to picture the mountains in this area. He had gotten lost before, proving he didn't know the terrain as well as he should, but the new rider had come from an area he knew better than the rest. "He rode in from Bisbee. That's the only town in that direction."

"Three? All of them heading in the same direction?"

"I'm not sure why they're on this trail, but two of them are after the map thief, just like us."

"We've got to hurry up and find what's going on!"

"We'll be facing three six-shooters. There's no reason not to believe all of them are fully loaded. Changing our tactics is all we can do unless we want to end the day as worm food." England Dan spat. "That's assuming they'd bother giving us a decent burial. More likely, they'd leave our carcasses for the coyotes."

"What are we going to do, Dan?" Cooley's voice rose in pitch until he almost sounded like a banshee.

England Dan didn't have an answer, but giving up now wasn't in his blood. They faced odds that almost guaranteed they'd die. Bile rose in his throat. Let Cooley hunger after the Lost Banshee Mine. His reason for getting the map back was simpler. It belonged to them, him and Cooley, and nobody had the right to take it.

CHAPTER TWENTY-SIX

LARS JENSEN TURNED the map around, then leaned back against his saddle and lifted the map to match patterns of stars. It took a few seconds for him to stop. There wasn't any obvious connection between the points and the Xs and the upside-down Vs on the map and anything he saw in the slowly lightening sky. Besides, his arms got tired fast. He half closed his eyes and realized how close to passing out he was.

The blood loss from his wound was worse than he thought. He should have eaten a couple more steaks to help replace the iron in his blood. The vet who had patched him up had recommended some rest before he hit the trail. Jensen knew he was tougher than the doctor thought, but the doc's suggestion was proving to be accurate. His hands still shook, and riding along in a stupor meant he relied more on his horse staying on the track than he liked. A rider had to be in control all the time. Lars Jensen was anything but in control due to his occasional light-headed wobbling in the saddle.

"Poke's going to be here soon enough," he said. Where his brother had gone was something of a mystery, but if Jensen had to guess, he'd gone to Bisbee. Jensen had passed the trail to the copper-mining town around noon. He'd considered camping there and waiting to see if his guess was right, but a nagging thought kept him moving.

"Miners. Them miners aren't going to give up easy." He drew his gun and opened the gate. A slow turn of the cylinder showed each chamber was ready to send a bullet into anybody trying to take the map.

If only Poke would show up, Jensen could give him the map and ride out. He'd gotten shot up and killed folks with whom he had no quarrel. That didn't bother him too much. Everyone died. They ought to have been proud that it was by his hand. But how he had failed to put the killing round into Alberto Gonzales worried him. The lawman had been like flypaper all the way from Mesilla. A small thing like getting plugged wasn't going to stop him.

"Leastways, we're in the same condition. It'll be a right interesting fight to see which of us wants the other dead the most."

Jensen chuckled at the idea of two invalids facing each other. It made life more vital. The showdown ought to be in the middle of a street, with the townspeople fearfully looking out windows as the two gunmen squared off. A piano player needed to witness the fight to write and sing a mournful ballad. Hands going for their weapons. Both slower than normal because of their injuries.

"I'd smoke him," Jensen said to himself. "Even all banged up, I'd take that deputy." He lifted his gun and pointed it at a big rock directly ahead.

"You won't get the chance. If I had an ounce of sense, I'd pull the trigger. Don't move!"

Jensen sat up so fast, his head spun. He tried to swing his pistol around, but the dizziness betrayed him. His eyes blurred, and when they cleared, he stared straight at Alberto Gonzales. The deputy marshal had a rifle trained on him.

"For two cents, I'll pull the trigger. No, that's wrong. I'll do it because you're the owlhoot who shot me."

"I'm getting sloppy. If I'd paid more attention to what I was doing, you'd be six feet under by now. Or buzzard bait." Jensen recovered enough to judge his chances of training his six-gun on the lawman as being almost exactly zero. Lying about being the deputy's attacker didn't hold water. The lawman knew he had been the one.

Gonzales wore a dark coat, and the sombrero's ornaments gave the best hint where the man's head was. The silver beads and sequins caught what little daylight remained. Or maybe it was starlight now. Jensen's mind spun all around. If he made a wish on one of those doodads on the sombrero, did that improve his chance of ending the deputy's life once and for all?

Instead of trying, he laid his six-gun on the ground and lifted his hands until his chest burned. "I can't get 'em any higher. I've been shot in the back and patched up by a vet."

"In Oasis?" The deputy spat. "Their doctor lit out for Bisbee with most of the rest of the town a month or more back. I had to get patched up by a whore."

"Did you enjoy it?" Jensen came to his knees, then rocked back and forth to get momentum enough to stand. He wobbled about, unable to stop. He hated showing such weakness, especially to a lawman—and one he thought he had already killed. "I hope she charged you."

"You shut your smart mouth."

Alberto Gonzales came forward slowly. Every step showed how difficult it was for him to stay upright. Jensen waited for him to get closer. The two could end their feud with a wrestling match rather than shooting it out. That wasn't as satisfying, but depending on how Gonzales died, it might be better feeling the life slip away as he tightened his grip around his throat.

"You should have given up a long time back," Jensen said. "You don't even know what you are arresting me for."

"Arson. You burned down a store, and the proprietor and his wife were inside. Both of them died. They were my friends." The deputy's face hardened. "I hear their screams in my sleep."

"That's your problem, then. You're not dead enough to little things around you."

"But what the marshal sent me after you for is mail robbery. You stole US mail. That's a federal crime. Turn about and put your hands behind your back. I've got shackles just the right size." The deputy lifted a set of handcuffs for Jensen to see. The rifle wavered until Gonzales tucked the stock under his arm to steady it.

Jensen waited for his chance. "I know you want the map. Go on. Take it and let me go."

"What map are you going on about?"

"This one." Jensen pressed the toe of his boot down on the map.

"What's it a map to?"

The deputy came closer. Jensen judged how to move. The rifle was held awkwardly. He was more likely to get whacked in the head than shot when the lawman moved to put the shackles on his wrist. He glanced down at the ground. If he pushed Gonzales away and off-balance, he could scoop up his gun, turn and fire. It hardly mattered if he wasn't his usual accurate self. Hitting the man in the chest would likely be a killing shot at this range.

"You know what it shows. That cavalry-payroll robbery six months back."

"I don't recollect any robbery. The army's close-mouthed about the men they lose and anything that transpires on their posts. Stick your hands out behind you and bend forward."

Jensen did as he was told. This made his play all the more dangerous. Off-balance, he was an easy target. But he dropped to his knees, twisted hard and rolled, fumbling for his six-gun. He flopped onto his back and started to shoot.

The night exploded with gunfire, and none of it was his. For an instant, he wondered why he wasn't racked with pain with a half-dozen bullets ripping into his body. Then Alberto Gonzales straightened, twisted about like a screw going into a piece of wood and fell to the ground. Jensen poked his gun at the lawman.

"Save your bullets. He's dead."

Jensen looked up as another shadow-cloaked figure came out of the murky twilight. White smoke rose from the muzzle of a six-gun.

"Thanks, Poke. I was about ready to take care of him."

"This the deputy marshal from over in New Mexico

Territory that's been dogging your tracks? I heard tell he was dead." Poke Jensen ejected the six spent cartridges from his pistol and reloaded.

"I thought I'd taken care of him, but he was tougher than he looked."

Poke Jensen nudged the body with his toe. "Not so tough now." He slid his gun back into his holster. "You got the map?"

If there had been any question who had saved him, that demand put it all to rest. Lars Jensen slipped his gun into its holster and picked up the map. He smoothed out a few wrinkles and held the map out for his brother.

Poke snatched it away and held it up to peer at it. "You sure this is it?"

That startled Jensen. He squared off in case he had to throw down on his brother. Poke had a way of keeping him confused, no matter how straightforward a thing was.

"That's the map the miners had. The one named Cooley bought it off a cowboy in Oasis, and he got it from the scum who stole it off Rivera. Or maybe Rivera gave it to him with a dying wish that he give it to you. Whatever the reason, it made its way into Cooley's hands, and there it is."

"You kill this miner?"

"There's nothing to think he and his partner will be any trouble."

"That's not what I asked. Did you kill both of them dead?" Poke Jensen hunkered down and put small rocks on each corner of the map so he could study it without the slight breeze blowing it around. He moved it a quarter turn, looked up at the sky to find the Big

Dipper, then adjusted the map a final time before running his finger along the dots toward the X.

"I answered," Lars Jensen said, his temper rising. Poke never thought his brother dealt with matters properly. Lars had reached the end of his rope now. He'd gotten shot in the back, and then Poke had come up and killed the deputy when he was fixing to end the man's life in a more satisfying manner. He'd been cheated, and it wasn't fair.

"We have to get through the mountains into New Mexico Territory. From Mule Springs, we can find where Beeman hid the payroll."

"I don't want any part of it, Poke. You go on. I'll ride a different trail."

"What's got into you, boy? This is the Fort Bayard payroll we're talking about. There has to be a thousand dollars in gold coins, gold bars and greenbacks. With Beeman and Rivera gone, there's no reason not to cut you in for a share."

Lars Jensen had heard this before. He settled down and looked at the map. It still made no sense to him, though he located the spot his brother said represented Mule Springs. From there, finding the way back into the mountains might not be that hard. All the trouble he'd gone through to get the map should make him a few dollars.

"A share? Half?"

"I said a share. Ten percent's a goodly sum. That's at least a hundred dollars. You can have it all in gold coin. Think of having five twenty-dollar gold pieces rubbing together in your pocket. You'd be rich."

"And you'd take the lion's share. I want half."

"You didn't risk your neck in the robbery. There were a half-dozen men guarding the payroll and we had only expected a couple soldiers. Our ambush went down fast, but it took longer than we expected. We had to blast open an armored wagon, too. Why, we barely got away when a patrol came riding up, blowing their horn and kicking up a powerful dust cloud." Poke Jensen spat and wiped his lips. "Beeman didn't get away, I reckon you'd say. I decoyed them away from him when he got hit. You know the rest."

"They couldn't prove you had anything to do with the robbery, but they sent you over to Yuma on other crimes."

"All trumped up, every last one of them. They had no idea how big a desperado they'd run to ground. Look, Lars, see this mark? Beeman put it on the map. It's a number. It means the distance to go along this here road before lining up the peaks. You'd never know that, and finding the payroll'd be impossible. Me and Beeman agreed on these things before the robbery. We were partners, Lars. His share goes to his ma. She's over in Hueco Tanks, outside of Franklin. Works in the stagecoach way station."

Lars stared at his brother. This was the first time he'd ever heard a charitable word from him, a single thought of another's well-being. It was worth the effort to retrieve the payroll to see if Poke meant it about giving some of the money to Barton Beeman's mother.

"How long will it take?" Lars felt drained from his encounter with Gonzales. He needed to rest up. Having a hundred dollars in gold would help him find a place worthy of a little vacation. There were several fancy spas farther east in New Mexico. Mineral springs, posh hotels. He'd heal faster taking the waters and eating exotic food.

"As long as it takes. I don't see it taking up more than a week of your precious time."

"A week," Lars Jensen said. "I can afford a week. For a hundred dollars."

"For a hundred dollars in gold," Poke Jensen said.

The tone his brother used made him wonder how the week might end. He'd keep his six-shooter close and never turn his back on Poke. He'd not make the same mistake Alberto Gonzales had. Not at all.

CHAPTER TWENTY-SEVEN

Tʜᴀᴛ's ɢᴜɴꜰɪʀᴇ!" ᴇɴɢʟᴀɴᴅ Dan Rutledge looked up, startled. "It's coming from farther up the trail."

"The two sets of tracks. Whoever's up there is shooting it out." John Cooley's eyes went wide, and he looked around, as if the next bullets would come his way. He got to his feet and put his arm around the mule's neck. From the difference in the way they responded, the mule comforted Cooley rather than the other way around.

England Dan wasn't so sure it was exactly that Cooley was right. Or not exactly. The rapid fire sounded more like a six-shooter being emptied. Then there was nothing. With no second gun firing, it was more an ambush than a fight. He touched his Webley and knew that was how he'd have to fight. Shoot first, a single shot, and make it count. But six rounds? Somebody was sorely angry.

"There must have been more than the sneak thief who took the map. If he had a partner, what we heard was a falling-out." He took a deep breath to settle his own jangled nerves. Sneaking up on one man was possible, even when all his Webley held was a single bullet. But two men? A completely different problem. Then he chewed on what little they did know in a different way.

"This might be to our benefit," England Dan said. Cooley stared at him as if he had lost his mind. "Two robbers. One kills the other. He's not expecting us to show up to take the map back. He'll be careless, thinking his partner was the only one who knew about the map."

"So you want us to keep going after them? After him?" Cooley looked around a tad wildly, as if hunting for a way to escape.

"It makes sense he'll be overconfident. He thinks he's won by killing his partner."

"Killing his partner," Cooley repeated dully. He fixed his gaze on his partner.

England Dan read the worry there. If the thief killed a partner, what about the only one with a bullet chasing after the map doing the same to *his* partner? "You've got your knife. We can take him by surprise."

Cooley touched the blade sheathed at his side. It was nicked and needed sharpening. He was more likely to use it to open airtights than in a fight. "How rich do you think it is? The Lost Banshee Mine?"

England Dan stared at his partner. The question carried an obvious intent. If he hinted that the hidden mine was played out or even lacked vast quantities of gold, Cooley had reason to back out. He'd rather eke out a meager living at the Trafalgar Mine than risk tangling with whoever had stolen the map. For a man risking everything to be a miner, Cooley lacked courage.

Or maybe it was more complicated. England Dan wondered if cowardice was his partner's problem or simply lack of faith in his own abilities. Taking risks every day was the life a miner accepted. No one in their right mind pickaxed hunks of rock, lugged them out, crushed and reduced the product and all for a few flecks of color. It took a certain bravery to work in a rock tomb, blow up mountains with dynamite, breathe bad air and endure sudden floods. But Cooley lacked the resolve to grab for the big prize.

"We can both get rich, John. Very, very rich, if the Irish Lord—your Lost Banshee Mine—is half as productive as stories say."

"Something happened to the old owner. What happened there? How'd the map come to be drawn?"

"Questions we'll never answer if we let someone else use the map. And remember. It's your map. You bought it." England Dan felt uneasy using such an argument to get his partner moving along the right trail. He wasn't all that sure there was any gold to be had. Secret mines, hidden treasures, all that was the exciting stuff of campfire tales. It sounded promising, but reality had a way of being less. A lot less.

And more dangerous.

"What you say makes sense. All right. Let's go, but should we wait until morning?"

England Dan considered this. They were tired from riding this far, but the rapid fire followed by eerie silence warned any delay worked against them.

"Let's ride. Slowly. That way we're not as likely to ride into an ambush."

"The shooter is looking ahead, not behind," Cooley said, nodding. The way he spoke told how he was trying to convince himself he wasn't being suicidal. "Let's go, Mabel. Don't you go making any of those braying noises you are so famous for."

The mule turned an unblinking brown eye toward its owner. Since evacuating the burlap, things had been just fine. Pressing on, even after a full day of plodding along, was part and parcel of a mule's life.

If England Dan spotted the gunman ahead of them along the trail, he had to act. He was the one with the bullet. The single bullet. He tried to keep a sharp eye on the tracks, and fifteen minutes into their hunt, he halted and pointed.

"Another rider," he said. "This is a road that goes straight to Bisbee."

"We'll face an army," Cooley said, his courage fading again. "Let them keep the map. We can make a living off the Trafalgar."

"Enough to woo Mandy?" That was all England Dan had to say to get Cooley thinking again. He wanted to get rich off the Lost Banshee Mine, but taunting Cooley was as much fun. His partner swiveled about in the saddle, as if he had been caught in a dust devil, swirled around, back and forth until he came to a halt, facing forward again. He gestured for Dan to keep on the trail.

England Dan rested his hand on the pistol, even if he wasn't going to do much damage. If he got off a shot, bluffing any opposition was easier. Running them off was all he hoped for, even if they took the map with them.

"There. Go check. There's a horse tethered to a tree limb." He heard the horse yanking hard, trying to get free. While Cooley checked, he dropped to the ground and studied the tracks.

The confusion of tracks told him nothing. Several horses had come through this spot, possibly milling about before riding on. He looked up when Cooley led the horse back.

"It's little more than a pony. That's the second horse, the one between us and whoever stole the map."

"From what's in the saddlebags, it belongs to Gonzales." Cooley held up a sheaf of papers. "Arrest warrants for Lars Jensen and a couple other road agents I never heard a whisper about. They're all dated a couple days ago."

"The telegraph had to hum to get the arrest warrants before he set out. He must have bought the horse back in Oasis and then hit the trail. But why here?" The deputy had had to buy a horse barely saddle-broken, maybe because he hadn't had much money or, more likely, it had been all there was to be purchased in town. Too many citizens had left with all their belongings and gone to find fame and fortune in Bisbee.

"Was he the gunman making all the fuss? Where'd he get off to?"

"Stay here," England Dan ordered. He drew his six-gun and started down the road. Here and there he saw the deputy's footprints along the path. When the stride shortened, he slowed. Only a few yards farther, he found a grassy patch where Gonzales had stopped. He took the deputy's cue and stood on tiptoe to look ahead past a tangle of brush.

He caught his breath at the sight. Dropping back flat-footed, he steeled himself to advance. Once he was through the undergrowth, nothing stood between him and the lawman's body. He strained every sense to be sure he was alone—or as alone as you can be with a corpse. A quick sniff of the air betrayed lingering gun smoke, but he heard nothing around him that sounded out of place. The gunshots had quieted the forest creatures. After a few minutes, they resumed their business of being animals, hunting and eating and being eaten.

Circling, he came up to Gonzales' body from the far side. The lawman lay facedown. The six holes in his back showed how he had died—and the source of the gunshots England Dan had heard back down the trail. He rolled Gonzales over. A look of surprise had been permanently frozen on his face. England Dan looked up and worked out what mistake the lawman had made. He had approached from the tangled undergrowth, only to have the killer come up behind him.

"Six shots. That's a powerful lot of hate."

"The gunman? Is he gone?" Cooley stood with the deputy's horse and Mabel. His voice quavered just a mite.

"Two men rode off."

"Chances are good it's somebody named in the warrants from his saddlebags. At least we know it's not Lars Jensen. Mandy shot him dead. She's one crack shot."

England Dan started to ask about that. Cooley had boasted of gunning down the outlaw. He pushed the question aside. It hardly mattered who had murdered the deputy, though being shot in the back screamed that Lars Jensen was responsible. The man was a stone killer. England Dan began stripping the deputy of anything useful. The gun belt and the ammo were the most valuable. He plucked one cartridge out and held it up, examining it closely.

"I don't know if I can use this. Gonzales used a forty-five and my Webley takes a four fifty-five." He broke open the Webley and ejected all the rounds. He snagged the one unspent cartridge and rested it over his right ear. With some trepidation, he slid six of the lawman's cartridges into the cylinder. There was a small amount of play around each cartridge. He worried that firing the smaller round would jam his barrel due to the slight mismatch in brass sizes sending the slug down the barrel in a crooked path.

"Will they shoot?" Cooley looked skeptical.

England Dan shared his suspicion that they might not fire properly. He considered trying it, then stopped before he pulled the trigger. Two killers weren't more than a few miles down the road, heading deeper into the mountains. Why alert them?

"I'll keep his six-gun. I know the rounds work there. The rounds will fire in my gun," he decided, "but ejecting them might be a problem."

"So you traded a gun with a single shot for one with six? That's some improvement," Cooley said. "Give me some of the bullets for my gun."

"What else did you find in his saddlebags? He wasn't the kind of man to ride off with only a couple dozen rounds."

Cooley fished around in the saddlebags. A huge

grin came to his lips. He held up a box of spare cartridges.

"We're better off because of him. The least we can do is give him a decent burial." England Dan chewed a bit on his lower lip as he struggled with the feeling that time was running away from them like stampeding cattle. Wasting even a second now let Jensen get that much more of a head start on them. But . . . but burying this varmint was the right thing to do.

"We don't have a spade. How are we going to dig the grave?"

England Dan held up his hands, then pointed to Cooley's. His partner balked, but a little persuasion got him rooting about, using a stick. England Dan found a broad, flat stone to scoop dirt. It took the better part of an hour to make the grave deep enough. A final search of his body for anything useful gave them nothing more, but England Dan unpinned the star on Alberto Gonzales' vest.

"I'll see that it's sent back to Mesilla so they'll know what happened to him."

Cooley mumbled something his partner didn't hear. He asked him to repeat it.

"I said I hope we get the chance to return the star. We have to take the map away from men willing to shoot a US deputy marshal in the back."

"Keep that in mind, John. It may come to us to do to them what they did to Gonzales." The look of fright on Cooley's face worried England Dan. How much good he'd be in a real gunfight was going to be a real problem.

Cooley dropped the last rock on the deputy's grave and stepped away, wiping his hands off on his vest. His lips moved. England Dan hoped he was saying a prayer, but more likely he was cursing his own fate. To be sure things were all proper, Rutledge said a few words, then pointed to the deputy's horse.

"You get to ride in style."

"No offense, Mabel, but you have been reduced to a pack animal again." Cooley thought a moment, then laughed. "Only we don't have anything to lash onto your back. You're the one with the most luck of all of us."

That idea sobered him again. England Dan led the way. The sun was working its way up over the peak to the east, making travel difficult. He pulled down his bowler and used what brim he had to block the blinding sun as he rode, but it was Cooley who saved his life with a frantic warning.

"Duck! Guns!"

England Dan lunged forward and tumbled off the stallion. He hit the ground hard, rolled and came to his knees, the deputy's six-gun clutched in his fist. For a second, he missed what Cooley had noticed. Then the long tongues of orange flame spitting from the gun muzzles showed him where to fire.

He fanned off a couple rounds, driving the ambushers back. His next couple shots were better aimed. He appreciated the gun's balance in his hand. Alberto Gonzales had gone with the best weapon available.

"Take cover!" England Dan need not have shouted the warning. Cooley had already scrambled for cover behind a thick-boled mountain mahogany tree. England Dan followed his own advice and rolled away. He flopped bellydown a dozen paces from his partner. He hunted for a tree like Cooley had found, but all he had was a low rock. More than one bullet whined off the top, forcing him to keep his head down. He re-loaded, took a breath and popped up to fire a couple rounds. He identified the two at the same instant his partner did.

"It's Jensen. And I swear he's got a twin with him." Cooley sprayed lead around wildly enough to drive the Jensen brothers back.

England Dan cursed his partner and Mandy. They'd claimed Lars Jensen was dead. Now he faced not only a known murderer but probably his brother, too. He fired into the bushes, trying to end the fight. A new fusillade came in response, forcing him to take cover behind a low pile of rocks. With bullets ricocheting off the rocks, he reloaded and worried over a plan to get out of this trap alive.

CHAPTER TWENTY-EIGHT

ENGLAND DAN SETTLED down and let the Jensen brothers expend ammo, trying to hit him. They chipped away at the rock shielding him, but blasting through it would require a mountain howitzer. In spite of their murderous attitude, he doubted they had one. He took a stick and balanced his bowler on the end. He carefully raised it so just the crown popped above the rock. The more bullets they expended, the fewer they had to actually shoot him or Cooley.

To his dismay, they didn't take the bait. He lowered the stick and put the bowler back on. He chanced a quick look around the side. The rising sun shone directly on the stand of trees where the two outlaws had taken refuge. He caught a glint of light off a pistol but wasn't in position to shoot.

"Dan, what are we going to do? They got you pinned down!" Cooley waved to him.

"Thanks for letting them know," England Dan grumbled. They didn't have to be geniuses to have figured that out, but even a small doubt on their part would have given him an advantage. Cowering behind the rock, an easy target if he tried to escape, stacked the deck in favor of the Jensens.

"I see where one of them's hiding. You want me to shoot him?"

England Dan hardly believed his partner. They'd end up a pound heavier from the lead if they exposed themselves, and Cooley wondered about shooting back. He motioned that he was going to decoy them out by making himself a target and that Cooley should take advantage of it. If the signal got confused, he was going to be ventilated.

He took a deep breath, then stood and started firing. One of the outlaws stepped out from behind a tree to get a better shot at him. For a brief instant, they stared at each other, taking the other's measure. This had to be Poke Jensen. He was taller, stockier and, if England Dan was any judge, uglier. Both had the same color hair and broad, wide faces, but Poke's intensity burned into him like a branding iron.

They trained their guns on each other and opened fire. They stood fifteen yards apart, a distance requiring some skill with a handgun. England Dan began firing methodically. The deputy's gun came up empty. He dropped it and slapped leather. He whipped up his Webley. To his surprise, Poke Jensen had emptied his pistol, too, and drew another six-shooter at his side. His reflexes were amazing. England Dan had always heard of lightning-fast draws but had never really seen one.

Until now.

But he had a small advantage. His Webley was far more accurate, and he had trained endlessly to stand in the middle of a hailstorm of bullets. Stiff upper lip, never retreat, for queen and country—all had been drilled into him for years. It had been a decade since he had served, but the training had etched itself into his mind and body. Poke Jensen fired. A bullet winged Rutledge, but he hardly noticed. His return fire was more accurate. When the Webley clicked on a spent chamber, he had driven the outlaw back to cover.

He dropped down behind the rock and panted harshly as he reloaded. As he had feared, the deputy's rounds did not quite fit his Webley. Bits of metal clogged the cylinder. He ejected the shells and saw shiny lead debris on the edge of the barrel. Carefully using the tip of his knife, he peeled away the lead. It wasn't useful to do this every time he reloaded, but he wanted the pistol to fire reliably for what he had in mind.

Waving to Cooley to lay down covering fire, he gathered his feet under him, then exploded outward. He pounded hard for the woods where Cooley wildly sprayed lead in all directions. He had almost reached the trees when a bullet hit his heel. He tumbled forward and landed flat on his back, staring up at the sky, stunned.

From some hidden reservoir of strength, he jerked himself around and rolled sideways until he fetched up hard behind a rotted log. The lead singing in his direction tore away huge chunks of the decayed wood. He felt the sharp sting as one slug tore all the way through the log and lightly caressed his cheek. Blood began oozing down to his chin. There wasn't time to stanch the flow. Getting to safety behind something that stopped the bullets was paramount.

To his surprise, Cooley ran from the woods, firing in the general direction of the outlaws. This took the Jensens as much by storm as it did England Dan. He rose, pumped his legs hard and threw his arms around Cooley, tackling him. The air above them sizzled with lead. They landed hard and crawled to safety behind a scrub oak.

"You stole my map, you miserable back-shooting sons of—"

England Dan pulled Cooley down. His outburst had drawn the fire of both gunmen.

"Settle down. You'll get yourself killed."

"Me? Who was it that ran from behind a perfectly good rock and made a target of his backside? You—"

"Never mind. We're stalemated."

"What's that?"

"Neither of us can gain advantage. We'll swap lead until someone runs out of ammo and the other side wins."

"You mean," said Cooley, "a side kills the other. I don't want that to be me. How much ammunition's left?" He checked his pistol and the box he'd taken from the deputy's saddlebags. Cooley looked up. "I've got a couple dozen rounds."

"I've got two full cylinders. One dozen."

Cooley turned pale. He started to speak, but no words came out. He sank down with the tree trunk behind him. "What are we going to do, Dan?"

"A flanking maneuver is our only chance. You stay here but only shoot if they stick out an arm or head.

Conserve your ammo. I'll circle and try to attack them from the side."

"That'd put them in a cross fire," Cooley said.

"If it works, we've got them. I'll try not to put holes in the map." He saw that his joke fell on frightened, deaf ears. Cooley wasn't in any mood to appreciate levity. "Get ready. I'll run for the trees over there in a couple minutes."

"Why wait?"

"The sun's coming up and will be above the trees. That's the spot that'll blind them. I hope it'll blind them." He took a deep breath and watched the bright line caused by the rising sun drop lower and lower. When it got to eye level for the Jensens, he lit out like someone had given him a hotfoot.

He hadn't gone ten feet when Cooley opened fire. He cursed his partner. There wasn't any chance Cooley had that good a target, but England Dan had no choice but to keep running. He reached a tight knot of trees and slid between them. They were hardly more than saplings but enough of them offered some small protection. He lowered his sights and braced his gun against one trunk. He expected one of the brothers to show himself. There wasn't even movement in the bushes where he thought they hid.

A twig snapped behind him. He dropped like a stone, rolled over and scanned the forest behind him. A flash of a blond-haired head a dozen yards away made him curse. Poke Jensen had had the same idea he had. Worse, both of them had chosen the same section of forest for their flanking maneuver. If he didn't stop Jensen, Cooley would find himself under fire and probably shot in the back.

He emptied his gun in Jensen's direction. How Poke Jensen reacted was hidden by the trees, but he guessed the outlaw's advance was stymied. With a quick motion, he opened the top-break Webley and ejected all the shells. He bobbled the cartridges, settled and then carefully loaded. He was almost out of ammo, but he still had the .455 cartridge lodged above his ear as a backup.

He got to his feet and worked his way back into the forest, hunting for any trace of Poke Jensen. A flash of movement set him off. Firing steadily, he chopped a bush to ribbons. Another quick move ejected the spent brass. He hunted for more ammo, then grabbed the one resting atop his ear and slid it home. The Webley snapped shut. With one round. As he faced Poke Jensen.

"I wanted to see who I was going to gun down," the outlaw said. He came from behind a tree to the left of the bush England Dan had "killed." With a contemptuous move, he holstered his piece. He began walking forward. His hand hovered over his pistol, ready to draw.

England Dan had no doubt the man's draw was spectacular. Not a hint of fear showed on Jensen's face. If anything, he was enjoying himself as he anticipated making another kill. If he had notched the handle of his six-gun, it'd look like a colony of termites had enjoyed a buffet.

"Come on out and let's shoot it out. You and me. Like men. Or is that asking too much of you?" Poke Jensen stopped when he came within ten yards.

England Dan backed away. Any showdown with Jensen would end badly for him. Worse, he had a sin-

gle round in his gun, not that he'd need more. Jensen
had to have been fast and accurate to have survived as
long as he had.

He stared at the outlaw and realized he was talking
himself into a grave. If he thought he'd lose any contest, he was half beaten.

Jensen's hand twitched. England Dan lifted his pistol
and fired. Poke Jensen cleared leather and fired. England Dan staggered and fell, but not from lead ripping
through his heart. His involuntary retreat had caused
him to catch his heel and lose his balance. Whether that
saved his life was a fact to be debated around many
campfires.

His bullet hit Jensen squarely in the chest. The gunman never got the chance to fire a second round. He
sank to the ground, his life draining from him fast. A
few gasping sounds came from his lips before he died.
England Dan wasn't sure if Jensen tried to speak or
whether those inarticulate noises were what remained
of his soul rushing from his body.

"You got him, Dan. You cut down one of the mean-
est gunmen in all Arizona." Cooley stood over him, his
six-gun aimed at the ground. As he turned, he covered
his partner.

England Dan reached up and pushed the gun away.
Grunting, he got to his feet and rushed to Jensen's side.
He yanked the gun from the killer's hand, then pulled
off the gun belt half filled with cartridges. He was once
more in the fight with ample ammunition.

"You killed him. You're going to be famous, Dan.
The man who killed Poke Jensen in a face-to-face gunfight."

"It wasn't like that." England Dan ejected the single

spent round and replaced it with a fresh round. "Keep
a lookout for the other one." He quickly searched the
body. Jensen had thirty dollars in folded, sweat-stained
greenbacks and a silver cartwheel. But he wasn't carrying the map.

"I saw it. Well, I heard it. And when I got here, you
were alive and he was dead, his gun in his hand. He
threw down on you and you beat him."

England Dan ignored his partner's ravings. The odds
had improved for surviving with Poke Jensen dead. But
his brother was as much a killer as Poke had been.

"Take a few cartridges so you can back me up. We're
going after his brother."

"He has the map?" It finally penetrated Cooley's
brain why his partner had searched Poke Jensen and
what he hadn't found.

"Let's hope they didn't hide it somewhere. Searching
around here would take days or even weeks. There're
too many ways to conceal a map." He failed to add what
was an even worse possibility. The outlaws might have
memorized the map, then destroyed it.

Poke Jensen's six-shooter in hand, England Dan
backtracked along the outlaw's route to this point.
Cooley crowded too close, but England Dan wasn't able
to shoo him away. At least his partner didn't babble
endlessly as they stalked Lars Jensen.

"Blood," England Dan said, poking at a muddy clod
on the ground. Just beyond he saw a smear across a
clump of grass. "We must have hit him."

"Horse," Cooley said. "There's where they left their
horses. Both of them are gone." He wandered around,
kicking at rocks and trying to look as if he read the
signs.

England Dan took it all in with a single glance. The gunfight had been more one-sided than he thought, but then he'd had to control his own fear as bullets whined around his head.

"They spread the map out on the ground here," he said. "They held the corners down with those rocks." He pointed to a perfect square. Each of the rocks had been moved into the position. Trying as hard as he could to hear hoofbeats, he gave up when only the wind filled his ears with soft whispers.

"What do we do now, Dan?" Cooley sounded apprehensive.

"I just mowed down half of the opposition. Lars Jensen has our map. I say we go take it from him."

"Even if it means we have to shoot him?" Cooley looked uneasy.

England Dan didn't answer because he would have said, "Especially if we have to shoot him."

CHAPTER TWENTY-NINE

"DOWN! WE'RE BEING ambushed!" Poke Jensen shoved his brother hard. Lars staggered and fell. He wasn't as steady on his feet as he should have been. He wondered why his brother had gone loco.

Then bullets tore past his head and whined off into the woods behind him. At the same time, Poke had his six-shooter out and fired steadily. Lars dragged out his iron and got to a sitting position. It took only a fraction of a second for him to find a target. A man wearing a bowler sprayed lead in his direction; Lars Jensen returned the deadly hail in kind. He growled deep in his throat when he missed. Nobody tried to bushwhack him and got away with it.

"Who are they?" Poke Jensen reloaded, then loosed a new curtain of death across the open space beyond the trees. "They can't be road agents. Nobody'd try to rob us."

"Not everybody knows you. Your reputation, sure, but not you by sight." Lars Jensen pinned down the one in the bowler and kept him cowering behind a boulder. "That must be the pair of miners that had the map." His six-gun came up empty, but he got a good view of the second man flinging lead in their direction. "That one. The one taking refuge behind the tree. That's Cooley. The other one with the bowler must be his partner, Rutledge."

"They aren't getting the map back."

"I agree. Over my dead body," Lars Jensen said. Then he laughed. "Over *their* dead bodies!"

"We're exposed. I'll circle and come at them from the side. You keep them busy."

Lars Jensen said nothing. He thought his brother was suicidal doing that, but then much of what Poke did struck him that way. Keeping the man with the bowler pinned down proved harder than he expected. Cooley opened fire as Lars reloaded, giving Rutledge the chance to retreat into the woods. Shouting to his brother that he had company out on the left flank was out of the question. That would warn Poke. It would also warn Rutledge. Poke knew how to take care of himself.

With that thought, Lars bent over and scooped up the map. He stuffed it into his pocket, then tried to kill the two miners out there. As he triggered the third round in his gun, he winced. A bullet left a deep groove in his left thigh. Lars Jensen half spun and grabbed the wound. Blood squirted between his fingers. He hadn't recovered fully from getting back-shot the last time he'd confronted Cooley. Unless he stanched this wound, he was going to lose enough blood to pass out.

Hobbling off, he got to the horses. His mind raced.

"He can fend for himself." Lars Jensen painfully mounted, bent and snared the reins to his brother's horse, then rode away. Two horses meant he would make better time getting to Mule Springs. If Poke killed the miners and got away, he'd know where to rendezvous. If he didn't, good riddance. His elder brother wouldn't be around to treat him like dirt. And when he found the stolen payroll, he wouldn't be given crumbs. It'd all be his and not a dime of it'd go to Beeman's ma or anyone else.

He pressed down hard on the gunshot wound on his leg. That money would serve him well down in Mexico while he recuperated. A thousand dollars bought a keg of tequila and a passel of lovely señoritas to wait on him hand and foot.

Galloping along jolted him and sent knife slashes of pain into his leg. Worse, he felt sick to his stomach. He hung onto consciousness with grim determination.

In less than ten minutes, his horse began to falter. He slowed, then stopped to transfer to his brother's horse. From here he walked both horses a half mile, then picked up the pace again. More than once in his criminal career, he had outpaced a posse using this very pattern. Gallop, swap horses, then build up speed again. The combination of riding one horse first and then the other put lots of miles under their hooves. Once Jensen had traveled over fifty miles in a single day, but the Superstition Mountains wore down both animals because of steep slopes and rocky terrain. Worse, he found himself wavering.

As sundown claimed the land again, he found a cave to put both horses in, built a fire just inside the mouth and fell into a heavy sleep that came close to being a coma. The sun was well up by the time he awoke. He tended his leg wound the best he could, washing it off using water from a nearby stream. Trail rations went down good, but jerky did nothing to restore his strength. When his horses had eaten their fill of grass and drunk enough water to get them on the trail, he repeated the prior day's travel, reaching Mule Springs after sundown.

Jensen longed to sleep in a bed. He had some money for the solitary hotel in the small town, but more than this, he wanted a good meal.

He put on a knee-length canvas duster to hide his gunshot leg and tried not to hobble as he went into the café next to the hotel.

The meal was decent, and he felt strength flowing back into his body after he finished. He leaned back and studied the waiter. The man was graying and had a world-weary expression of someone trapped in a dead end.

"You live here in Mule Springs very long?" Jensen asked.

"Most all my life. My ma and pa moved here when I was six."

Jensen estimated that was more than thirty years back. He knew better than to make himself stand out too much, but he needed information.

"I was told to meet a friend in the hills west of here. You recognize a pattern of mountain peaks like this?" He drew a fair copy of the map on the tablecloth, using what remained of the gravy on his potatoes.

"You ain't a miner," the waiter said. "We've seen an army of them through here over the years. The last bunch came two, three years ago. Why do you want to find this place?" He tapped the sketch.

Jensen almost lost his temper. He asked questions, he didn't answer them. Pistol-whipping the old man would get him nowhere. For all he knew, Mule Springs had a marshal. The town wasn't all that far from Fort Bayard. Tangling with the army when he was hunting for their stolen payroll was a fool thing to do.

"A friend's up there. He gave me a map that's not too good."

"That might be Prickly Pear Pass. If this hill's moved farther off, I'd say it definitely is."

"I'm not much of a mapmaker. Let's say this is Prickly Pear Pass. How do I find it?"

The old man laughed. "It's hard not to find it. Get up 'fore sunrise and wait. The sun lights up the two peaks on either side of the pass like they was made of gold. Somebody told me they have quartz faces on them. I don't know about that. But after the sun's up more than a half hour, they look like plain old brown rock."

"Much obliged." Jensen got to his feet, trying not to wince. His left leg had stiffened on him. "Time to get these bones into bed."

"I'll get you a room. The hotel's mine, too. If you want, I'll see that you get a second-story room that looks out toward the mountains. All you'll have to do is pull back the curtains to see where to ride."

Jensen grunted as he followed the waiter to the hotel desk to register. If he had read Beeman's map a'right, he'd find the payroll before sundown the next day.

All night long he tossed and turned in the uncomfortable bed. Waking before dawn proved no problem. He realized he was het up over finding the money. It took all his willpower not to let out a whoop of joy

when he propped himself on the windowsill and saw
how the rising sun set two of the peaks on fire. He
spread the map out, located the line of inverted Vs
showing the peaks and carefully counted. The two on
the map matching what he saw were the last two Rivera had sketched in. That made remembering which
they were easier.

Breakfast, the trail, the two peaks and Prickly Pear
Pass. His leg ached dully, but the promise of finding the
payroll let him ignore it as he rode on. The trail through
the pass proved steep and treacherous, but he pressed
on. He used both horses to the best advantage, always
switching to the other when the one he rode began to
flag. Eventually, his efforts paid off. On the far side of
the pass, he found a spider web of roads. There had
been considerable mining activity in the region once.
Now silent testimony of the weed-overgrown, double-
rutted road and the empty hills showed that the miners
had moved on to better claims. Straight west through
the Superstition Mountains, Bisbee had become the
new boomtown. That suited him just fine, not having
nosy miners or prospectors watching his every move.

Using the map got him turned around, but he
pressed on. The lure of the cavalry payroll set his heart
to pounding a little faster every time he thought of it.
The stolen money promised him more than he'd ever
had on his own, and all he had done to earn it was get
shot a couple times. Poke was like a bad penny and
always turned up. Since he hadn't, he was probably
dead. Nothing else explained why he hadn't caught up
since he wasn't likely to surrender to anyone. Losing
his brother along the way was unfortunate, but not
overly so. Poke had gotten what he had deserved for

most of his life. It struck Lars as ironic that Poke had
been cut down by a miner wearing a bowler and a bat-
tered British Army uniform coat.

Someone who was as big a maverick as Poke had
done him in. All this time Lars had thought the law or
a bounty hunter would cause his brother's demise.

A final study of the map gave him a tiny trail mean-
dering up the side of a tall peak. He forced himself to
take the slope slowly for the sake of the horses. His
occasional dizziness moderated his excitement even as
he swayed to and fro. The map's dotted line showed
where Barton Beeman had gone. Lars Jensen blinked
at realizing there was only one possible trail, then rode
on because that meant he had found the mine where
the outlaw had hidden the loot.

He popped over the rim of a low mesa. At the far
side rose another mesa. Jensen let out a whoop. The
distant rock face had a mine shaft blasted into it. All
around the stretch of mesa leading to the mine shaft,
deep pits made riding dangerous.

"Where'd you hide the goods, Beeman? Where?"
Lars stared at the mine. It would have made sense to
stash the payroll there, out of the weather. But Beeman
had been severely wounded. That would have made
tossing the gold into one of the pits a better choice.
"Dump it in the nearest hole, then beat a retreat."

He looked around and saw how several narrow
trails onto the mesa presented ways for Beeman to
leave after hiding the payroll. Jensen considered which
of the westward trails would best have connected Beeman with Poke. If he'd known of those other pathways,
he'd have used them and saved himself a couple days'
travel.

"So he went west from here after drawing the map, then passed the map to Rivera as he was dying, and the cowboy found him on the far side of the Superstitions." Jensen nodded. It all fit. Now for the real question. "Where'd he hide the money?"

He dismounted and went to the first of the pits. Carefully peering over the side, he saw sunlight reflecting off ripples in the pooled dirty water. It wasn't quite a cistern, but Beeman hadn't been dumb enough to throw the money into a well. Even if it had filled up from the rains after Beeman had prowled around here, the outlaw was smart enough to know how hard it'd be to recover the loot in such a deep pit.

Working across the mesa, saving the mine for the final search, he peered into each of the pits. Some were little more than shallow bowls blasted in the rock. Jensen painfully jumped down into a couple of those to examine the bottoms. The loose rock littering these pits betrayed him. No hidden payroll. After clambering out, he looked around. Two more pits.

Jensen took another look at the map and positioned the paper to mirror the layout of the mesa. The mine had been bored into the solid rock of a towering cliff. Above the mine stretched a second mesa.

"Stairsteps," he muttered. He had no desire to scale that cliff and hunt on a second mesa. Beeman had been wounded. That argued against him going to such lengths. Jensen checked the next-to-last pit.

Nothing.

Going into the mine looked more and more like the only way to find the payroll. He limped to the final pit, expecting to give it a cursory search before going into the mine. Jensen stopped, toes at the pit rim. His eyes raced over the shallow bowl. He half turned to enter the mine and then stopped. Wheeling back, he stared hard into the pit again.

He dropped to his knees and examined a tiny pile of rocks. There wasn't any way the stacked rocks had set themselves one on top of the other through natural means. Wind or rain? Never.

"Ah, Beeman, you marked it so it was easier to find." Jensen tossed the rocks away. At the bottom of a depression lay a canvas bag marked with US ARMY and an insignia telling the world it belonged to the Fort Bayard paymaster.

He let out a whoop of glee and bent over to drag the payroll up so he could see how rich he was. Stones rattled back into the pit. Wind whistled past the cliff face and sucked the musty breath out of the mine shaft behind him. With a strong tug that sent new agony into his body, both in chest and leg, he dumped the bag onto the ground.

Eager hands reached to open the bag.

"You're a dead man if you go for your gun."

Lars Jensen looked into the pit. He had been so eager to get rich, he hadn't seen the long shadow of a man coming up behind him. The shadow figure held a six-shooter in a steady hand. Lars had been caught dead to rights.

CHAPTER THIRTY

⌒

"Not that way," England Dan Rutledge said. "We're going this way." He pointed to a steep mountain trail.

"But, Dan, the sign says the road to Mule Springs is that way." Cooley pointed to another road leading from the crossroads. "We got lost before. This time, we should follow the signs."

"Unless I miss my guess, Jensen went that way. We can't travel fast enough to catch up with him, even if he is wounded."

"You found plenty of his blood along the trail. He must be riding with one foot in the grave."

"He's got two strong horses." England Dan patted the black stallion's neck. "We've got decent horses, but they're all tuckered out. We have to rest, or they'll die under us. Jensen jumps over to his spare and keeps riding."

"I heard tell that's the way a lot of bank robbers escape. They steal horses ahead of the robbery, then ride their horses into the ground, switch over and keep riding. No posse can keep up with them that way." Cooley looked longingly along the trail to Mule Springs.

England Dan wondered if Cooley was losing his nerve again. He had survived the shootout and boasted about his part in it. Every telling made him more into the hero who killed Poke Jensen and chased off his outlaw brother. It didn't bother England Dan too much. If anything, he wanted to be a fly on the wall to hear what Cooley claimed as his role when he explained it all to Mandy—if he ever did. The woman saw him clearer than he saw himself, but then her work as a Cyprian forced her to size up her customers or pay the penalty. Blowhards and braggarts were her customers.

"This way gets us to the Lost Banshee Mine faster. Jensen is riding to Mule Springs. Then he has to double back, going uphill. We can reach the same place faster because it's shorter, and we only need to climb a little bit since we're already in the mountains."

"You said you had no idea where the mine was, even after you saw the map." Cooley sounded like he was accusing his partner of a crime.

"I thought real hard on it. I never explored this part of the Superstitions, but more'n once I heard prospectors talking about it."

"Why didn't they claim the mine, then? Tell me that."

"They might have found the Irish Lord, but the owner shooed them away. On that, maybe the owner's in cahoots with Jensen. If he is, we'll have both Lars Jensen and the owner to deal with. It's a good thing we have some ammo."

"Not that much. We should get on back to Oasis and stock up before tangling with Jensen again. After all, the mine's not going anywhere."

England Dan knew that, but something else had made the Jensen brothers so eager to get the map. They weren't miners. Even if the Irish Lord—the Lost Banshee Mine—was the richest mine in all Arizona, he doubted they'd pick up rock hammers and go into the mine to chip away at the blue dirt. In his experience, men who held up stagecoaches and banks avoided real work. His big question was how much stolen money was hidden here.

"You think we can get to the mine before Jensen?" Cooley asked.

"The only way to find out is to try. If you want to go on back to town, now's the time." He saw Cooley wrestling with the decision. Then Cooley made his choice.

"Why're we standing around jawing like this? Let's ride."

England Dan tried not to laugh. They were riding into more trouble, no matter what they found. Deep down in his gut, he worried they had bought a pig in a poke. The Lost Banshee Mine might not be abandoned at all. The Jensen brothers had some reason for searching for it, for not knowing where it was and having to rely on the map made by somebody else. Too many details were left to the imagination. In that, England Dan knew both he and Cooley had built up fairy tales all too easily.

As they rode, he almost wished that the banshee would screech again, just so he could see Cooley's reaction. His partner still refused to believe he had scared off Big Ear and his hunting party mimicking Big Owl.

"It's a steep climb, Dan. Are you sure we ought to go on?"

England Dan eyed the incline. They had ridden long enough to be near the mine. If Jensen needed a day to travel twice the distance and still faced a climb matching this, they would arrive ahead of the outlaw.

"The trail's not been traveled in a spell," he said. "I don't know if that's good or not, but let's see what's at the top of the hill."

"It goes onto a mesa. I've seen the mountains do this before. And a mesa rises out of this one, like giant steps. That can expose gold. I've seen that, too."

England Dan let his partner rattle on. He urged Whirlwind up the slope. The horse picked its way slowly but never stumbled. Cooley's horse was less sure-footed. Mabel brought up the rear, never missing a step. The strange line of travelers struggled along and finally crested the track. Cooley had been right. This mesa was broad and flat, but the north side had another peak growing from it. A mine had been blasted in the rocky face.

"Why'd anybody dig all those pits?" Cooley took off his hat and scratched his bald head. "You don't get gold out of the ground like that. You find a vein and follow it until it peters out."

England Dan had no idea why the pits existed. He rode to the nearest one and looked into it. A little water pooled there, left over from the recent rains. Catch basins because the mesa was so flat? The miner wanted to keep the rainwater from flooding his mine? Whatever the reason, more than a half dozen had been dug in an otherwise featureless mesa.

"There it is," Cooley said with a hushed reverence. "The Lost Banshee Mine."

"There's plenty of evidence it's been worked for a while," England Dan said. They went to the mine. He stopped just outside the mouth and stared. "There's why nobody's recently heard from the owner."

A mummified body sprawled just inside the mouth. England Dan edged forward and nudged it with his boot. The arm fell off. The wind and weather had taken its toll on the body.

"How long?" Cooley's voice cracked with strain. "How long's he been dead?"

England Dan examined the body. "There's a pair of bullet holes in his chest." He reached across and picked up a rusty six-gun. He tried to open it to see if any rounds had been fired. The corrosion was too thick.

"Dan, here's another one. Another body." Cooley had walked a yard deeper into the mine. "He's been shot, too. Just once. I don't see his gun, though."

The coat crumbled into dust as England Dan searched the pockets. He pulled out a leather wallet and opened it. The leather had protected the contents. The stub of a pencil had been shoved into a leather loop. He ignored the writing device because something more inside held his attention. Unfolding the page inside, he slowly read it, then looked up.

"This is a bill of sale. This fellow was the owner and signed away his right to the Irish Lord."

"The Lost Banshee Mine," Cooley corrected automatically. He started searching the other body.

"There isn't a buyer's name entered. Something went topsy-turvy before the deal closed. They shot it out, and both died. There is no owner of this mine." A crazy thought came to him. If he signed the bill of sale, he'd be the mine's owner.

"There might have been a third one who took care of both of them." Cooley held up a wad of greenbacks. They were crumbling around the edges from the weathering, but what remained totaled a hundred dollars. He tried not to be obvious about it as he stuffed the roll into his pocket, but England Dan saw. Rather than demand his partner split the money, he tucked the wallet with the bill of sale into his coat pocket.

"Check a bit deeper in the mine. If there was a third one, he'd likely have crawled into the shaft."

"I'll not stray too far." Cooley inched along, trying to use the light from the mine mouth as long as he could. He abruptly stopped a few feet from the second body. "We might want to clear out, Dan. There's enough dynamite stacked here to blow us all to kingdom come."

He heeded Cooley's advice. His partner joined him, shaken.

"There's at least ten cases of dynamite. If it's been there since these two shot it out, it's a year old. You know how old sticks leak nitroglycerin. Sneeze in there and it'd all go blooey!"

Walking a safe distance away from the mine, England Dan looked over the mesa and everything around. The mine had been blasted into the side of a cliff that rose to another mesa. The pits scattered around made dangerous traps if a soul was inclined to sleepwalk. He pointed some distance away to a shack.

"There's where he lived. Let's see what we can find there."

He and Cooley led their mounts to the cabin. A

tinge of jealousy hit him. The miner had lived better than the pair of them ever had. The cabin was downright palatial compared to theirs back at the Trafalgar Mine. He tethered the animals behind the cabin and went in. Cooley was already rummaging about. A stack of rocks on the table drew both their attentions.

After examining the pile, they looked at each other and shook their heads in unison.

"The mine's all played out if these were recently taken. There's hardly a fleck of gold to be had." Cooley dropped the rocks in disgust. "That might have caused the shootout. The owner tried to sell a worthless mine, and the two of them exchanged lead."

"There's no telling what went on, but these rocks— you're right. Our dross at the Trafalgar has more gold in it than these."

"Our luck's played out, just like at the Lost Banshee Mine." Cooley dropped to the bed. It had a decent mattress, but he didn't notice it in his dejection. "After all the shooting and killing, we don't get anything."

England Dan noticed how Cooley touched the bulge in his pocket. He was keeping the greenbacks as his due.

"We can work the mine to see if we're right about the quality of ore," he said. But in his gut he worried that what had once been rumored as the richest mine in the Superstition Mountains had become the most worthless. "At least we can keep working the Trafalgar Mine a few months more until it looks like this." He picked up a rock and dropped it on the table.

It landed with a thunk, but England Dan heard something more. Something outside.

He went to the door and peered out. A quick arm held Cooley back. "Lars Jensen's finally showed up."

"What are we going to do, Dan? Let's shoot him from ambush. There's no way we can have another showdown with him. He's a killer."

"So are we," England Dan said. He closed his eyes and pictured the dead Poke Jensen. Then he opened his eyes and watched as Jensen moved from pit to pit. "What's he looking for?"

"He's not interested in the mine. It's as if there's something in a hole on the mesa that's got him hunting so eagerly."

"I was going to enjoy it when he saw there wasn't anything in the Irish Lord, but look! He's studying the map."

"My map," grumbled Cooley. "I paid good gold for that map."

"He's checking every pit against the map. Whatever he's hunting for has nothing to do with the mine. Something else has been stashed here." A dozen plans flashed through England Dan's head. His speculation about the Jensens hiding something here had to be right. But what? He fingered his Webley, but it was out of ammo. He had Poke Jensen's six-gun. It struck him as fitting to get the drop on the outlaw's brother using the gun he had died with. "Let's ask him what he's hunting."

"It's not gold. Not in this worthless mine," complained Cooley. Then he realized what his partner intended to do. He grabbed Rutledge's arm, but England Dan jerked free.

England Dan stepped out, Poke Jensen's six-shooter clutched in his hand. He never took his eyes off Lars Jensen as the owlhoot dropped to his knees and began digging about in the pit nearest the mine. Boots crunching, making more noise than anyone could miss, he kept a steady approach. When he got close enough that his shadow fell over Jensen and into the pit, the outlaw reacted.

Too late.

"You're a dead man if you go for your gun."

"Who are you?" Jensen rocked back, his hands resting on the edge of the pit.

"I killed your brother. Killing you'd be a real pleasure."

"You tried to kill me before. We shot it out back on the trail here."

"Too bad I only hit you in the leg," England Dan said, edging around to look into the pit. He saw the canvas money bag with the Fort Bayard paymaster insignia on it. "Since you needed the map, I'd say it was your brother who stole that."

"It's been a chore getting the map. I didn't mind shooting a few people along the way to get it, though. And I won't mind shooting a few more to take the payroll."

England Dan fired the instant he heard the threat, but he was a fraction of a second too late. Jensen threw a handful of dirt and rock into the air. At the same time, he jerked hard away from where the six-shooter was aimed. England Dan missed by a country mile. Then Cooley piped up, shouting and complaining and firing at random. One of the slugs barely missed Dan. He swiped dirt from his eyes and dodged to keep his partner from shooting him.

Trying to avoid every danger caused him to take a step forward into the pit. He lost his balance and tumbled down. He landed hard on his belly. The jolt rattled him enough to give him double vision. He tried to call out, "Stop!" to Jensen, but dirt choked him. The outlaw limped for the mine.

England Dan never considered the danger. He began firing. Jensen reached the mine, whirled about and unloaded his six-shooter. Cooley added his wild discharges to the firefight. And then someone's bullet sailed past Jensen and hit the small mountain of unstable dynamite.

The explosion lifted Cooley off his feet and threw him twenty feet back. Rutledge fared better, being hidden in the pit. Lars Jensen simply evaporated in a bloody haze that was quickly replaced by what seemed an endless dust storm as more dynamite in the mine detonated.

When the last of the explosions died down, England Dan was deaf. He decided the blasts were over when the ground stopped shaking. Pulling himself out of the pit, he stood on wobbly legs and looked around. The Lost Banshee Mine no longer existed. Half the mountainside had collapsed into the shaft. He staggered back, wiping dust from his eyes, and went to his partner. Cooley kicked and writhed about, sputtering. He spat a mouthful of dirt out and sat up, taking his partner by both shoulders.

"That was some explosion. I wish I'd seen it!"

They stared at each other for a heartbeat, then laughed hysterically. Tears ran down their cheeks, leaving dirty tracks. They clutched each other until the shock passed. England Dan's hearing returned, and shouting at Cooley wasn't necessary.

"We showed him," Cooley said. "What was it he was pawing out of the pit?"

"Let's go see."

They walked back to the pit. England Dan let Cooley dig the canvas bag out of the ground. Cooley let out a whoop and sat cross-legged. He emptied the bag and pawed through the money.

As his partner caressed the greenbacks and made stacks of gold coins, England Dan went to the collapsed mine. He tossed aside a few rocks and picked up a hunk of stone the size of his fist. Judging from the way the explosion had shattered the cliff face, this came from higher up toward the other mesa. Using his thumb, he scraped away the oxide.

"We're rich, Dan, we're rich! There's more'n a thousand dollars here, and it's ours!"

"That's not ours, John." He walked back with the rock in his right hand. His grip on it was so tight, he came close to crushing it. "There might be a reward."

"What's the army going to do with it? This must have been stolen months back. They already got more pay for their soldiers. They're not going to miss this. It's ours, Dan, ours! Think of everything we've been through."

He saw how Cooley moved his six-shooter a little closer. Arguing with him over the stolen payroll might get messy. This was more money than either of them had seen since staking claim to the Trafalgar Mine.

"We return the money to the army and work this mine. The owner's dead, after all, and not going to complain."

"I'm not giving up this up." Cooley picked up his six-shooter. The determined set to his jaw showed the direction any argument would go.

They both whipped around as an inhuman screech filled the air.

"Big Owl," England Dan said softly. The screech came from the upper mesa.

"Banshee," Cooley said. "That cinches it." He began stuffing the money into the bag and slung it over his shoulder. "We keep the money and vamoose."

"It's not right keeping the US Army's money," England Dan insisted. "But"—he held up his hand to keep Cooley from using his six-shooter—"let's dicker a mite over this. We're partners, right?"

"What are you getting at?" The wild look on Cooley's face put any partnership in doubt. Greed was drowning out friendship.

"We can return the gold for a reward and work this mine." He glanced up, wondering if Big Owl would howl. Silence. "Partners. We split fifty-fifty as we did back at the Trafalgar."

"No."

"Or we go our separate ways. You keep the money. I keep the mine. We call it even." He saw Cooley thinking on that. He added a little extra to the pot. "Mandy wouldn't have gone back to Oasis, but she'd fit in just fine at a town like Bisbee. You can find her there."

"This much gold'd win her over." Cooley clutched the canvas bag to his chest.

"It's been good being partners. Maybe we can team up again later," England Dan said, knowing that'd never happen. "You take the pony, but leave me Whirlwind and Mabel."

"The mine and Mabel?" Cooley laughed. "You deserve each other. Both of you are muleheaded."

England Dan nodded, not trusting himself to say any more. Cooley backed off, just to be sure he didn't get shot in the back. He strapped the money bag on the pony, mounted and trotted away, heading west toward Bisbee.

He disappeared over the mesa rim in a few minutes. England Dan ran his thumbnail over the gold in the rock. After walking to the rubble from the explosion, he began sorting through it until he found the underlying stockwork. He followed the veinlet back to a larger exposed section of the cliff face. If he saw this much promise on the newly blasted surface, there had to be thousands of ounces of gold waiting for him to dig out.

He pulled out the leather wallet and opened the signed deed. Using the stub of pencil in the wallet, he carefully wrote in his name as the purchaser.

"I'm the new owner of the Irish Lord Mine," he said with some satisfaction.

His attention snapped up when Big Owl wailed again.

"All right, all right, I'm the new owner of the Lost Banshee Mine."

The cry rose, then faded as the wind died. England Dan Rutledge didn't mind having a banshee for a not-so-silent partner, as long as Big Owl kept his distance.

Ready to find
your next great read?

Let us help.

Visit prh.com/nextread